Hidden Moon

Book 1
The Keeper Saga

K.R. Thompson

Cover Design: Alchemy Book Covers/Keri Knutson

ISBN-13: 978-1489569967

ISBN-10: 1489569960

DEDICATION

This book is dedicated to my husband and son.
Thank you for letting me play in my world and for never failing to
bring me back to live in this one.

You are my heart.
I love you.

ONE

IF ANYONE HAD told me that my life was going to change this drastically, I would have rolled my eyes and told them where they could put that prediction. Everyone's life changes, that's what makes life what it is. But if I had been told the reason for this life-altering change was that I was part of a legend and an important key to a secret that had lasted hundreds of years, I would have thought they were insane. Myths, legends and fairytales were only stories found in books. I didn't believe in them.

And I was beginning to doubt happy endings existed, too.

I watched tree after tree whip past the window of the passenger seat window. There wasn't anything magical about us driving down the interstate, dodging amongst the endless range of mountains that stretched out as far as the eye could see.

If I had to describe this move, I would have said that it felt like a death sentence, which was kind of ironic since death was what brought us here in the first place.

My dad died two months before in a car accident. We were left with nothing but a small insurance claim and just enough money to move north to my great-grandmother's house. My great-grandmother, whom I'd never met, had died the year before and left us her big, rambling estate.

"We're gonna be okay." The words that came out of my mom's mouth were not convincing. "This is going to be good for us."

Neither one of us believes that, I thought, listening as her tone fell flat.

"Yeah, we'll be fine." I tried to sound optimistic as I kept my face to the glass so she wouldn't see the tears that filled my eyes.

The road curled, and then plunged us into darkness as we started through a tunnel carved into a mountain.

When you head through Big Walker Tunnel, Nikki, you've almost made it into the heart of the mountains. That's when you'll find the forest.

I couldn't remember how many times my dad had told me that, as if he were giving me directions should I ever need to find my way. Not directions to the town or even to the house, but rather to the millions of acres of national forest that ran for miles, surrounding everything. The town, the house, even the interstate were tucked

6

away in that forest, so I never knew what he had been telling me to find. My one regret was that I hadn't ever asked him what he'd meant. Now it was too late. He was gone and I'd never know.

The exit was coming up with a small green sign pointing the way. Bland.

You can say that again, I frowned. Not even a *welcome to* in front of it, or a guess at the population size. That sign did not seem all that welcoming.

As the car slowed down for a stop sign, my little sister woke up from her nap in the back seat.

"Are we there yet?" Emily brushed her dark brown curls from her eyes. Fred, her raggedy teddy bear and constant companion, was clutched in her other hand.

"Almost," Mom answered, "Just a few more minutes."

The road curved, taking us away from town and civilization. The mountains became taller and the trees came to the pavement.

After another mile or two of nothing but forest, a small building popped into sight.

As we turned down the gravel road beside it, I saw a carved wooden sign with an emblem of a howling wolf. "The Village," I read aloud, "I wonder what that is?"

"The Indian reservation runs behind it, so it has to belong to them. Maybe it's an old sort of trading post of some kind. I'd say that the school takes field trips there."

My mother's words sunk into Emily's brain. "Indians," she squealed. "I like it here. I wonder if they'll teach us to shoot arrows?"

I grinned. Six year-olds were not hard to please. Placate the kid with Indians and she loved the place, sight unseen. I caught the smile tugging at the edge of my mother's lips. It was the first time since we'd left that I'd seen her smile.

The ruts in the road made for a slow, bumpy ride and gave us plenty of time to look at a small two story house near the road. "That's a cute house," I said as I took a closer look and Mom navigated us around a huge pothole. The house was small, but seemed well kept. The windows had little boxes where bright, cheery flowers bloomed in bursts of pink and yellow. The swing on the porch swayed in the breeze. Whoever lived there had taken pride in their home.

"Your great-grandmother gave a half an acre to a woman a few years back. She told your father that she was a nice woman who was just down on her luck and needed a place to call her own. I think she called her Anita, but I can't remember a last name. It's been too long. But anyway, the house must be her place. Maybe we can go introduce ourselves once we get settled in."

Our house doesn't look as loved as that little house a mile back, I thought. Paint was peeling from every visible inch and the sagging roof over the porch gave the house a sense of foreboding. One downstairs window had duct tape across it, making it look like the house had lost an eye.

Awesome. We've inherited a horror house, I thought as I got out of the car to take a look around. The house had been in the care of a real estate agency since my great-grandmother's death and I had overheard my mother talking to them, being reassured everything was in good condition and ready for us to move in. Apparently, whoever she was speaking to liked to live in spooky, broken houses.

I made a circle around the house and came back to the car. My mom still hadn't gotten out yet. She was gripping the steering wheel so hard her knuckles had turned white.

"Mom. Hey." I tried to get her attention as I opened the driver's door and attempted to tug her out of it. She felt as if she was concreted into the seat. I was beginning to think I would need a crowbar to pry her out. After a couple seconds of hard tugging, I managed to get her standing and decided now was the time to point out every possible good thing I could find.

"Look how huge this house is. Emily will have tons of room to run around. We'll get it fixed up, and then think of all the cookouts we can have in the yard. And hey, if it's raining, then we'll just eat on the porch. We'll get us some rocking chairs, maybe even a hammock. And we could sit here and drink lemonade in the summer." I was wracking my brain trying to think of things that people would do in the middle of nowhere. I should have Googled this place before we came. We weren't anywhere close to civilization. I felt like a real estate agent trying to sell something that no one in their right mind would want.

I could strangle that real estate agent, I frowned. This was all her fault.

"Do you think it's going to be okay, Nikki?" She turned to me, with a look on her face that was half-hopeful and half-skeptical, as if she wasn't sure she should believe me.

I stretched my fake grin back across my face as far as it would go. I figured I was showing her every tooth I had. Once in grade school, I had smiled like that and a boy told me that I looked like the jack o lantern that his dad carved him every year at Halloween. I didn't figure it to be my most convincing smile, but it was all I had at the moment. It must have worked a little because she calmed, and began looking at the front of the house.

"Can we go in, Momma? Can we please? Can we go pick out our bedrooms now?" Emily begged as she hopped from one foot to the other. Her little brown curls bounced around her big brown eyes like tiny brown corkscrews.

Mom bit her bottom lip for a second, and then she smiled, "I guess we may as well see how bad it is. Then I'm going to call that real estate woman. I know we had a clause in that agreement that everything would be kept up, and this definitely isn't kept. I guess we should see what's inside."

The first thing that caught my attention when we stepped inside was the big staircase that spiraled to the upstairs. Emily ran up the steps and started claiming her room as soon as she hit the top step. I followed her up as Mom finished looking through the downstairs rooms. I found Emily in the room she had claimed and walked down the hall into a bedroom that looked out to the woods on the side of the house. In an effort to be as happy as my sister, I played along and announced my choice.

"This one's mine," I said at the top of my voice.

Emily ran across the hall to see which one I had picked. She crinkled up her little nose in disgust.

"That's the little one," she said slowly, as if she needed to explain it to me, since it was obvious that I didn't understand. "The one down that way is a lot bigger. Don't you want that one?" She pointed a finger down the long hallway toward the other end of the house.

"No, I like this one. It's plenty big enough. It's twice as big as my old room."

"Yeah, I guess so." She wandered over to my window, went up on her tiptoes and pressed her face to the dirty glass to peer out. "I know why you like this room. You can look for Indians easier over here, right?"

"Yeah, kid, that's right. And I'm not trading, so get on out of here. Go find something to explore." I swatted her butt as she giggled and ran past me.

Yep, I can watch for Indians. I smirked. I had the room closest to the upstairs bathroom. I walked in and turned the knob and expected nothing. The water that came out in a steady flow surprised me. It was cool and clear, so I splashed my face and looked into the mirror above the sink.

Water droplets clung to my eyelashes as I inspected the reflection staring back at me. A wild, blonde mass of chaos rioted around my head, but my brown eyes were clear and stared back at me with the complete calm I felt in spite of the circumstances.

I decided to try the rest of the faucets in the bathroom. The hot water chugged out a brownish goo before it ran clear. All of the faucets and the toilet were in working order from what I could tell. I ran down the stairs and looked up to make sure the water I had just sent down the pipes wasn't going to leak on my head.

So far, so good.

My mom finished up a conversation on a pink phone attached to the wall. She hung up and turned to me, "That was the real estate agent, she claimed that they didn't know the house was in that bad of shape. They're going to fire the man who was in charge of it. She's going to send someone out in the next day or so to take a look." She nodded toward the pink phone. "The landline is all that's working, I don't have signal on my cell."

I pulled my own phone out of my pocket. Nothing. Not a single bar of service.

"Well, that's lovely," I muttered, then looked back up at Mom. "I'm going to see if I get anything on it outside."

I walked in circles in the yard. I held my phone over my head and I twirled it around my knees, but I couldn't find the slightest hint that it was ever going to work again.

You'd think this place would have a cell phone tower, I thought irritably, as I headed toward the back yard to try my luck there.

But as I walked along the edge of our yard that bordered the forest, the fine hairs on the back of my neck started to stand on end. It felt like something was watching me.

THE FOREST CALLED to him. He felt the whisper of the wind against his skin, the caress of the tall grass that brushed his legs. The forest was green before, but now it seemed vibrant. He reveled in his body. His sight was so much clearer when the animal took over. He could see every leaf in detail, every bit of moss that grew on each tree as he ran.

Am I running? He wondered. It didn't feel like it as it didn't take much effort at all.

It seemed the forest wanted him. It belonged to him, welcoming him like a long lost friend.

He knew she was here, too. But this hiker didn't belong—not like he did.

He heard her. Her running steps seemed to echo through the trees, but he wasn't worried. She couldn't escape him. He was faster, and he was in no hurry. He would savor every second. Adrenaline coursed through his body, making him want to give chase. He smiled.

No, he would do this slowly—it would be special. She was special, after all. She was his, only his. No one would take her away from him.

He could taste her fear in the air and it excited him, coursing through his veins like a drug. He longed to take her essence, to make her part of him forever. He wished this feeling would last an eternity.

She had stopped. She wasn't running anymore. He didn't see her, but it didn't matter. The animal in him sensed her. There wouldn't be any hiding, at least not on her part.

Finding her would be child's play, he thought, as he crept through the trees as silent as a ghost. Every instinct told him she was close, and his muscles grew taut in anticipation. With effort, he made himself slow down and come to a stop. His cold, dark eyes scanned for his prey. He could hear her, her labored breaths coming fast and hard. He was close now. So close.

A slight movement to the right caught his eye. He spotted her then, cowering behind a tree like the pitiful, helpless prey she was. He noticed she hadn't seen him and so he stood still, watching her with eyes that weren't human.

She was shaking, small tremors ran the length of her body, her eyes darting back and forth, searching until she saw him. He stepped toward her, forming an evil smile that became a snarl. Her eyes widened in terror as she watched the fur grow over his arms and legs, as his eyes slanted into those of an animal, and the last traces of humanity vanished. She backed up, never taking her eyes off his.

"Please. Please don't..." She tripped over a vine, falling down hard on the forest floor. Her eyes squeezed shut. This final, pitiful act drew him toward her. The temptation was just too great now. He could resist it no longer. He could no longer play the game. It had to be now. This was their moment. It belonged to him and this woman in front of him. And he knew in that instant, she was his, and would stay his forever.

Her final cry echoed through the trees.

Disposing of the body wasn't quite as much fun, he decided. They always seemed to run the opposite direction of where he wanted them to go. He always had to backtrack anytime he made a kill.

He sighed, heaving what was left of her on his shoulder as he walked through the forest. He had to be careful as the tree branches were swatting at him now. Nature never did like it when he hunted the hikers. He knew in a day or two it would forgive him and welcome him again as if nothing happened. That was one of the perks of being a creature of nature. It always forgave him.

His journey led him along the edge of the forest. Usually, he didn't mind this part of his walk since it brought him close enough to see the two houses that sat near the dirt road. He didn't notice anything unusual as he passed the first one, but when the second one came into view, his blood ran cold.

The house that should have been vacant held a small car in its driveway. He dodged farther into the underbrush and felt the briars dig into his clothes. He cursed under his breath as a single thorn scored the flesh of his upper arm. It was a small, quick pain that scabbed and healed before the thorn ever left his body.

He shifted his burden around on his shoulder as he ducked down behind a bush. There, in the back yard, he saw the girl. Then the fury came. His body covered in mist as the animal awoke, ready to hunt. She was close enough to the woods that he could get her without anyone knowing. She was staring into the woods as if she knew he was there.

He was almost ready to grab her, when a woman came out on the porch.

"NIKKI, GRAB SOME of the cleaning stuff out of the car when you come back in."

"Okay," I answered, running back to the front yard in record time since the back yard had just freaked me out.

There isn't anything there but trees. You're just being silly, I chided myself as I grabbed one of the boxes out of the truck. You just have an overactive imagination.

Once I was back inside the house, the weird feelings left and I trudged the box upstairs to my mother, who stood in my room.

"The moving guys are supposed to be here tomorrow, so we'll worry about cleaning more when we get up in the morning. Besides, it's going to be dark soon. We'll all stay in your room tonight since it's the smallest," Mom said as she grabbed some cleaner. "I'll take the bathroom. You take this one."

When she left, I started cleaning some of the grime off the window. Then I saw him.

A boy that seemed to be my own age stood just inside the edge of the woods, staring up at the window. He wore a pair of jeans that fit snugly over his long legs, and a black tank top showed off the lean muscles in his arms. Those arms also happened to be folded across his chest as if he didn't like what he saw. His long, straight hair hung to his waist and was so black that it gave off a blue hue in the places where the sunlight touched it.

No emotion showed on the boy's face. He just stared at me. Thinking he might be waiting for me to make the first move, I pressed my hand to the glass in a wave.

But he didn't move.

"Nikki, I need some more floor cleaner. That bathroom's a mess. What are you doing?" Mom stopped as she came around the corner through the door.

"There's a boy outside. Right there at the edge of the woods. He's looking up at me," I said, moving away from the window so she could take a look.

"Oh? Where? I don't see anyone." She peered through the dirty glass.

"He's gone. He was right there a second ago." I squinted at the trees. There was nothing that looked as if someone stood there seconds earlier.

"He was probably just curious, honey. After all, we are the new neighbors now. They just like to keep an eye on who is moving in around them. Now, how about helping me find some more stuff to clean with, eh? I'm starting to think that sleeping bag is going to feel comfortable tonight."

THAT NIGHT, I dreamt of the Indian boy.

I could see him sitting with others in a circle around a fire. They were all talking. I couldn't hear what they said, but it didn't seem to matter. I was floating around the fire, trying to get closer to the one I had seen outside my window. He was the one I wanted to see. He was laughing and talking to the boy beside him. He didn't look as intimidating as he had out the window. He seemed at ease here. I floated closer to get a better look. I saw the muscles in his shoulders tense as he turned and stared straight into me. He looked shocked for a split second the same guarded stare that I had seen on his face earlier, returned. I should have backed away, but I was frozen as I stared into the most unusual eyes I had ever seen.

They were the color of liquid amber, with small black flecks spotted here and there. It was as if someone had melted gold, and flicked small shiny bits of onyx around in them. They were beautiful.

It was too bad this was a dream, I told myself. He wasn't close enough for me to see his eyes earlier, but no one had eyes like that. I knew I was dreaming. I looked at him again. He was angry, the muscles in his jaw tightened, making his high cheekbones even more pronounced. His eyes narrowed in suspicion as he stared back at me. I backed away, floating back away from the circle, away from the fire and into the darkness.

I awoke to the sound of a wolf's mournful howl in the distance. Cold chills ran down my spine as I burrowed down deeper in my sleeping bag, and stared up into the faint moonlight that fell through the window.

TWO

I AWOKE WITH a start the next morning, bolting straight up in the sleeping bag. The sun was shining through the window. It seemed minutes ago that I had been lying there watching the sliver of moon through the trees, thinking of my dream and his eyes. I shook my head. I had too good of an imagination. Only I would dream something like that.

I looked over and found Mom's sleeping bag empty. She must have risen earlier and went downstairs. Emily still slept, curled up in a little ball on her side. Fred was squashed up under her cheek as she hugged her pillow. I slipped out of my bag so I wouldn't wake her, and went downstairs. I found Mom sitting on the front porch, her knees tucked under her chin as she stared out into the yard.

"Good morning."

She turned and smiled up at me. "You're up early, Nikki. I was going to leave you alone for another hour. Did you sleep okay?"

"I'm fine. How 'bout you? Are you okay?" I sat down beside her and dangled my legs off the side of the porch.

"I was just remembering the last time we were here. This porch and I have a history, you know." She gave me a rueful smile, "I went into labor with you here."

"No, I didn't know. I thought you had me in Florida." This was news to me. It was startling. It felt like I had just found out I had been adopted, though there wasn't any chance of that. I was nearly a replica of the woman sitting on that porch. Normally, I don't think this news would have mattered, but as everything else had changed in such a short period of time, it left me shaken.

"We came up to visit a couple weeks before I was due to have you. We hadn't been here an hour and my water broke. You were born in Bland, Nikki."

I returned her smile, though it felt pretty weak to me. I had roots in Bland County. This was a shocker. I could no longer consider myself a Florida native.

"So why didn't we ever come back to visit?"

She shook her head. "I don't know. You were only a couple of days old when we left to go back home. Your dad never wanted to come back, but he called your Gran every day or two to check on her."

I kicked my bare feet against the wooden lattice on the bottom of the porch. Life had just pulled the rug out from under me and my mother didn't seem to notice.

"I hear Emily up and running around. I'm going to go check on her," she said as she got up to go back inside, "The moving guys should be here in a little while, so I'm going to start cleaning. Come in and get some breakfast in a few minutes, okay?"

"All right." I listened as the screen door slammed. It was just me on this porch now. This porch that once heralded the glorious day of my arrival. Did it matter where I was born? Virginia or Florida, I was still alive either way. And I was here, whether I liked it or not.

Sometimes you just don't get a choice. What matters is how you are going to react, I decided as I got up to follow her into the house. I was going to make the best of this new life, no matter what.

"Donuts are on the table," my mother called out from the living room as the screen door slapped shut behind me.

I found the box, and crammed one in my mouth. Definitely not a healthy breakfast. I drowned the sugar with a huge gulp of milk. Then I heard the crunch of gravels outside. Someone was here.

A young-looking woman with short, chocolate-brown hair was getting out of a small blue car. She looked up at me and smiled.

"Hello. I'm Anita. We live down the street, so to speak. We're your closest neighbors, so we took it upon ourselves to be the welcoming committee." She gave me a bright grin, showing lots of straight, white teeth.

"I'm Nikki," I said, smiling back at her. "Come on in. My mother is in here somewhere."

As if she had heard us, my mom came out the door, wiping her hands on the sides of her jeans. "You'll have to excuse us, we've been cleaning. I'm Brenda, and you've met Nikki. The little one running around here somewhere is Emily."

"I'm Anita, and this is Brian, my son," Anita said, nodding towards a dark-haired boy who was getting out of the other side of the car. "We just wanted to see if you guys needed anything. We saw you drive by yesterday evening, so we thought we'd drop by this morning and introduce ourselves."

"Come on in," Mom urged, holding open the door and bumping me out onto the porch at the same time. "Overlook the mess." They both went inside and left me and the boy to stand there looking at each other.

He grinned at me. "So, I think they've hit it off rather well, don't you?"

I laughed. "Yes. My name is Nikki."

"Yeah, I think I've been introduced to you three times now." His blue eyes sparkled "Are you ready for school?"

"I'll be a junior this year, and no, I'm not ready," I said, offering him a half-smile. "I hate being the new kid."

"Oh, it won't be too bad. At least you won't be starting in the middle of the year. Don't worry about it, I'll show you around. You probably are in most of the same classes that I am. It's a small school. Listen, the bus doesn't come up this far, so if you want, you can catch a ride with me. I mean, if you want to," he added quickly.

"Yeah, that would be great."

"So are you guys related to Aunt Mae? I mean, I know she wasn't your real aunt, or mine, for that matter, but that's what we always called her."

"Aunt Mae? Do you mean my great-grandmother?" I asked. When he nodded his head, I added, "I didn't know her. We never came to visit."

"That's a shame. She was a nice lady," he said, "and I'm not just saying that because she helped us out when I was little. She was like an aunt to me. I'm glad that you all are going to be staying. Some of the people that rented the house out after she passed away were college guys. They were always partying, and well, you can see what they did to the place. Not to mention, I think they had the reservation on its toes. The tribe was keeping a pretty close eye on them, especially after they decided to have a bonfire one night and it got out of hand and spread towards the forest."

"Do they come close? The Indians, I mean. I saw an Indian boy at the edge of the woods yesterday. He didn't look very happy. He just stared at me," I said, pointing toward the back yard.

"A boy? You mean, about our age?"

"Yes, I think so. Who was he?" I asked.

"I think it might have been Adam," he said, "There are only a handful of Indian guys about our age, and they all stick close together at school. They're pretty close anywhere else you see them. But it's Adam that always seems to be in charge, and if he didn't look very happy, I would bet it was him. He's not too friendly and he takes everything seriously. Too seriously, I think. But I don't know why he would be here unless he was just checking everything out."

"Oh," I said, not sure if I should ask what color eyes Adam had.

"So, do you know anything much about them?" he asked.

"Other than you, they are my only neighbors. That's all I know." I said.

He grinned at me, and pushed his dark hair out of his eyes. "Okay, that's a no. Our *neighbors* as you call them, are the tribe called the Wighcomocos. They are one of the oldest tribes in Virginia, historically dating back to 1607. In case you're wondering why I sound like I'm quoting this, the school takes field trips there every year, and Mrs. Graham says the same thing every year. You'll get off the bus and the first thing you'll hear," he cleared his throat, then assumed a high pitched, nasal voice, "'The Wighcomocos were one of the six tribes encountered by John Smith in 1607...'"

I laughed as he kept up his repertoire for the next few minutes, and applauded as he finished. His face flushed with embarrassment.

"Well, you just wait. You'll see," he said, trying to clear his throat back to normal. "You'll have it memorized in no time. I had it down verbatim by the time I was in first grade."

"Oh, well. At least if there's a quiz on it, I can get you to help me since you seem to be an expert."

"You've got it," he grinned. "The tribe is friendly when you are on the reservation, even Adam for the most part. They are very proud of their heritage, and they love to teach. Some of the stuff they'll show you is pretty cool."

Then Brian turned, as if he had heard something in the woods behind us. "Oh, yeah. I should warn you. You'll probably hear wolves howling, but don't worry about them. I've lived here my whole life, and I've never seen them."

"Oh, okay." The hair stood up on the back of my neck as I remembered the feeling of being watched the day before.

Brian looked over my shoulder as our mothers came back outside, still talking. They said their goodbyes and Anita started toward the car.

"Well, I guess I'll see you later. I think that's my cue that we're getting ready to leave," he laughed.

"If you see the guy in the woods again and you're close enough, look at his eyes. Adam's got some weird eyes, kinda gold colored with black specks in them. You'll know if it's him," he called over his shoulder as he made it to the door.

"Okay," I stuttered, making a rather feeble attempt to wave as Anita started up the car and started down the driveway.

"Those eyes," I murmured to myself, as the little car crunched in the gravels, turned and disappeared around the bend.

"Yeah, he does have some pretty blues, doesn't he?" Mom teased, coming back up the steps.

"I guess so," I smiled. "So what did Anita have to say?"

"She asked where I was working, and I told her I was going to start looking around for a job when you guys started school Monday. She told me that they were looking for a dispatcher down at the sheriff's station where she works. She said if I was interested, she'd put in a good word for me. Can you believe it? We haven't been here a whole day yet and I may have already found a job."

"That's awesome. So what does Anita do? Is she a dispatcher, too?" I asked.

"No, she's a deputy. You wouldn't think it to look at her, would you? She's so petite and so friendly, you wouldn't think she's law enforcement," she said. "But she said she loves her job and that it's her way of helping people in the community. I asked her why she decided to be a deputy since it seemed like a dangerous job. I wish I hadn't asked her. I didn't know her well enough to put her on the spot like that."

"Well?" I prodded, wanting her to finish her story.

'She said when she was a teenager she had gone to a football game. After the game, she started to walk home since she didn't live far. She only made it as far as the bleachers when a man pulled her behind the bleachers and raped her. No one saw the attack. Anita was so frightened, she had kept her eyes squeezed shut until she knew her attacker was gone, so she didn't see him either. The police never found the man. Later, she decided that she could help other women like herself, she wasn't going to be afraid anymore."

"Wow, it's great that she could turn something horrible like that around into something good," I said. "What does her husband do?"

"She isn't married."

"What about Brian's dad?" Then it dawned on me and my mouth fell open. "Oh."

"She's a very strong woman. I'm glad to have met her and I'm very glad she's our neighbor. But just the same, don't go wandering around when no one is around, okay?"

"Sure." I watched as she went back into the house, and remembered Brian's long locks of nearly black hair that fell toward his bright blue eyes. I wondered if there was a reason, other than my grandmother's goodwill that caused Anita to choose to move so close to the reservation.

THE WEEKEND FLEW by. The real estate agency had been as good as their word. There were workers at the house all weekend putting a new porch on the house, replacing windows and doing all sorts of odd jobs that needed to be fixed. We watched them in fascination as the house seemed to transform in front of our eyes. They said by the end of the week all the work would be finished. I thought it should make it into the Guinness Book of World Records at the rate of speed that they worked. The only thing they weren't going to fix was the paint on the house, which would be our job. My fingers itched to grab a brush and get started, but I couldn't until all the rest of the work was done and the workers left.

Brian came by on Saturday as he promised, and Mom had agreed to let me ride to school with him. She dropped me off at his house on Monday morning on her way to check on the job at the sheriff's office. She was going to drop Emily off at the grade school on her way.

Brian was leaning against an old blue truck with his hands shoved in the pockets of his jeans, waiting for me. When I jumped out of our car with my backpack, my stomach was in knots.

"Good morning. Shall we?" He opened the door to the truck and waited for me to hop in.

"Good morning," I smiled. "Yes, I suppose we shall."

He jumped in the driver's seat, and turned the key in the ignition. Smoke billowed out behind us in a huge cloud when the old truck fired and rumbled to life.

"Sorry," he said, his face flushed. "It's old, but I promise it will get us there."

"Hey, it runs. It's cool you have your own car."

"Your mom doesn't let you drive her car?" he asked.

"I've got my learner's permit. I never got around to getting my driver's license. I didn't need it down in Florida. We lived right in town, so everything was within walking distance. I never thought much about it until now," I explained.

"You want to drive?" he asked, gesturing to the wheel. "I'll let you if you want. Practice makes perfect. And trust me, you'll want to get your license There isn't anywhere you can walk to where we live, unless you want to start out a day or two early."

"No, I don't think so. I can't drive one of these." I pointed at the manual gearshift. "I've only driven automatics."

"Well, I'll have to teach you. Whenever you decide you want to learn, just come on up to the house and I'll have you driving in no time," he grinned. When he saw the shocked look on my face, he changed the subject to my cell phone that was lying on top of my backpack. "You get anything on that?"

"No. I don't think my carrier covers this area."

He laughed. "Don't take it personally. None of them work here. It's like the dead spot of the United States. You know those little maps they have with all the little red dots that show there is coverage where you live?"

"Yeah?"

"Well, we don't live anywhere near one of those little dots. And it isn't because they haven't tried. Someone is always putting a tower up in this county trying to be the first to get his company to work here. So far, Bland County is a dead zone and they can't figure out why. The mountains have been catching all the blame so far," he shrugged.

"Lovely." I cradled my useless phone in my hand. My old life seemed even farther away now. My lifeline was broken. It was as if the final thread that could have held me to everything I had known had just snapped, and now I was floating farther away into the unknown with no way to ever go back.

Brian glanced over at me as we slowed and made the turn down a small street. "Don't worry, eventually someone will figure it out. Technology is always making leaps. Maybe they'll find out how to make some kind of turbo-charged tower and that phone will be working again in no time." He gave me a sympathetic smile. His blue eyes sparkled the exact color of his flannel shirt.

I tried to smile back, but figured I was giving him my Halloween smile. I unzipped my backpack and stuffed my phone in it. It felt like I was burying a friend.

"Ah, the tribe's here," Brian said, pulling into the school's parking lot, nodding toward a beat-up looking Jeep where a pile of tall guys with dark hair were getting out. I noticed the one I saw before as he got out of the driver's door. He had his back turned to me as he talked to the pair that had just pulled up beside him on a motorcycle.

"That's Erik, with the black leather jacket. He's on the bike. He's the friendliest of the lot. Kinda goofy sometimes, but he's cool," he frowned, looking at the girl whose back was turned to us. She was pulling off her helmet, shaking out her long hair that fell seductively down her back in a thick, silky wave.

"Oh. That's Penny, his girlfriend, sitting behind him. Everyone from the reservation carpools, but there's always someone who doesn't fit, and they end up on the back of the bike behind Erik. Looks like it was Penny's turn again."

We got out of the truck. I slung my backpack over one shoulder, and we started walking past the group on our way to the front doors of the school. The one named Adam stopped talking to the others and turned to look at me, as if he had heard me speak. I hadn't said a word. His eyes glowed with the same amber I had seen in my dream. Even though I had been expecting it, I still stopped and stared at his eyes.

"Come on, Nikki, we have to get your schedule from the office. Then I'll show you where to go." Brian tugged on my arm, apparently thinking I was just stopping to gawk at the local people.

I realized that when he had turned to look at me, five other dark heads had turned, too. They were giving me curious looks. I felt warmth creep up into my cheeks. I lowered my eyes and was starting to follow Brian again, when I saw him smile, laughter filling his eyes. The one on the bike with the short hair and a roundish face started whistling at me. His girlfriend swatted the back of his head in an effort to hush him.

I caught up to Brian and we went through the front door, then down a small hallway on the right, and through a door where the word *OFFICE* was written in large letters.

An elderly lady with snow-white hair sat behind a desk, bifocals perched on the end of her birdlike nose. She looked up over her glasses and smiled at us when she noticed us come in the door.

"Good morning, how can I help you?"

"Good morning, Miss Ratherby. This is Nikki." Brian turned to me. "What's your last name? I never thought to ask."

"Harmon. Nicole Harmon." I smiled at the receptionist. Her stiff, arthritic fingers shuffled through a stack of papers, until she found what she was searching for and pulled a single sheet free and held it up for closer inspection.

"Ah! I've got your schedule right here, young lady. I think you have most of the classes that Brian has. You can show her around, can't you, dear?" she asked, peering over at Brian.

"Yes, ma'am. I'd be glad to." He nodded, causing dark locks of hair to fall towards his eyes.

"Okay, you two run along. The bell will be ringing in a few minutes, so you'd better go to your first class," she said, then smiled. "Welcome to Bland High, Nikki."

We looked at my schedule as we walked to our first class, which happened to be math. I had literature, history, anatomy, and Spanish classes with Brian. The only ones I didn't have with him were art, English and Phys Ed. I could find those without him.

The school isn't that big, I thought.

Math class went by without a hitch. I managed to find a seat in the back and was surprised to find that I had covered the same material before. The teacher was impressed and kept me afterwards for a few minutes to ask me questions about my other school. It put us later getting to the next class. Brian half-ran/half-walked me down the hallway to my English class and left me at the door with a quick grin and a reassurance that he would be there when it let out. I smiled at him as he ran back down the hall. I felt like a kindergarten kid getting ready to get on the bus for the first time. I wasn't sure why I felt that way. *Get a grip, it's just an English class*, I chided myself as I twisted the knob. I took a deep breath and went in.

The class hadn't started yet, though it looked like it was going to at any minute. The teacher smiled at me, asked my name and then told me to have a seat next to Mr. Black Water. I turned to see which seat she was talking about.

It was next to the boy with the golden eyes.

He stared straight ahead, ignoring me as I took the seat beside him. The air around him sparked and snapped, startling me so that I smacked the girl who sat behind me with my book bag.

"Hey, watch it," she exclaimed, rubbing her shoulder.

"Sorry," I muttered under my breath, easing the bag off my shoulder, and under the seat.

As I slid in beside him, I looked at him from the corner of my eye. He had a long, straight nose and high, sharp cheekbones, and looked every bit like the serious Native Americans I had seen in history books. As I watched, a tiny frown mark deepened between his brows, though he never looked at me. His long, black hair was darker than the black t-shirt he was wearing. It fell forward, hiding his face in a thick, silky curtain as he leaned over his book. I took the gesture as a hint to quit staring at him, and turned back to my own book.

A collective groan came up from the whole room as we were instructed to turn to page forty.

Sentence diagramming, I thought happily. Piece of cake.

"First of all," said the teacher, who had introduced herself as Ms. Barker. "I know some of you had problems with this when we ended the year last year. So we will be going over this material again, and you will learn this before I pass you. For this reason, we decided to have seats with shared desks this year. Quiet, please." She clapped her hands in an effort to quiet the murmurs. "The person you are sitting beside is going to be your study partner."

I felt him tense beside me. The air seemed to grow hot, popping and snapping.

"I expect you to take it upon yourselves to study together at least a couple times a week. By the end of the year, I expect you to know the difference between adverbs and verbs, prepositional phrases and the like. Although we will be covering other material, we will be going over this often to make sure everyone learns it." She shot a pointed look at Adam, who ignored her. She sighed, frustrated. "Who wants the first try at diagramming the sentence on the chalkboard?"

After another forty-five minutes of basics, an uncomfortable heat and crackling air that was starting to sound like Rice Krispies cereal, the bell rang. Adam jumped out of his seat and left the second it went off. I was still picking up my books when Ms. Barker came over and smiled at me.

"Nikki, I was wondering if you could make a good effort in trying to help Adam with this class. I've got your manuscripts from your previous school. I know you've already had sentence diagramming and that you excelled at it. Adam needs help with it. I nearly didn't pass him from last year. I won't pass him this year if he doesn't get it down, and that would be a pity, as this is the only class he has problems in. He is a very bright student. He just hasn't committed himself to learning this," she smiled.

"Yes, ma'am. I'll help…if he'll let me," I added, thinking about the way he stormed out. The way he was acting, I didn't think he'd let me help him do anything at all. For someone I had never met before, he seemed to dislike me. The knots in my stomach tightened again.

"He will let you if he expects to pass this year." She stared at me over a pair of wire-rimmed glasses. "You'd better head to class. Just please do your best to help him."

I managed a quick nod and rushed out the door.

Brian, true to his promise, was leaning against the wall, outside the door.

"Hey," he grinned. "What did you guys do to Adam in there? He looked like he was ready to kill somebody."

"He found out I was going to be his study partner. I don't think he likes me very much."

"How could he not like you? He just met you. Sort of. Don't think anything about it, he's just being Adam. He'll come around. Let's head to the cafeteria. I'm starving," he said, taking my books from me. Then he grunted, "A quick detour first to find your locker. I was planning on being chivalrous, but even my charm will dwindle after lugging these things around."

I laughed and laced my arm through his. "Okay. Let's go."

A pretty, petite blonde girl was putting her books into the locker beside mine. She had big, green eyes that sparkled with mischief when she saw us walk up.

"Hey, Brian. It's about time you found a girl you liked," she teased.

A locker slammed at the end of the row, and I saw a flash of long, black hair going around the corner.

"Hi, Ronnie," Brian grinned at her. "This is Nikki. She just moved in the old house up the road from me. I'm just showing her around."

"Oh, so that's what it's called now, is it?" she laughed as he blushed, "Nice to meet you." She extended a dainty, small hand and smiled.

"You, too." I grinned, and shook her hand.

"You look like just the person we need in the cheerleader squad," she looked at me as if she were sizing me up, "We had a couple girls quit from last year. Tiffany made them mad, like she does everybody. Anyway, we're having tryouts today after school. If you can stay that would be great."

"Um, I don't know," I began as I tried to think of a way to get out of it.

"I can wait, it's not a problem. I don't have anything pressing at home. Besides, I think you could give Tiffany a bit of competition and that would be entertainment at its finest." Brian laughed at my discomfort.

I shrugged. It looked like I was stuck, so I may as well make everyone happy. "Okay. So, where's the cafeteria? I'm hungry."

We made it into the cafeteria and Brian took a big sniff.

"Smells like spaghetti and mystery meatballs. It's official. School is back in," he announced, and then whispered to me, so the cafeteria lady wouldn't hear. "We're safe, it's the first day of school. They use whatever meat is leftover from earlier in the week to make their meatballs. So today, at least it's fresh meat." He shot a very large innocent-looking grin over to the cafeteria woman who was giving us a suspicious look.

We found a table with some of Brian's friends. There was a blond-headed guy named John, who happened to be Ronnie's boyfriend, and a small, chubby brown-headed girl named Beth. Both smiled at me after introductions were made. I noticed all the Indian guys were sitting at the same table across the room from us. Each of them had two plates of food, though none of them were eating. They looked like they were having a serious conversation and by the quick looks in my direction, it was about me. I stared down at my plate. My appetite left me.

"I wonder why those guys keep staring over here," John said, running his hand through his short blond spikes.

"I think Adam's upset that he has to pass English class this year. And Nikki here, got elected to be his study partner," Brian explained.

"You poor thing." Ronnie giggled with amusement.

I looked back up and noticed that the girl named Penny, who had been riding double on the motorcycle, was looking over at me, smiling. I smiled back and went back to eating my spaghetti, listening to the conversation about people I didn't know.

A few minutes passed when I heard a soft voice speak. "Excuse me?"

I looked up to find Penny standing next to me with a shy smile. Her pretty brown eyes darted toward the floor and her brown cheeks flushed in embarrassment.

"Hi, I'm Penny. Adam isn't happy about having a study partner, but we all think he needs one if he's going to pass English class. I think we might have talked him into being a little more cooperative." She shrugged, lifting one shoulder. "Anyway, what I'm trying to ask is, could you come over to the reservation today after school and try to help him?"

"You're setting up his study dates?" My mouth opened in astonishment.

"I kinda got nominated. Since I was the only girl here today, it was unanimous and they decided to send me over." Her face flushed darker and she bit her lower lip.

I looked back over to their table, and saw Adam looking sullen while the one named Erik grinned from ear to ear with amusement. The other three boys just smiled politely at us.

Angry, I stood. "Come on, Penny. They're not putting this on you. He has to talk to me if he wants help."

"Don't forget the tryouts," Ronnie mumbled through her teeth.

I walked over to their table with Penny in tow. I stopped in front of Adam and stuck my hand out.

"I'm Nikki, your appointed English study partner."

"I know. I don't think that's a very good idea," he said in a low voice.

"Well if you want to fail, that's up to you."

"No, that's not what I meant." He was looking at my still offered hand. He shrugged and took it in his. A spark leapt between our hands and the air sizzled.

"I'm Adam," he said, still holding my hand. The air still sparked, although it seemed no one but the two of us felt or saw anything.

I dropped his hand as if it were on fire and resisted the urge to rub mine on the leg of my jeans. He was looking at me as if he thought I was the one who caused all the little sparks.

"I am unavailable to tutor you this evening," I said primly. "However, tomorrow evening if you wish, I will be available."

He nodded, his beautiful amber eyes never left mine. Feeling awkward, I nodded and started toward my table.

"Good luck at tryouts," his voice whispered so low I thought I had imagined it.

I resisted the urge to turn around and see if he had spoken as I kept walking and took my seat next to Brian.

"That's weird," Brian frowned as he looked at the table I had just left.

"What?" I asked, letting out the breath I hadn't realized I had been holding.

"The way he was staring at you as you walked back over here. I think he likes you," he murmured, not looking the least bit happy.

"Look out, Brian. You may have competition." Ronnie grinned. "And you do have a point. I've never seen him look at anyone like that before. It's kinda weird."

I looked back at the other table, but no one was looking at us now. They had finished eating and seemed to be talking about something else. The bell rang, making me jump in my seat. The cafeteria came alive in a rush of food and trays that everyone shuffled around and made their way out of the door to their next class.

The rest of the day went by fast. Brian took me to art class as the last period of the day. I fell in love with Ms. Hayton, the instructor. She introduced herself in front of the class in a smock that once had been white, but now was covered with every color of the rainbow. She looked like she had been in a water balloon fight, with paint being the water. She had bright, blue eyes and short, frizzy brown hair that looked like a perm job gone wrong. Strangely enough, it looked perfect on her. She looked like abstract art.

She told us to draw anything we wanted. As long as we stayed busy, we could talk to each other as long as it didn't disturb anyone. I started sketching out the trees I had memorized out of my bedroom window. I thought I was doing pretty well until I looked over and saw the lifelike image of a young Indian woman the boy beside me was drawing. He was one of the guys that had been sitting at Adam's table at lunch. Like the others, he had the same dark black hair with a subtle blue tint, but where Adam's hair came to his waist, this boy's only came past his shoulder. He tucked a loose strand behind his ear as if it were a habit he did many times a day.

"That's amazing," I said, smiling. "I wish I could draw like that. The eyes are beautiful. She looks so real."

He returned a polite smile. "Thank you. Ms Hayton is a wonderful teacher. You'll be doing this is no time."

"Who is the woman in your picture?"

"Mother Earth," he replied in a matter-of-fact tone. "She is always depicted in our culture as a young, beautiful woman. She is full of life, and the giver of life. Most pictures painted or drawn by Native Americans that have a young woman in them are pictures of Mother Earth."

"I never knew that," I murmured, then shook my head and introduced myself. "Sorry, I'm Nikki."

"I know. I'm Ed," he grinned. "And that idiot over there is Erik." He pointed to motorcycle boy with the short, spiked hair and a big goofy smile on the other side of him.

"Since we're giving a lesson in Native American tradition," Erik said, "Ed is not his given name." His dark eyes sparkled with mischief.

Ed gave him a dirty look, and then pretended to be busy with his art.

"Nikki," Erik said as he leaned forward to peer around Ed, "in case you didn't know, some Native Americans still practice the traditional beliefs when naming their children."

Ed scowled.

"Marianne, Ed's mom, is one of those people. Plus, it doesn't help that she has an odd sense of humor. In the old days, mothers wouldn't name their children until they were a few years old. The reason was because so many of the children died when they were infants. Anyway, when they were sure the child would survive they would pick a name, based on what the child did or liked," he explained in what I was guessing was his most serious face.

"Ed seems like a nice, reasonable name," I said, trying to reassure Ed, whose brown face was starting to flush.

"It seems our good friend here had a certain fondness for only one thing when he was two years old. He loved playing in the dirt. He would have it from his head to his feet, even in his mouth. No matter what Marianne did, she couldn't keep him out of it. She warned him that he would regret it if he didn't stop, but he wouldn't mind her. So she named him 'Eats Dirt'. We've sort of shortened it to Ed. I think it becomes him more," Erik grinned, trying to duck as Ed smacked him on the head with his binder.

"Not much fun writing Eats Dirt Young Eagle in those little blocks for your SAT test. I'm going to get it legally changed when I turn eighteen next year, whether Mom likes it or not," Ed mumbled under his breath.

I smiled at him. "I think it's unique."

"Your trees are looking good," he commented, as if he wanted to change the subject.

"Thanks, they're the ones outside my bedroom window," I said. The ones where Adam had stood, I added silently.

Seeming to read my mind, Erik popped his head around Ed again. "Nikki, thanks in advance for helping Adam. We want him to pass so that we can all graduate together next year, so if we can help at all just let us know. He's really smart. I just don't think he likes English class all that much. I guess he figures if he can speak our native language and English, then having a class to teach him something he already knows is a waste of time. He doesn't like the idea of a study partner, but I have no idea why. I think he's more open to the idea now. At least I hope so, since we bullied him into it."

"Well, we'll see how it goes. I'll try, but he'll have to try, too," I said, resigned.

The bell shrilled again, announcing the end of the first day of school. I found Brian standing in his customary spot, leaning against the wall outside the door, his hands shoved in his jeans pockets.

"I'm beginning to feel like a stalker," he joked, grinning at me. "Are you ready to see what the cheerleading squad has to offer? Ronnie has spent the last half hour in chemistry, pestering me about making sure I get you to the gym after school."

"I hope I don't disappoint her. I've never been a cheerleader," I said, still trying to find a way out of it and not succeeding.

"You may not have been a cheerleader, but I saw trophies sticking out of one of those packing boxes the mover guys left in your living room when I was over Saturday. You've been in some kind of athletic something-or-the-other," he prodded.

"Gymnastics and tumbling," I sighed. I knew as soon as the words left my lips I'd lost the argument. I may as well get ready to be a cheerleader.

Brian gave me a triumphant grin. "Don't worry, it will be easy. They never do anything complicated that I've ever seen. You'll be a pro at this, no problem."

He steered me into a large gymnasium lined with bleachers down one wall. Beth, Brian's friend from lunch, was the only one sitting in the bleachers. She had a notepad in her hand. When she saw us she waved.

"Beth's on the school paper. She must smell a story." Brian returned the wave.

I groaned. Great, that was just what I needed. More trouble.

Ronnie came running up to us, grinning from ear to ear. "Great. I'm glad you're here. Brian, go sit with Beth or something. Come on, Nikki." She took my arm and tugged me toward a group of cheerleaders. Bland Wolves was stamped across the front of their green and white outfits.

The tallest girl stood in the middle of them, her hands crossed in front of her chest. She gave us an aggravated look. She had long blonde hair pulled back in a silky ponytail which swayed back and forth as she shook her head to the question one of the other girls had asked her.

"Tiffany, this is Nikki," Ronnie said. "She wants to try out for the squad."

Tiffany looked at me. "You're new. It doesn't matter; you won't make the cut anyway."

I had been tempted to throw the tryout. But now she had made me mad and I was determined to show them things I was sure her little backwoods squad had never seen before. I'd show them someone who wasn't going to back down.

Tiffany sighed and walked out onto the floor. "Well, let's get this over with. I'll lead. You just try to copy what I do when I get finished. Got it?"

I gave her a curt nod and waited for her first move.

She started with a jump split in the air. Her legs kicked to either side, and then she landed on the balls of her feet. She looked at me and lifted a perfectly arched eyebrow. I jumped higher up than she had, before I kicked out my legs, landing as easily as she had.

Next, she did a series of cartwheels that landed in a split. I duplicated the movement and added two back flips to the end, before I landed beside her in a split.

The cheerleaders clapped. Tiffany scowled and got up off the floor. She didn't look at me. "You'll do," she muttered.

Ronnie flew over to me as if she had just grown wings, nearly knocking me to the floor in a big hug. "I knew you were going to be great. That was amazing. Where did you learn those back flips? Tiffany never has been able to do those. You showed her up. I think this is so cool." She chattered nonstop beside me as Beth and Brian got up and came over to us from the bleachers.

"Awesome," Beth grinned. "I love seeing Tiffany get showed up. I'm glad I came and watched. It's too bad I didn't get Bernie over here with his camera, that last flip would have looked great at the top of the page."

"Oh, you're going to put it in the paper." I suddenly felt less sure of myself.

"What's wrong, Nikki?" Brian teased, "Afraid of a little publicity?"

"Do you have to put that in the paper?" I asked Beth.

"Well, no," she frowned at me. "I don't have to, but I think it would make a good article. It would give some of us a boost around here, to know that some people can make Barbie doll over there look bad."

I remembered Tiffany's attitude and my temper flared back up. I grinned a little too widely. "Do what you want. If it helps, I'll do another flip for the camera."

"I'll take you up on it another day," she promised. "I think Bernie has already gone home. I'll make sure he's around next time, even if I have to drag him here by his camera."

Brian threw an arm around my shoulder. "Are you ready to go home? I don't want to worry your mom."

He dropped me off at my house and told me he would come pick me up in the morning for school. I waved as he drove back down the road, and then opened up the front door, throwing my backpack on the couch as I went by.

"Is that you, Nikki?" Mom called from the kitchen.

"Yeah, it's me," I said. I found her sitting at the old Formica table, sipping a glass of tea.

"How did your day go? I was getting ready to call Anita and ask if she saw you guys, when I heard you come through the door."

"Not too bad. I met some of the guys from the reservation, I have to be study partner with one of them a couple times a week, so don't worry if I'm late tomorrow. Oh, and I made the cheerleader team." I went to the old refrigerator and pulled out a coke, then went back over to the table to sit across from her. "So, how was your day? Any luck with the job?"

"I got it. I start day after tomorrow. Tomorrow I have to go in for drug testing, a physical and all that mess." She waved her hand as if dismissing the mundane details. "So, cheerleading, and on the first day, too. I am so proud of you. I bet you're going to make a lot of new friends with those girls."

"Sure, Mom." I tried to smile. I thought of the one enemy I was sure I had made with the human Barbie. "I'm going to go up to my bedroom. Call if you need me."

I curled up in the chair in front of my window and put my sketchpad in my lap. I stared out at the trees. Their thick branches made a canopy above all the small, delicate plants that thrived around their gnarled roots. I opened my pad and started sketching.

I drew everything but the place where I had seen Adam stand. I stared at the paper. It looked like a frame of trees and plants, as if it waited for someone's picture to be framed inside. It was empty. I frowned and lifted my eyes up to look out the window to decide what to draw in the empty space.

The smallest bush beside the trees was moving. It swayed the slightest bit, as if someone had brushed past it as they walked away. I jumped up from the chair and ran out of the room and back down the stairs, pulling on my shoes before I hit the landing.

"Mom, I'll be outside," I yelled, not waiting for a reply.

I ran to the edge of the woods and stopped. I hadn't been so close to the edge of the yard before. Now I could see there was a small path in the exact spot, where I had been staring. It wasn't very noticeable, just worn down grass that showed someone or something

49

had traveled the same steps, back and forth a few times. It looked recent. The grass was still green. It stopped at the edge of the brush in the exact place where I had seen Adam.

I thought I heard the sound of someone moving a few feet away and stepped into the shade of the trees onto the path. I walked a few steps, then stopped and listened again. Absolute silence. Even the birds quieted. The small hairs on the back of my neck were standing up again. I jumped when I heard Mom call for me to come back inside to eat. As I turned and started to walk back out, I felt eyes staring at me.

I swung back around, looking for anything out of the ordinary. I saw nothing.

I went back into the house with the unsettling feeling that someone was watching me.

A voice seemed to whisper in my head, *Close. Much too close. Be more careful next time.*

THREE

THE NEXT MORNING, I heard Brian's truck pull up in front of the house. I glanced at the clock. He was early. He was at the front door by the time I grabbed my books and shoved my feet into my sneakers. I opened the door. His hand was raised up in front of him, ready to knock. He grinned at me and pushed his hair out of his eyes.

"Good morning," I said, "Sorry you had to come all the way up to the door. I tried to catch you before you had to come this far."

"It's okay. I'm a little early." His eyes sparkled with unexplained humor.

"Okay." I watched him warily. "I'm ready if you are."

"I'm ready. I thought we might try something different today if you're game."

"You tell me what it is first, and then I'll tell you if I'm in or not." I stopped walking and stood still. The last time he had badgered me into something, I ended up being a cheerleader. I still wasn't happy about that.

"Well, I know how you feel about driving," he began. My mouth opened to protest, but he hurried on before I could speak, "It's just that I know you're going to need a way to get around, you know, to study with Adam a couple times a week. Don't get me wrong, I don't mind taking you anywhere you'd like to go. Actually quite the opposite, but I'm getting off track. What I'm trying to say is, if you had a vehicle you wouldn't have to worry about me waiting for you. You could come home whenever you wanted to. Besides, what if your mom has the car and you need to go somewhere else? You never know what might happen. Anyway, I thought if you wanted, I could let you borrow the truck a few days a week. We could take turns driving to school. It would be good practice." He stopped for breath and smiled.

I chewed on my bottom lip. The offer was sweet and well-meant, but we were talking about an extra pedal and a gearshift. How was I supposed to keep both hands on the wheel? And what about coordination? I had to use both hands *and* both feet to drive this thing. Nope, I didn't see that happening in the near future.

I opened my mouth to say no thanks when I looked back into his hopeful face and said the opposite, "I'll try."

"Great! You don't have anything to worry about. I'm a great teacher and nothing bad will happen, I promise. Here let me take those," he chattered as he took my books from me and walked over and opened the driver's door.

He jumped in the passenger side and handed me the keys. After a deep breath, I put them in the ignition got ready to start down the road to disaster.

"Okay, put your left foot on the clutch and start her up. Good. Now put it in first and ease up on the clutch pedal," he instructed.

The truck lurched three times and tried to die before it started down the road. I made it up to the third gear before I had to stop at the stop sign at the end of the road. Then, I forgot to push the clutch in and the truck shuddered and died.

"Don't worry, you're doing great. Just put it in neutral and start it back up," Brian coaxed.

I hoped he was going to say that was enough for one day, but it seemed he wasn't going to let me off that easy. I ground my teeth together and started the truck up again. I was paying rapt attention to applying the clutch at every stop until we made it into the school's parking lot. Then I saw Adam and I forgot everything.

He was leaning against the front of his car with his arms folded across his chest again. He was watching me. All the other guys had already walked to the front of the school.

"Okay, just pull in right there. Slow up a bit," Brian said as he scoped out a parking place.

I slowed down too much. The old truck coughed, shuddered, and died just as I pulled in. I set the parking brake, leaned my forehead against the steering wheel, and said a silent prayer of thanks.

"You only killed it twice. That's great for a first try." Brian beamed a grin that stretched from one ear to the other.

"I don't think I can handle anymore today. You get to drive us back after school," I groaned.

"Not a problem," he smiled. "We'd better head to class."

I grabbed my books off the seat and got out of the truck, slinging my backpack over my shoulder. The little voice was whispering inside my head again,

Good job, Nikki. It'll get easier, I promise.

I looked up and saw Adam smile at me before he turned and started to run to catch up with his friends.

That was weird, I thought, was he waiting on me to show up? I frowned. I was beginning to think the guy was bipolar. One minute he snapped at me, the next he smiled. Prescription medication was in order.

He wasn't in any of my other classes. Only English. I made it through the morning's classes, and found myself standing at the classroom door again. He was sitting in the same spot as the day before when I slid in next to him. He was wearing black again. He always seemed to wear dark clothes. Maybe I would buy him a white shirt for a present if he passed this class.

"Hello, Nikki." He turned and gave me the full effect of his golden eyes.

"Hi," I tried not to stare at him, so I looked down at my open book in front of me.

"I wanted to apologize for my attitude yesterday. I know it's not your fault we got paired up together for this class."

Well, that was rude. Medication wasn't going to fix that.

"If you'd rather pair up with someone else, I'm sure we can get Ms. Barker to switch us around," I said as I tried to keep my temper in check. I took a deep breath and looked up at him.

The air had warmed again, but instead of being uncomfortable, this time it circled us like a warm breeze.

"No, that's not what I meant at all." He frowned, as if he was trying to decide how to say what he meant without getting into bigger trouble. He started again, "I meant that I just don't like this class, and that I had no place getting angry at you. For that, I am sorry."

The air started sparking.

"This place needs to get their ventilation system checked out. Maybe their heat pump has gone bad," I mumbled, moving my pencils in a neat line above my book.

Adam frowned for a second, causing the little frown mark to dent between his brows. He must have taken my rambling as an acceptance of his apology. "So Brian is teaching you how to drive."

"Yeah, he's trying. I keep forgetting the clutch and then I kill the blasted thing."

"I saw you. You did a good job. It'll get easier, I promise," he whispered as Ms. Barker called the class to order.

Weird coincidence, my brain told me, as I fumbled with my book to get to the right spot. Maybe I was the one needing medication.

As we went out the door at the end of class, I remembered I hadn't asked directions to his house. I turned around only to plow straight into him. His hands came out to steady me. I put a hand out to catch myself and it landed against his chest. We both stood as if we had frozen together. His hands were on either side of my waist and I felt his heart hammer hard and quick beneath my palm. I looked up to see him staring down at me in awe. His face was only inches from mine. I took in his high cheekbones and his long straight nose. He had the slightest cleft in his chin that I hadn't noticed before. I felt his breath catch as my eyes slid back up to his. His eye seemed so warm.

I jumped when I heard someone clear their throat behind me.

"Mind if I cut in, Adam?" Brian's voice was cold.

Yes, an angry voice whispered in my head.

Adam looked over at Brian and dropped his hands from my waist. "Sure, no problem. Did you forget something, Nikki? You were heading back in the room."

"No, I was just going to ask how to get to your house to study later," I said as I felt the blood rush back up to my cheeks.

"I know where he lives. I'll get you there." Brian's blue eyes flashed and the muscles in his jaw clenched.

"I have a better idea," Adam said, "I'll just come over to your house. That way you don't have to worry about holding Brian up until we get finished."

"I don't mind," Brian interjected as he gave Adam a cold stare.

I put a hand on Brian's arm and smiled up at him in an effort to diffuse the situation, "I know you don't mind, but you're already stuck with me playing chauffeur twice a day now. Besides, if I'm home I can keep an eye on Emily if Mom needs to go out."

Adam smiled. "Okay, it's settled. I'll come to your house."

"I live right past Brian."

"Don't worry, I know where you live," he said over his shoulder as he walked away from us.

I've found you before, the whisper echoed in my mind.

Brian frowned as Adam walked away, as if he didn't like the idea of my spending time with Adam alone. I had to hand it to him. If I had seen what he had seen a few minutes ago, I might be thinking the same way.

He affirmed my suspicion when he said, "Maybe it's not such a good idea. You did say you saw him outside your window. If you want I can come hang out while you help him. It wouldn't be a problem. Mom's working late today, so I'll stop by the house and leave her a note in case she makes it home before me."

"No, I'll be fine, honest. You just drop me off at the house and then go home and get your nerves ready for tomorrow's driving lesson. You'll need your rest. I may make it into fourth gear tomorrow morning!" I laced my arm through his and grinned up at him.

"Are you sure? I don't mind to come up."

"I'm sure." I smiled and tried to change the subject, "So I wonder what they've got to eat for lunch today?"

He laughed. "That wasn't very subtle, but I'll let you off the hook if you promise you'll call me if you need me."

"I promise."

John and Beth were sitting at the same table as we got our plates and came over to sit with them. The table across the room was empty. I felt panicked, though I didn't know why.

Beth looked over at me and smiled. "They go back to the reservation at noon, two or three times a week to learn their 'traditional' stuff. Penny explained it to me last year when I did an article for the paper. It's part of how they keep their tradition alive."

"I'm surprised they talked to you. I didn't think they would like outsiders."

"Quite the opposite. They are a very proud people and they like to share their way of life with others. They like to teach, you'll see. I overheard Mrs. Graham say that we'll be going over to the reservation soon for a field trip. I'll have to get ready to write the article for that, although it should be the same as it is every year." She frowned as if thinking of different ways to describe the same thing that happened year after year was going to be a challenge.

"Speaking of articles," I said, "thanks for not putting me in one."

"Don't get too comfortable. The only reason you're not is that I know that now you're part of the squad and something better to write in the next few days may pop up. I've seen Tiffany give you some evil looks today. I'd watch out if I were you."

"You could take Tiffany, hands down." Brian grinned at me, and then he added, "but all kidding aside, you may want to watch your back where Tiffany is concerned. She's sneaky, so keep your eyes open."

I sat there staring down at my half-eaten burger and wondered what on earth I had gotten myself into. I now had an arch-enemy and it was only the second day of school.

The rest of the day went by at a snail's pace. I realized that I was looking forward to seeing Adam after school. I kept replaying the moment outside the door of English class. Thankfully, none of the teachers called on me to volunteer any answers even though a couple of them looked at me as though they suspected my mind was elsewhere.

The bell rang and Brian drove us home. He hesitated when I thanked him and jumped out of the truck. I leaned back in to grab my book bag.

"You're sure you don't want me to stay?" he asked in a worried tone.

"Yep, I'm sure. I will be okay."

"Promise me again. You'll call if you need me, right?" he asked, catching my hand. "I can be up here in just a minute, you know."

"I promise. You worry too much."

"I don't think so," he muttered. "I'll see you in the morning."

Reluctant, he turned loose of my hand and put the car in gear, leaving me to stand and watch him drive down the road. I shook my head. I could take care of myself. After all, it was only Adam.

Mom had left me a note to say that she and Emily had gone out shopping for paint for the house and that they would stop and grab a pizza on the way home. I went upstairs to tidy up my room. I caught my reflection as I went by a window and decided I was the one who needed tidying up. I went into the bathroom to inspect my reflection.

My hair was doing its usual chaotic blonde frenzy around my head. I turned on the water, using my fingers to flick little drops of water in my hair to tame down the flyway curls. I gathered the mass up and pulled it through a scrunchie at the base of my neck. It was as good as it was going to get, I decided. I shrugged and went back outside to see what the construction workers had fixed that day.

On the porch, I noticed a new window that looked better than the previous one that had sported the duct tape. I walked around the side of the house, inspecting all the little changes. I smiled at the thought of the paint that my mother was bringing home.

"It's looking good." Adam stood next to me, looking at the house. His thumbs were tucked in the pockets of his jeans as if he had been standing there for hours.

"I didn't hear you drive up."

"You wouldn't have. I walked."

"You walked? Isn't the reservation a couple of miles from here?"

"It is," he grinned.

"Did you walk down the road or come through the forest?" I asked, interested in the location of his arrival.

"The forest, of course," he nodded toward the little path I had discovered earlier.

You didn't think I was going to walk past Brian's house, did you?

He was frowning. The small wrinkle formed between his brows. He saw me looking at him and his face went blank.

"So, did you bring your book?"

"No."

"That's fine. We can use mine," I said, trying not to stare in his eyes again. "Let's go inside and get started."

We went upstairs to my bedroom so I could grab my textbook. Adam looked at the chair that I had placed in front of the window. A small smile twitched on his face.

"You like watching the woods." It seemed more of a comment than a question.

"Yes."

"I didn't think I would like you when I saw you the first time." His voice was a barely audible whisper. He turned back to stare at me again.

The air was getting warmer again, hugging me in a warm heat. I walked over to the window and tried to tug it open. It stuck after a couple inches, leaving me to yank on it with all my strength.

I felt him before I heard him. Adam's arms circled around me as he put one hand on either side of mine. "Here, let me help."

The window slid open. A cool breeze hit me full in the face and I took a step back. His chest was solid against me and I could feel his sharp intake of breath as soon as I touched him. It startled me enough that I tried to turn and take a step back toward the window at the same time. I toppled backward and once again his arms were there catching me, steadying me back on my feet. I flushed, feeling like an idiot. A warm hand came up to push back an errant curl that sprang free to spiral next to my cheek.

"Okay, English," I said, ducking around Adam to grab my textbook off the bed. I held it in front of me like a shield.

"Okay, English," he repeated, smiling.

I sat down cross-legged on the top of the bed and pointed, indicating I wanted him to sit, too. I opened the textbook as he sat down. Then I put on my best teacher face.

"I think we should start at the beginning," I said, giving him my most serious look.

He smiled at me. "That sounds like a good idea."

"Nouns," I started. "What are they?"

He shrugged, and stared at me, waiting for me to answer my own question.

"Nouns are the subject of the sentence," I explained, "for example, if I were to say, 'the tree is green,' then *tree* would be the noun."

He frowned, and then nodded. The little wrinkle of concentration was back again, crinkling between his eyes as I gave him another sentence and he tried to guess the right noun. I found myself staring into his eyes again, getting lost in their depths. He cleared his throat and I found him staring back at me.

"Well?" he asked.

"Well, what?"

"I asked if that was the right word."

I looked back down at the book, trying to find the sentence I had given him, "Yes, that's it."

I concentrated back to the task at hand and gave him more sentences. I started with the easier ones, then made them harder, as he guessed every one of them right. I stared down into the book, searching for the hardest ones, when I felt him reach up and pull my scrunchie free. My hair cascaded around my shoulders and down my back.

"You are beautiful," he whispered. He gave me a shy smile as I looked up at him, "*You* would be the noun."

"Um, yes. I mean no," I stammered, then looked at the floor. "That's a pronoun." My face started to flush, and I started to feel the air begin to snap around us again, even though the breeze still blew through the window.

I heard a car pull up and hopped up off the bed to look out the window.

He was still smiling at me when I turned around. "That's my mom and my sister. Let's take a break and go downstairs."

He nodded and followed me down the staircase.

"Hi, Nikki," Mom said as I came around the corner of the kitchen. "I didn't think you would be home yet. Didn't you have a study date?" She stopped and smiled as she saw Adam come into view, "Hello."

"Mom, this is Adam," I introduced him.

"It's nice to meet you, Adam. I'm sorry the house is such a mess. I thought Nikki was going over to study at your house, or I would have cleaned up more."

"That's okay, Mrs. Harmon. We thought it would be easier if I came here instead, so Brian wouldn't have to wait and Nikki wouldn't be rushed," he explained.

Emily came from outside and into the kitchen in her usual full speed, not seeing Adam by the door. He must have heard her coming, and stepped ever so slightly to the side to keep her from running full into him. She stopped in front of him and her eyes widened.

"You're a real Indian," she whispered in awe.

He grinned at her. "Yes, I am."

"Wow." Emily's face flushed in excitement. "Did you come from the woods? You know, Nikki thought she saw someone outside her window the first day we were here."

His smile froze for a second, and then warmed up again. "Yes, I came through the woods. You will have to come visit us sometime. I hear that the school is bringing everyone on a field trip soon."

"I know. I can't wait," she beamed at him.

"Emily, you need to go up and get started on your homework. You can talk to Adam later. Here, take some pizza up with you." Mom herded Emily to the door, and handed her a paper plate.

"'Bye, Adam." Emily waved around our mother's legs.

"'Bye, Emily," he grinned at her.

As she left, Mom turned around and smiled. "Sorry about that. She's your typical six year-old. She would have pestered you the whole time you were here. I didn't see your car outside. Do you need us to give you a ride back?"

"No, ma'am. I'll be okay. I'm used to walking. It won't take long to make it back home."

"Make sure you're careful when you head back. I think they're calling for rain tonight." She smiled at him and then turned to me. "I saw Anita today. She was telling me about Brian's scheme to get you into driving."

I snorted. "Yeah, it's a scheme."

"Well? How did it go?" she prodded.

"Ok." I shrugged.

"Once you get the hang of it, we'll have to find you a decent car. I think Brian is sweet to be taking you to school every day, but I'm sure you would like a little freedom of your own. Now, you guys grab some pizza and go study." She stuck half of the pizza on a plate and shooed us out of the kitchen.

Back upstairs, I nibbled on a slice as I looked through the book. Adam scarfed down two pieces, one after another, as he peered over my shoulder to see what I had planned for him next.

"No cheating." I pushed his face back over my shoulder.

We worked until dusk. Loose sheets of notebook paper covered the bed with our notes. It would be dark soon. I stretched and rubbed the crick I had gotten in my neck.

"I think we've made quite a bit of progress today."

"I think so, too. Thank you for helping me. I couldn't have done it without you," Adam said. His eyes narrowed an instant later.

I heard the phone ring and my mother answer it, though I couldn't hear what she said.

"Brian is calling to check to see if I have smudged your reputation," he said dryly.

"Nikki, phone. It's Brian," Mom called up the stairs.

I groaned as Adam smirked at me.

"Tell him I'll call him back in a few minutes," I yelled back to her.

"I need to go," Adam stood, and then walked towards the door. "Thank you again for the help."

"Wait. Hold on." I jumped up from the bed, trying to pull my shoes on, half-running, half-stumbling, as I tried to catch up with him. "I'll walk out with you."

"You should call Brian back. I know the way out." His amber eyes seemed to flame with contained rage.

I looked up at him, perplexed. I didn't know what I had done to bring this sudden tirade on, so I said, "I would like to walk you out, if that's okay with you. I will call him back later. He can wait."

He snorted. "You'd better not make him wait for too long, I can hear him pacing all the way up here. He's trying to decide whether to come up or not."

"How do you know that?"

"Lucky guess. It's what I would do," he shrugged, and then gave me a small, reluctant smile. "Come on then. Walk me out."

Once we were outside, I didn't realize that I was leading us to the path that I had found at the edge of the woods.

"We could drive you home," I said, looking at the shadows that lurked a few feet beyond us. "You're not going to make it home before it gets dark. It could be dangerous in there." I stared at the ominous darkness that seeped toward us.

He laughed. It was a short quick burst that lit up his face. "You're worried about *me*?"

"Yes."

"I know this forest better than anyone. I'll be home before full dark and I'll be fine. I'm not Little Red Riding Hood, you know," he grinned. His eyes gleamed with humor at some joke that he only knew.

"Are you sure?"

"Yes." He reached out and gently touched my cheek. "Good night, Nikki." He turned and walked into the woods out of sight. The darkness enveloped him.

"'Goodnight," I whispered into the dark, empty stillness.

I walked back to the house and found Mom sitting in the living room. She grinned at me and tossed the cordless phone into my hand. "Good luck. You're going to need it."

"Thanks," I muttered as I took the phone upstairs with me.

I flipped to the back of my binder where Brian had sketched his number in bold numbers with a big smiley face in place of the zeroes. I dialed and waited for him to pick up. It didn't make it through the first ring when I heard him pick up.

"Well?" he demanded.

"Well, hello to you, too."

"Hello. I've been waiting for forever. What happened?"

"We learned nouns." I yawned into the phone, trying to sound bored.

"Oh." He seemed mollified. "Well, when is he coming over again?"

"I don't know, Brian. We didn't get around to setting another one up. You called, so he went home and I called you back."

"Oh. I'm sorry." He didn't sound sorry at all. In fact, he seemed to like the idea that he had made Adam go home.

I grinned, trying to keep the amusement out of my voice, "Not a problem. So are you picking me up early again in the morning?"

"You bet. It's your turn to drive again, you know."

"Yeah, don't remind me," I groaned. "Listen, I'll see you in the morning. I think I'm going to head to bed early tonight."

He laughed. "Okay, good night, Nikki."

"'Night, Brian."

As soon as I clicked the phone off, it rang. "Hello?"

"Hey, it's me again," Brian said. "I'm sorry, but I forgot to ask you something. There's a group of us going to hike up on the Appalachian Trail this weekend, would you like to go with me?"

That sounded like a date, I thought.

As if he had read my mind, he continued, "Just as friends, I promise."

"Sure, it sounds like fun."

"Okay, great." There was a smile that came through the receiver in those words. "I'll see you in the morning."

The phone clicked off again. As I set it down, I wondered when the next call would come that ended up being a date. Even though he had promised to stay as friends, something told me that he wouldn't want it to stay that way much longer.

FOUR

I HAD A plan. I'd spent half the night thinking about it. If there was a group of us hiking, who was to say I couldn't invite more people? There was only one person that I wanted to see.

"Hi, Adam." I smiled, as he slid in the seat beside me. English class was almost ready to start, so I had to hurry.

"Hi," he answered. He seemed preoccupied. This could be harder than I thought.

His long black hair was pulled back into a tight braid that ran down his back, leaving his face open. The lines of his jaw and cheekbones were more pronounced. So far, he seemed to be trying to ignore me, looking around everywhere but at me.

"So, there are some of us going on a hike up the Appalachian trail this weekend," I began. I stopped when he turned and pinned me with his piercing eyes. I took a breath and went on, "I was wondering if you were going."

His eyes never wavered from mine as I watched different emotions well beneath their surface. Then, his face became guarded again.

"It isn't safe," he said and turned away.

So much for my big plan, I thought, as Ms. Barker came in and started the class.

"Okay guys. You've had a couple days to get in your first study date. I want to see if you know the basics. We're going to start at the beginning. I'm going to write a sentence on the board. I want a volunteer to tell me what the pronoun is." she walked over and wrote on the chalkboard, then turned and asked, "Who wants to volunteer?"

No one spoke up; everyone's eyes flitted back and forth, as if they hoped they wouldn't be called on.

"Come on, people. It's only a sentence. It won't hurt you."

I almost fell over when I felt a hand come up from beside me. I turned and looked at Adam, who gave me a small grin.

Let's see if I learned anything, a voice whispered in my head.

"Yes, Adam," Ms. Barker said, "thank you for volunteering. What is the pronoun?" She pointed up to the black board where she had written *You should have studied* in bold letters.

"You," he said quietly. "'You' is the pronoun."

"Wonderful."

As she turned back to her board, Adam whispered under his breath, "I guess I learned something yesterday evening." His eyes sparkled with mischief.

At the end of class, he shocked me by reaching over and taking my books from me. He shrugged, smiling. "I'm heading towards the lockers, too. Let me take them."

I walked beside him to the lockers, unsure of what to say until we reached them.

"Thanks," I said taking my books back and putting them in the locker.

Adam leaned against the lockers. "You need to be careful in the woods when you go on that hike. Stay with the others and don't separate. I'll try to make it, but I don't know if I'll be able to. If I don't go, promise me you'll stick close to Brian. He'll look out for you." He waited as I stared at him, and then gave me a rueful smile. "Yeah, I know. I may not like him, but I know he won't let you out of his sight. So, promise?"

"Okay," I wasn't sure how the conversation had gone this way. One minute he didn't want to look at me and the next he was worried about me.

He smiled and walked off as Brian came running.

"Sorry, Nikki. Class went over and I couldn't make it in time over to yours," Brian huffed.

"It's okay, I know my way around now."

"What did *he* want?" He jerked a thumb over his shoulder at Adam's retreating back.

"He just wanted to tell us to be careful and stick together if we went on a hike this weekend."

"Is he coming, too?" He grimaced.

"No, I don't think so."

With Brian in much better spirits, we went to the cafeteria and sat at our usual table. I set my tray between Ronnie and the wall, forcing Brian take the seat next to Beth. The guys at the table across the room were deep in conversation, sending occasional glances my way. Ed and Erik both waved and smiled when they saw me looking back at them. There was one girl I hadn't seen before. She didn't look very happy with whatever the conversation was about.

"That's Hannah," Ronnie whispered to me. "She tries to hang all over Adam. I don't know what they're talking about over there, but she's giving you some pretty bad looks. Looks like she's jealous."

She's not the only one, I thought, as I caught the look on Brian's face. His blue eyes seemed to be shooting darts at Adam.

Adam got up and walked toward us. He stopped and smiled down at me. "Nikki, I was wondering if you would eat lunch with me today."

"S-sure," I mumbled as I picked up my tray and followed him back over to his table.

Hannah stood up and took her tray, dumping its contents in the trash as she left, her long hair swinging wildly behind her. Everyone else at the table seemed oblivious to her and smiled at me as if my eating lunch with them happened all the time. Chairs scooted around the table, as they made room for me to sit next to Adam.

Erik gave me his usual huge grin. "Hey, Nikki."

Leave it to you to be the icebreaker, I thought as I smiled back. "Hey, Erik."

The other two boys I hadn't met smiled as Adam introduced them as Michael and Tommy. They were cousins. They could have been twins, I realized, as I looked into two very similar faces. Each had a dimple on their left cheek when they smiled. They were younger than Ed, Erik, and Penny by a year or two, which made them sophomores. That was the reason why I hadn't seen them in any of my classes. Next to the others, the cousins looked younger and smaller. Even more so since they sat next to Ed, who was taller than Adam by an inch or so.

"When are you available for another English lesson?" Adam asked me.

"Whenever you want."

"He needs all the help he can get," Erik teased, "He is available tomorrow evening. If you want, I can take you over after school."

"If she wants to go, I'll take her." Adam shot him a look, but Erik only grinned wider.

"I can get a ride. It's not a problem," I said, trying to calm the tide of testosterone that seemed to be rising.

Ignoring Adam, Erik turned to me. "I've seen you driving Brian's old jalopy. When are you going to get your own wheels?"

"Whenever I can find a cheap car," I assured him. Soon wouldn't be soon enough.

"I talked my mother into letting me get rid of my old car. It isn't much, but if you're interested, I'll make you a great deal on it."

"Yeah, he'd rather ride around on his bike. If you bought the car, I could tell you where the money would go, straight into parts for the 'cycle," Ed snorted, as if the idea of getting rid of a perfectly good car to ride a motorcycle was insane.

"He's just jealous," Erik said. Then shot a grin at Ed. "Don't worry, buddy. I'll still give you a ride to school when Adam's Jeep is too full."

Ed turned up his nose. "You couldn't pay me to ride on that deathtrap. If the Jeep's full, I'll either stay home or hitchhike."

I laughed. "How about call and ask a neighbor for a ride? If I buy Erik's car, I'll have extra room."

Ed puffed out his chest and grinned at Erik. "She offered to give me a ride."

Erik feigned disappointment. "But I did, too." He tried to frown, but the sides of his mouth kept quirking up. He gave up and grinned.

Adam had been quiet, listening to the banter between the two. He leaned toward me. "So, are we on for tomorrow after school? You can ride with us. We have room regardless of what these two idiots say. I'll make sure you get home before dark."

"Sure, that's fine, unless you'd rather study tonight," I offered.

"I can't tonight," he said without explanation, then stared straight ahead.

"We have a missing hiker on the trail," Erik explained. "Whenever one of them goes missing, we scout out the woods and try to help find them. Adam's dad is the sheriff so he lets us know when someone goes missing. We help search. The national forest runs from here all the way up to Roanoke so it's a lot of territory for the police to cover. They appreciate all the help they can get. Since the forest wraps right around the Res, we help whenever we can."

"Oh, I hope you find him safe."

"Her," Adam whispered. "It's a her. A young woman in her early twenties. When she didn't make it to her checkpoint yesterday, her parents reported her missing. She had made it this far because the store clerks remember her from where she had bought supplies in town a couple of weeks ago."

"The trail killer," Ed mumbled under his breath.

"We don't know that," Adam's voice was sharp. "She could just be lost, and if she is, we'll find her."

"The trail killer?" I asked, "Who's the trail killer?"

"No one knows," Ed shrugged. "Its pure speculation that there's a killer at all. In this area, over the last five years, a number of young women have been reported missing from the Appalachian Trail and have never been found. It was as if they just disappeared into thin air. Only their gear is found, always by the trail. Of course, there would be a small chance that they saw something they wanted to check out and then just wandered off and got lost. But without their gear? No way."

"They never found any of them?" I asked as cold chills ran down my arms.

"No," Adam whispered.

Now do you understand why I don't want you in the woods alone? the voice whispered as Adam's eyes seemed to stare into me, their onyx specks shining dark against the gold.

"I understand," I said. He looked shocked for a second and then a smile tugged at his mouth.

The bell rang and the usual rush of confusion ensued. The boy behind me shoved his chair into the back of mine, sending me into the table. Adam caught the back of my chair and stopped it just as I was about to be pinned.

"Are you okay?" he asked, as he glared at the back of the boy who was heading toward the trash can.

"Yeah, thanks," I mumbled, getting up from the chair he still held.

An arm came down to help pull me up from the chair. "Are you all right?" Brian asked.

"Yeah, Adam kept me from getting smashed."

He nodded at Adam. "Thanks."

Adam gave a slight nod in return as Brian picked up my tray with his free hand.

"Good luck tonight, I hope you find her," I called over my shoulder as we walked toward the door.

After school, much to Brian's delight, I offered to drive us back home. I managed to get us back to my house in one piece without killing the engine even once. After waving to Brian, I did a little dance through the front door, happy that I had done so well. Mom grinned at my enthusiasm.

"Good day? I don't think I've ever seen that dance before," she teased.

"Great day. I'm getting the hang of driving Brian's truck." I leaned in and kissed her on her cheek.

"That's wonderful, honey. We'll have to look into getting you a car. Whenever you want to go take the test for your driver's license, just let me know."

"One of the guys from the reservation is selling his car. I have to go over tomorrow after school and help Adam study so I thought I'd check it out. I've got money saved up and I don't think he wants much for it. Whatever day you don't have to work late and aren't busy, I'll be ready for the driving test."

"I have dayshift all the rest of this week. I should be home whenever you get here after school. Whenever you're ready, I'll be here."

"Okay," I nodded and sat down beside her, "How was work?"

"Adam's father is the sheriff so he's in charge. He's very nice. And there are two other deputies besides Anita, so there aren't many people there, but everyone is patient and helpful. I think I will like working there."

"Adam was telling me about the woman that's missing from the trail. Have they found her yet?" I asked.

"No, not yet. They're still looking. It seems she had a spat with her boyfriend a couple weeks ago, so they're trying to find him to see if he knows anything," she broke off, as the phone rang. She got up to answer it in the kitchen.

I thought about Adam and the other guys searching the woods looking for the lost woman as I went upstairs. I sat down and stared out to the woods, imagining the group of boys scouring the forest.

A sudden flash blinded me. When I opened my eyes, trees were flying past me as I ran.

There were wolves around me. One gray, one cream, and two a sable brown. The brown wolves weren't as muscular, yet they moved with the same fluid grace as the others. I led them on the trail. They sniffed the air around them, their nostrils flaring as they searched for a scent. I looked at the trees around us. The woods were silent. The birds had quieted. Six giant wolves slowed down to a walk as they searched.

The cream colored wolf reared back his head, and let out a mournful howl that was full of sorrow and anguish. He sat back on his haunches and stared at something in front of him as the rest rushed over to see what he had found.

I came up beside them and saw what caused him to cry out. A hiker's backpack, in a dark green color, was lying against a tree. I looked closer where one of the carrying straps had a name scrawled into the worn leather...Meghan. Two aluminum walking sticks laid beside it. I bent down and sniffed the end of one. I breathed in a sweet, copper smell. I snorted, trying to shove the scent back out of my nostrils, as my eyes registered the sticky, dark red stain. It was blood.

We would never find her, he had found her first. I set back on my haunches and howled, my mournful cry echoed in the air as my brothers joined me in my anguished song.

I blinked back out at the trees through my window, shaking my head to clear it. Cold chills swept up my spine as I heard a pack of wolves howl in the distance. The sun had set as I sat there daydreaming. I got up from the chair and changed into my pajamas. Leaving the window open, I crawled into bed as a soft breeze played on my face. I lay there in the dreamy place between sleep and awake, wondering if Adam had found the girl or if the wolves had.

THE MOON CALLED to him. It stirred his blood, waking him from a peaceful sleep. Even stronger than the pull of the moon, was that of the wolves. He could hear them in the distance as they searched. He listened to their quick footfalls. They were running, trying to save the missing girl. He walked along the edge of the forest as he fought the urge to join them. His skin felt as if a thousand tiny electric currents were running through it. The moon beckoned to him. He fought back the growl that tried to rise from deep inside his belly. Something furred slid against his bones, as if searching for a way out. He fought it, thinking it was simply a matter of will to keep himself whole. He felt the graze of teeth and the slash of claws. The creature snarled inside of him. It was frustrated, becoming angrier and more determined to get out as it charged against him, as if his very body were a cage to be escaped.

The force of the blow threw him to the ground. A single howl split the night air, giving the creature more strength. It forced him to submit. He watched in horror as the fur flowed over his body and changed into the nightmare from which he hoped to wake. He heard the wolves' cries as they sang their sorrowful song to the moon. Somehow, he knew they called to him. They were waiting for him.

The animal wanted to join them, to answer their call. The boy trapped inside the creature cried as despair washed over him. He threw back his head and howled, cursing the moon. He didn't want to be a monster. He only wanted her, and now he knew he would never have her. He ran, faster than his human legs had ever carried him, as he tried to outrun the anger that built inside him and the rage that pushed him farther and farther.

FIVE

I TRIED TO look cheerful as I looked at Brian's bloodshot eyes. "Good morning."

"Morning," he mumbled as he buckled his seatbelt, then pulled the hood of his jacket up, covering part of his face.

He must be cold, I thought as I reached over and flipped on the truck's heater. "Did you hear the wolves last night?"

I saw the edge of his eye narrow. "No."

"Oh. I figured you might have heard them. There must have been a pack of them out there howling last night. I lay in bed and listened to them most of the night."

"I didn't hear anything," he said in a hushed whisper.

I shrugged and started up the truck. If he didn't want to talk, I wasn't going to make him. We traveled in silence all the way to the school and I pulled in our usual spot without any problems.

"Good job. If you don't mind, I'm going to let you take yourself to your classes today. I'm not feeling well. I may leave early and go back home. If I do, I'll call Mom at the police station and tell her to let your mom know you need a ride home."

"Are you okay?"

"Yeah. I just didn't sleep well."

"Don't worry about me. If you need to go home, I'll be fine. I'm supposed to go over to the reservation to help Adam with his English after school. He's already offered to drive me," I reassured him as I reached over to squeeze his hand. "Just get better, okay?"

"Sure." He got out of the truck and walked into the school without waiting for me.

Adam was in his usual spot against his Jeep. The rest of the guys were waiting with him today. I started to walk past them, but one look into his eyes froze me in my tracks. His eyes looked older somehow. I noticed the rest of the guys had the same look to them, too. Even Erik's usual smile was gone today, but Ed looked the worst of them all.

"You didn't find her," I whispered. "You didn't find Meghan."

I saw the answer in his face before he shook his head. "No, only her gear."

We all walked into school together in silence. The day went by slowly. Adam didn't speak as I slid in next to him for class, he only gave me a sad smile. He followed me afterwards to the cafeteria and stood behind me in line.

I looked over and saw John and Ronnie sitting at their table. Beth and Brian were nowhere to be seen. I figured Brian had gone home to rest and that Beth was probably digging up a story somewhere. John and Ronnie were snuggled up next to each other, looking cozy.

Adam leaned forward, whispering into my hair, "Come sit with me today, I could use some cheering up."

I followed him over to their table, and sat down next to him. All the guys had two plates of food each, piled full. They seemed to be shoving food in their mouths as quick as possible, though they didn't seem to be tasting any of it.

"So did you find anything else other than her gear?" I asked Adam, who seemed to be eating with even less enthusiasm than the others.

He swallowed hard. "Her walking sticks—and some blood."

"Was the blood hers?"

"The police think so. They are sending it off for testing to make sure," Ed's voice was grave.

The table fell silent again.

Adam stopped eating, and sat back, staring into space. The look on his face seemed to call out to me. I reached under the table and took his hand without thinking. His warm fingers entwined with mine, and the air warmed around us like a big hug. We sat in silence as everyone else finished eating and the bell rang. When we stood together, our hands were still together. Adam noticed it and dropped my hand. A warm flush crept up the side of his neck.

I thought we hadn't been noticed until I walked over to the trash with my tray and happened to catch Ronnie staring at me with wide eyes.

Hold on a second, Adam's voice seemed to whisper to me from across the room.

He dumped his plate in the trash and walked over to me. "I'll walk you to your next class."

His hand found mine this time and he seemed oblivious to the openmouthed stares that seemed to come from every direction as we walked down the hall. He stopped at the art class' door and gave my hand a slow squeeze as he released it.

"Thank you for letting me walk you and for cheering me up," he smiled.

"No problem," my voice came out in a squeak.

"Are we still on for our study date? I saw Brian leaving earlier. My offer of a ride to the reservation still stands. Hannah didn't ride with us today so we have plenty of room."

"That sounds good," I said, my voice stronger. "I'll meet you outside after school."

"Okay." His amber eyes sparkled as he turned and walked back down the hall.

Ed and Erik had kept a respectable distance behind us. Once Adam passed, they walked up to me and smiled. We all went in together and sat in the back of the class.

Ms. Hayton came in and started the class. She told us to pick up a pencil and start doodling. As I started sketching a pair of eyes in the corner of my paper, I thought of Adam. My mind turned to the daydream that I had of the wolves that searched for the lost girl. I drew the backpack lying against an old gnarled tree. Then I filled in the walking sticks, setting them in the spots where I had seen them. Then I began drawing the side profile of the cream-colored wolf I had seen. I wasn't paying any attention to the paper or my drawing, I concentrated on what my memory held. My own mind seemed lost within itself as it replayed over and over, hearing the wolf's sad cry as he threw his head back to howl at the moon.

"That's very interesting, Miss Harmon. It's very unique." I was shaken back into reality by Ms. Hayton's voice as she walked past.

I looked over at Erik, who had turned to look at my drawing. His mouth dropped open and he stared at me in astonishment. I looked back down at my sketchpad. I had drawn the scene out of my daydream. I caught the deep shadows in the trees beyond the wolves with the moon full and round above them. *Meghan* was scrawled in a feminine hand on one of the straps of the backpack. I looked down at a very realistic looking wolf with his head leaned back, his eyes shut as he bayed at the full moon which hid amongst the treetops. Beneath the wolf, I had written *Hidden Moon*. The things that looked out of place were the pair of muddy brown eyes that sort of looked like my own, farther up the path, which seemed to stare down at the wolf.

Erik seemed to be trying to get Ed's attention when the bell rang. I flipped the pad shut and put it inside my binder. I got up and started for the door, leaving a still wide-eyed Erik and confused-looking Ed in the room.

I ran down the hall toward the lockers and smashed into Adam as soon as I rounded the corner.

"Hey," he said, startled. "I was just coming to see if you would let me walk you to Phys Ed since that's my next class, too. We're sharing the gym today."

"Sure, I just need to stick this in here," I wheezed, breathless, as I opened my locker and shoved the binder as far back under all the other junk as I could make it go.

"What is it? Top secret?" Adam teased.

I frowned at him and slammed the door.

"Okay. Sorry," he said quickly, "Are you all right?"

"I'm fine." I closed my eyes and took a deep breath, then opened them and started to walk. "But we're going to be late."

"No, we won't. And even if we are, what will we have missed? A couple jumping jacks?" He snorted.

I smiled. It was nice to know I wasn't the only one who dreaded Phys Ed. But I was betting Adam didn't have to worry about jumping around in a little green and white outfit, while keeping an eye on Psycho Barbie.

Maybe I would get lucky and she wouldn't be there, I hoped as we walked in the gymnasium.

"It's about time." Tiffany scowled at me. "You're late. Didn't anyone tell you that we show up ten minutes early to warm up and stretch out?"

"No, you didn't," I replied as I walked past her. "And that would be *your* job, since you're the captain. So if anyone is to blame, it is you."

I heard Adam chuckle as he went over and joined the guys at the other end of the basketball court. Tiffany's face was turning the color of a boiled tomato as she tried to ignore me and turned to chastise the next girl that had come in after me. At least we weren't in our little uniforms today. Everyone was comfortable in their gym shorts.

"It's too bad we can't vote," Ronnie murmured beside me. "Ms. Jenkins, our coach, doesn't think there are any of us that are better than Tiffany. That's why she made her captain for the last two years."

"Things change," I muttered.

I noticed Beth up in the bleachers watching us. A little scrawny guy with thick glasses and a dark thatch of brown hair was with her. A big, clunky camera hung around his neck.

"She's got Bernie with her this time. She's hoping you show Tiffany up again—and I for one hope she's right."

A willowy woman with graying, blonde hair came up in front of our group. She smiled as she looked over her group for the year and took in the new faces. Her green eyes locked onto me.

She hasn't looked at anyone else that way, I thought, panic flaring up inside me as I returned her stare. I wonder what Tiffany told her about me.

She quit staring at me and smiled, clasping her hands behind her back as she walked back and forth in front of us.

"For those of you who haven't met me yet, I am Ms. Jenkins, your cheerleading coach. I see some new faces among us, so I know that some of you passed Tiffany's tryouts. I trust her judgment, and welcome you to our squad. However, please know that rules must be followed." She stopped in front of me and continued, "Many of our exercises depend on the cooperation of the entire team. Even the slightest change in one person's position, can injure someone else. So please work as a team, pay attention and follow directions."

She smiled at me. "Being as we have enough girls, I thought we would split you up in two groups and we'll work on pyramids today."

No problem, I thought, Ronnie will be the top of one. There are other girls smaller than me that will be the top for the other. She'll put me at the base.

She split us up, putting the shorter girls with Ronnie to be bases. I ended up with Tiffany and the taller girls in my group. I looked at the tall legs around me. This didn't look good. I was inches shorter than anyone else in this group.

"Nikki, you will be the top for the other group," Ms Jenkins smiled.

I groaned. I was going to have to trust the rest of these girls around me to keep me from hitting the ground, and there was one of them in particular that I didn't trust even when I was *on* the ground.

I stepped up on thighs and shoulders to get to the top of the pyramid, wobbling and trying not to hurt anyone on the way up. I could tell the rest of my group had done this many times before as they gave me tips on where to place my feet and how to stand. I made it up to stand on the top two girls' shoulders. I stood still trying not to breathe or move any kind of muscle. I saw the boys on the other end of the gym playing basketball. It looked like the reservation guys were playing against all the others and that they were winning.

They were fast, I realized, watching them run around the other boys, passing the ball back and forth. Every move they made seemed choreographed. When one turned to pass the ball, the other seemed to already know they were supposed to be there. They seemed to glide across the floor, making the other team look clumsy and slow. I noticed Adam was facing me the biggest part of the time, only turning his back when he had to. It looked as if, somehow, he was watching me, too.

Ms. Jenkins told us to get back down and start again. The object was for the pyramid to get up within a certain amount of time so that it fell in time with the music. I climbed up and down my little human mountain several times, getting more confident with each try.

"Wonderful," she clapped, pleased. "No one has gone up that many times without having some kind of difficulty. You're doing a wonderful job, just wonderful." She beamed up at me.

I tried to smile at her as I started back up again. I had made it halfway to where Tiffany was standing with her knee bent, waiting for me to go up again. I stepped up, and felt her shift, just the smallest bit, as she straightened her leg. I lost my footing and fell backward. Knowing I was falling fast, I relaxed my muscles and tumbled, rolling into myself as I hit the hard floor.

Wipe out, I thought, as I sat up to take note of any damage.

I realized I was surrounded, but not by the girls. Adam was crouched down beside me. He was flanked by the other four guys, who had made a tight circle around us. They all looked worried.

"You're bleeding," Adam told me, his nostrils flared as if he could smell it.

"Elbow," Erik frowned, looking at the back of my arm.

"Yeah, I guess I scraped it when I rolled." I turned my arm to see what he was looking at. I watched the blood that ran down toward my wrist.

"Is anything else hurt?" Adam asked, as his eyes still searched me.

"No, I don't think so."

"Okay, boys, move out of the way." Ms. Jenkins pushed at Michael, who was shoulder to shoulder with Tommy and seemed to be as unmovable and solid as a brick wall. Neither boy paid her any attention. She finally squeezed around them to get to my other side, "Oh dear, just when you were doing so well, too. We need to get that cleaned up."

"I'll take her to the nurse," Ronnie's voice came from behind my head as she ducked under Ed's arm.

"Thank you, Ronnie. Okay, boys, back to your side of the court, everything is fine. The rest of you girls, keep working," Ms Jenkins said in an effort to get everyone moving.

None of the boys acknowledged her. They stayed still until Adam gave them a barely perceptible nod. His eyes were still on me. As the others started back across the court, he helped me up to my feet.

"Are you sure you're okay?"

"Yeah, it's just a scrape. I'll meet you after school." I said as Ronnie started tugging my good arm.

"Come on. You're bleeding all over the floor."

I let her lead me out of the gym and toward the nurse's station.

"Those guys were fast. I don't think you had been on the ground but a half-second when they came over. I saw you fall and I swear they were like a blur. Then all of a sudden, they were surrounding you," she giggled. "I didn't think they were going to let Ms. Jenkins in to see about you."

"Yeah, that was kinda weird," I admitted.

"So are you and Adam an item?" she asked, taking me off guard. "He seems protective of you."

"N-no," I said, feeling my cheeks start to burn.

Ronnie laughed. "You don't sound so sure, Nikki."

"I'm not sure of anything right now. I'm not sure I'm cut out for this cheerleading thing." My elbow was starting to throb as it bled, leaving tiny splats of blood to follow us down the hall as if we were Hansel and Gretel with breadcrumbs.

"What are you talking about? You're a natural, you heard Ms. Jenkins. You did great until you lost your footing and fell."

We made it to the nurse, who cleaned up the scrape and put clean gauze around it. She put my other hand on top, told me to keep pressure on it and sit there until it quit bleeding. Then she told Ronnie to head back to class. Ronnie gave me a sympathetic smile and left.

I sat on the table in the sick room for the next twenty minutes, keeping the gauze on my arm. Various posters on the walls informed me that cleanliness depended upon me while others warned me of the dangers of STDs. I memorized every letter on the eye chart and thought I was about to go nuts with boredom, when the nurse came back to check on me. When she seemed satisfied that I wasn't going to leave a trail of blood all over the school, she let me go.

I had just opened the door when I saw Adam leaning against the wall across the hall, his arms folded across his chest as he stared at the door, as if standing guard.

"I thought you were supposed to be in class," I said, trying not to look happy to see him.

"After you fell, no one felt like playing ball anymore, so they dismissed us early. I was worried, so I came to wait for you." He shrugged, then touched my arm, inspecting the bandage. "I think we should go skin Tiffany for that little stunt she pulled. Does it hurt much?"

"It's getting sore, but I'll live. How did you know she did anything? I could have just gotten clumsy and fell."

"She moved her leg just as you stepped on it. And anyone that can fall on that hard floor and not get hurt worse than a scraped elbow, is not clumsy," he retorted. His golden eyes blazed as he swung his long hair back over his shoulder. "I saw her. She was jealous after the teacher gave you a compliment."

"How did you see and hear all of that? You were on the other side of the gym."

The fire in his eyes dampened, and he gave me a weak smile. "I pay attention. Let's go get your things and get out of here. I've had enough of this place for one day."

"But school isn't over yet, the bell hasn't..." I was cut off by the shrilling bell as Adam took my hand and pushed through the other students, leading me to the lockers and then out the door.

Ed, Michael and Tommy were standing around the Jeep. Penny was behind Erik on the motorcycle. Her arms were wrapped around his waist and her cheek rested against his shoulder. She smiled as she saw us walking hand in hand toward them.

"How's the arm?" she asked.

"It's okay." I smiled at her.

"Tiffany shouldn't be allowed to be on the squad, if she's going to act like that," Ed said, shooting a murderous glance at the back of a blonde ponytail that was getting into a little blue car near the front of the school.

"We saw her move, we know she's the reason you fell," Tommy informed me.

"All of you saw her move?"

The four dark heads in front of me nodded in unison, leaving me speechless.

"Let's go," Adam said, opening the passenger door for me. Ed, Michael and Tommy piled in the back, backpacks and books flew over the seat into the cargo space as everyone buckled in.

"You want to drive?" Adam offered, as he looked over at me and started up the Jeep.

"Huh-uh." I shook my head. "I'm happy where I am, thanks."

He grinned and we pulled out of the parking lot. A few minutes later, we pulled onto the gravel road leading us towards the reservation. We pulled up behind Erik's motorcycle in a driveway beside a little white house that sat beside the woods. Everyone piled out of the Jeep, splitting up in different directions to go home. Erik was leaning against the hood of an old blue Wrangler as he watched everyone go. He grinned as I looked in disbelief at the car.

"I thought we'd stop here first, and then go study at my house," Adam said. "I hope you don't mind."

"Not at all." I said, and then stared at Erik. "This isn't the old beat up car you're getting rid of."

"Yep, good ol' Bessie," Erik patted the hood, and then looked down to speak to the car. "Don't take it to heart, love. I never said you were beat up."

"You've got to be joking. That's a nice car."

"I know, but I can only drive one thing at a time, and the insurance on both the 'cycle and the car is pretty steep. I wouldn't dream of getting rid of the motorcycle, unless it was to get a better one, of course."

"Of course," I murmured as I took in the Jeep's flaking powder blue paint, the black rag top, and the big knobby tires.

"You wanna take her for a spin?"

"Sure."

He tossed me the keys and hopped into the backseat. Adam got into the passenger seat as I looked over the interior. It was clean and well-loved. A tie-die colored peace sign hung from the rearview mirror. I grinned as I looked at the cigarette lighter and saw where he had put a sticker with a slash over the cigarette lighter to suggest that he didn't allow smoking in his vehicle.

"Ok, so the heater knob sometimes sticks, you have to jiggle it a little. She burns a little oil, but not bad. I just check it once a week. I gave it a tune-up a couple of months ago, but I haven't driven much since the weather warmed up. The four wheel drive works great, so you shouldn't have any trouble getting out in winter." He frowned, trying to think of anything else important. "I think that's about it, start her up and let's go."

I turned the ignition, and was thankful that Brian had taught me to drive a manual transmission as I pushed down the clutch and put it in first gear. The Wrangler was easier to drive than the truck. It shifted smoothly as we went back out to the main road. I fell in love with the sound of the tires humming down the road. We went a couple miles and turned around to come back.

"What do you think?" Adam asked. I noticed he had been quiet during the entire exchange.

"It depends on the price, but I think I'm in love." I smiled as I tried not to get my hopes up.

"If you want it, I'll work with you," Erik promised, going into salesman mode. He came up with a low figure and watched my eyes widen in the rearview mirror.

"Are you sure?" I asked, "That doesn't seem like enough."

"It's enough. I got it for a good deal, so I'll give you a good deal on it, too. Maybe karma will work in my favor and I'll find the 'cycle parts I've been looking for cheap. She's all yours, if you want her."

"Deal. We can stop by the house and I'll get you the money."

"Don't worry about it today. Dad's got the title locked up so I'll have to wait until he gets home to get it. When you get back, I'll get my junk out of here and you can just drive it home tonight. We'll do the other stuff tomorrow," he said as I pulled back into his driveway. "Wait. That won't work. You can't drive it home by yourself. You haven't got your driver's license yet."

"I'll ride with her when she goes home if she wants to take it tonight," Adam offered, as we parked and got out.

"I want it," I said, giving Erik a huge hug.

"Easy, you'll make Adam jealous. Maybe Penny, too," he joked as he watched his girlfriend and another woman come out the front door.

"I told you, Penny. You can't leave him alone for a minute. Trouble finds him," the petite little woman said, her dark eyes sparkling.

"Mom, this is Nikki. She's buying the Wrangler," he said, sticking his head back in the vehicle to search the glove compartment. His voice came out muffled, "Nikki, that's my mom."

"Hi, I'm Jenna," she said as she held out her hand.

"Nice to meet you." I shook her hand.

"I hate to break this up, but if we're going to study…" Adam interrupted.

"Go ahead, I've got to get all of my stuff out of here." Erik's hand waved outside the car, shooing us away. "I'll be done before you're ready to go."

"Nice to meet you, Mrs.…."

"White Hawk, but just call me Jenna," she smiled as Adam led me back to his Jeep. "Come back anytime and visit, Nikki."

We pulled up in front of a house that sat close to the road. A basketball goal was attached to the back of a shed that served as a garage. Adam parked near it, then hopped out of the Jeep and came around to my side and opened the door.

"Dad must have had to work late," he murmured.

"Maybe they found a lead on the missing hikers," I said, trying to fill in the awkward silence with some kind of conversation.

"I hope, but I doubt it," he said as he took my books from me and led me to the porch.

He opened the front door and held it for me. "Come on in. I'm going to grab us something to drink, then we can go out on the back porch. I'll be right back."

"Okay." I looked at the pictures that lined a shelf in the living room.

Most of them were of Adam as a little kid. One of them was him with a man I guessed to be his father. A young Adam sat on a red bike with training wheels. His father looked just as happy as the little boy, and looked proud as he smiled down at his son.

I walked to the end of the shelf and found an older picture. His father looked younger in this picture and was hugging a very beautiful, very pregnant woman. A pair of brilliant amber eyes smiled up into the camera, a startling contrast against the mass of dark, long hair that hung over her shoulder.

"So there's where you got those eyes," I murmured.

"My mother," Adam said, startling me, as he came up behind me with two glasses in his hands.

"She is beautiful." I said, still looking at the picture.

"Yeah, she was. She died when I was born."

"I'm sorry," I said, trying to think of what else to say.

"It's okay. Erik and I have been best friends for as long as I can remember and Jenna is just like a mom to me. She's the closest thing I've ever had to one," he shrugged and gave me a small smile. "Let's go out on the porch. We need to get started. I promised I'd have you home by dark."

Once we studied, we walked back over to pick up the Jeep. True to his word, Erik had his things out of the Wrangler and made me promise if I had problems to bring it back and he'd either fix it or buy it back. I drove us back toward my house. I noticed Brian's truck was pulled in its usual spot, but the house was dark.

"He must be out with his mom," Adam said as he saw me staring at the house.

"Must be," I murmured, making a mental note to call and check on him when Adam went home.

Adam was frowning at the woods that ran along the road, a small wrinkle furrowed between his brows.

"What is it?" I said, slowing down.

"We're being watched," he said as he watched the tree line.

"By what?" I asked, straining to see what he saw.

"By whom," he corrected, using his newly-found knowledge of English grammar. "I don't know, but it feels like I should know. It feels…familiar."

I pulled in front of my house, parking next to Mom's car.

"Would you like to come in?" I asked.

"No, I need to get back. There's something I need to check on back at home."

"I can get Mom and we'll drive you back. If there's something in the woods you shouldn't go back that way."

"There are lots of things in these woods, but I'll be fine. Walk me out?"

We got out and walked towards the path. We reached the edge of the trees where he picked up my hand and brushed a light kiss against my knuckles.

"Thank you again for the study date," he whispered, then turned to walk into the shadows of the trees.

"You're welcome," I spoke to the empty place where he had stood.

I wish he would quit doing that, I thought, as I walked back to the front porch. He always seemed to melt right into the trees. One minute he was there, the next he was gone.

Mom was on the porch waiting for me when I made it there.

"Did Adam have car problems? We could have taken him home." She glanced at the blue Wrangler sitting next to her car.

"No, that's my car," I grinned. "He was just riding back over with me so I could bring it home. I told him we'd take him back, but he wanted to walk."

"Your car? It looks nice. I'm impressed." She smiled and then frowned. "He should have let us drive him back. I didn't like the sound of all that howling last night. I talked to Anita about it. She said she thought it was wolves. She said we'll hear them a lot, but that they've never bothered anyone."

"I'll give him a little time, and then I'll call over and make sure he got home. What about Brian?" I asked. "Did she say anything about him?"

"No. Should she have?"

"He left school today not feeling well. His car was home when we went by. I need to go call him." I ran into the house and grabbed the cordless phone, kicking off my shoes before I ran up the steps.

I curled up in my chair and dialed his number. I listened as it rang and rang. No one picked up.

Maybe they went into town for something, I hoped, as I sat gripping the phone in my hand as if it were a lifeline.

I sat there worrying about both Brian and Adam. One was sick; the other was in a forest that was full of wolves and other things that went bump in the night. I looked up at the clock. Adam had only been gone fifteen minutes. There was no way he had made it home yet. I jumped up, unable to sit still, and paced back and forth in front of the window.

I went down and grabbed the phone book off the kitchen table and started back upstairs, flipping the pages as I went. My fingers skipped through B's, until I found Black Water. There were two listings, one for an Evan Black Water, Sr, and one for an Evan Black Water, Jr. I picked the latter's number and poked it in the phone as I plopped back down in my chair. I knew he wasn't going to be there, but maybe I could leave a message with his dad to call me when he got home. The phone rang twice and then I heard someone pick up.

"Hello?" the voice answered.

"Hello, Mr. Black Water?" I asked, hoping I got the right number.

Laughter crackled over the phone into my ear.

"Well, sort of. But not the one you thought you were talking to," Adam sounded amused.

"Adam, how did you get home so fast? You haven't been gone twenty minutes," I asked, looking at the clock again to make sure I wasn't losing my mind.

"Oh, I know shortcuts. And I ran a little," he said, nonchalant.

He ran? He didn't even sound winded.

"Nikki, are you okay? Did something happen after I left?"

"Yes, I mean, I'm fine. Everything's okay. I was worried about you and wanted to make sure you got home safe."

"Oh," his voice came over the phone in a whisper. "I didn't mean to worry you. I'm sorry. I'm home and everything is okay."

"Did you see anything in the woods on your way back?"

"No, everything was quiet, which means something was there earlier. Promise me you won't go into the woods by yourself, Nikki. There are things in there you wouldn't understand. Some of it's dangerous."

"Like what?"

"Just promise me."

"Okay, I promise."

"Thanks. Did you happen to call and check on Brian?" he asked.

"Yeah, I don't know where he is. He isn't answering." Worry clouded my brain again.

"I don't know where he is either, but I'm sure he's fine," he tried to reassure me. "Nikki, I need to make a couple phone calls. If you want, I'll call you back later."

"No, I think I'll try calling Brian again. I'll see you at school tomorrow." I said, glad that I had found Adam safe. Now I was ready to put my mind at ease about the other one.

"I'll be there. Goodnight, Nikki."

"Goodnight."

I called Brian's number two more times, but he never picked up. I looked over at the clock. It was getting late. Maybe he just didn't feel like talking to anyone. I would take the Wrangler out to his house early in the morning and check on him, I decided. I clicked off my bedroom light, put on my pajamas, and sat down in the chair at the window I propped my elbows up on the windowsill. I listened to the stillness and wondered what had watched us, and if whatever it was, was still out there.

HE HAD BEEN watching the little house on the dirt road when the vehicle drove by. He had come in the hopes of catching a glimpse of the woman and boy who lived there, but the house was dark. No one was there. He still sat there, hidden in the shadows of the forest, hoping that maybe they would come back soon. He had been there for quite awhile when he saw the light blue Jeep roll past him.

He spotted the boy in the passenger side and caught a small glimpse of the girl driving. A fresh wave of anger flooded him and his body covered in a silver mist as the animal pushed his way into his mind.

The Jeep was heading to the house at the end of the road, the one he had been in charge of. The wolf took over his body as he watched it disappear around the curve.

He sat for a moment, playing out different scenarios in his head. If he followed them, he would have to wait until the boy left and hope that he wouldn't be caught. Not an easy task as he was certain that the boy had noted his presence as they passed him. He had caught the shine of golden eyes that sparkled in the moonlight when he had looked in his direction.

There wouldn't be any way to reach the girl, he decided, not on this night. Better to try another day when the boy wasn't around. It would be much easier that way.

The glow of red taillights reappeared for a moment before they turned another curve. They would be at the house soon, and then the boy would be in the forest with him. He sighed, which came out as an aggravated snort through his muzzle.

The silver wolf stood up and turned to run. He would need a bit of a head start. After all, the boy was fast, too—and if there was one person that he didn't want to confront, it was Adam.

SIX

I WOKE UP the next morning in the chair by the window. It was early. The sun hadn't quite risen yet, but the sky seemed to be getting lighter.

Dummy, I thought crossly, you could have at least crawled into bed.

I ran down the staircase and grabbed the keys to the Wrangler. I was ready to yell to Mom that I was going to run down and check on Brian, when I realized she wasn't up yet. I scribbled a note and left it on the table as I ran out the door.

I pulled up in front of Brian's house. Anita's car was still gone, but the truck was still in the same spot it had been in the night before. I ran up the steps and pounded on the door. When Brian opened it, still in his pajamas, he looked startled.

"Nikki? What's wrong?" he asked as he grabbed my hand and pulled me inside.

"Are you feeling better?"

"Yes," he said, looking at me as if I were insane. "Nikki, what's wrong? It's not even six-thirty in the morning. You're in your pajamas. You don't even have shoes on!"

"Oh," I said, noticing that everything that he had said was true. I looked down at my bare feet. "I was worried about you."

"I'm okay," he reassured me. "Honest. Mom and I went out to a movie. I saw where you called on the caller ID when we got home last night, but I thought it would be too late and I didn't want to wake you. If I knew you were worried that much I would have called you no matter what time it was, I swear." He pushed my hair away from my cheek.

"Oh," I murmured. I felt like a big fool.

He smiled. "I'm glad someone worries about me that much, it's a nice feeling. I was getting ready to pour myself a bowl of cereal. Come have breakfast with me?"

"Okay."

We sat across from each other, both in our pajamas, eating the crunchy cereal and sipping our milk at the little table in the kitchen.

"You know, I thought something horrible had happened when I found you at the door." Brian shook his head, and then smiled. "Don't get me wrong, I love spending time with you, but people may get the wrong idea if you show up with your bedclothes on."

"I forgot. I was still worried and had to see if you were okay." I looked over at the bright blue eyes that glimmered under the mussed, dark hair.

"What are you doing in Erik's car? Not trying to change the subject, but it is his car, isn't it?"

"It's my car. Or rather it will be, after today."

"I hadn't heard he was going to sell it," he mused. "It will be a good car for you. He takes good care of his stuff. Plus, he's a good guy. He wouldn't sell you a piece of junk. Speaking of the guys at the Res, today is the field trip. It should be fun…"

The clock in the living room chimed. Startled, I jumped.

"I guess I need to head back and get ready for school. Or at least to go get clothes on," I said as I got up.

"I'll come pick you up in an hour or so," Brian said as he walked me to the door.

His eyes were warm as they looked down at me. "Thanks for coming by to check on me. It was sweet of you."

"I'm glad you're feeling better, I was worried about you. Thanks for breakfast." I smiled up at him as I walked passed him and out onto the porch. He stopped me, grabbing my arm.

"Wait a minute, take these." He handed me a pair of flip-flops. "Today's lesson. Always drive with shoes on."

I pushed my feet into them and smiled. "Thanks."

He reached over and tucked my hair behind my ear before he leaned forward and kissed me on the cheek. "Drive safe. I'll be up to get you in a little while."

"Okay," I whispered, not sure what else to say or do. I walked back down the porch steps and got into the Wrangler. I backed it back out onto the road and started back home. I looked in my rearview mirror. Brian stood on the porch, watching me as I drove away.

I drove back home wondering what I had gotten myself into. Part of me seemed to get lost in Adam anytime he was near. With him, it was as if I had found the other half of myself. But I had been far more worried about Brian being sick than I had been about Adam as he walked home alone. I was always comfortable with Brian. We hadn't known each other that long, but it felt as if I had known him forever and that I could tell him anything.

Mom choked on her coffee as she watched me come back in the door. Small splats of brown caffeine dotted the front of the paper she had been reading.

"You went out like that?" she asked, astonished.

"Yeah, I forgot to get dressed."

"You were still worried about Brian. I know you had the phone with you all night. I found it in your bedroom after you left. So was he all right?

"Yeah, he's fine. He and Anita were out late, and he didn't want to wake us. I guess I need to get in the shower and get ready for school."

"Yes, I do believe that would be a good idea," she said as I started for the stairs, "And next time you make sure you tell me in person where you're going. Just because you have a vehicle now, doesn't mean you can just go anywhere. I still need to know where you are, understood?"

"Yes." I mumbled. It wasn't even eight o'clock yet, and already I was getting into trouble.

Brian picked me up, his usual happy self again. We rode to school and I updated him on what he had missed the day before. The cheerleading escapade, the trip to the nurse, and the enemy that I had in a certain blonde cheerleader. I left out anything that pertained to Adam. I wasn't sure why, but I felt guilty. It wasn't like either of them had asked me out.

Brian pulled into our regular spot. Then he saw Ronnie over by the door.

"I need to go catch up with her before she goes in, she has notes I need. I'll see you in there," he said, jumping out of the truck.

"Sure."

Adam was in his same spot, waiting for me.

"I take it you found him alive and well."

"Yes," I frowned. He was acting as if I had done something wrong. "Okay, I give up. What's the problem?"

"No problem," he said. His voice was at odds with his eyes. They were burning with anger. He was lying to me.

I shrugged, and started walking. If he wasn't going to talk to me, I wasn't going to worry about it. He kept up with me easily. His nostrils flared and his nose scrunched up as if he had smelled something he didn't like. He still didn't speak, only stepped to the side to let me go through the door first.

I can smell him. He touched your cheek. Did he kiss you? Why did you let him? What about me? Don't you care? The voice whispered in my head.

He didn't say a word when we split and went down either side of the hallway toward class. I didn't see him again until English and still he stayed silent, not acknowledging me as I slid in next to him.

Fine, if that's the way it's going to be, I thought. I moved as far to the edge of the desk as I could get without falling out into the floor. I bent over my book, ignoring him. My hair bounced over my shoulder, shielding me in a thick blonde wall as I tried to concentrate on my book. I heard him take a deep breath.

"I'm sorry," his voice wasn't much more than a whisper. It made me wonder if I had imagined it. I ignored him and sat there contemplating the fact that I might be going crazy. After all, normal people don't hear voices in their heads.

Ms. Barker came in and started class, and I stayed at my little corner of the desk, as if I had never heard him or anything else that whispered through my mind.

After class, I felt the desk move as he got up. He hesitated for a second, as if trying to decide whether or not to wait for me. I didn't say anything, so he left. I followed a few seconds later and found Brian outside the door with a big scowl on his face. It vanished when he saw me and a smile took its place. "Hey, are you ready? They're loading up the buses for the field trip."

We found a seat in the back of the last bus and it ambled down the road. It stopped just shy of turning on to my road and turned instead into the parking lot behind the carved, wooden sign of a howling wolf.

We had arrived at The Village.

"Okay, children," a nasal, high-pitched voice shrilled through the air like a siren the second we got off the bus." Your attention, please."

The clatter and noise subdued. I looked to the front of the group to the thin, bird-like woman with facial features so pinched, it gave her the appearance of one who had eaten sour grapes.

Hmm, so far Brian has Mrs. Graham pegged, I thought, smiling to myself, maybe there's a reason they gave her the job as school librarian. I don't think she's meant for many speaking roles. Maybe that's why she takes her role as field trip leader so seriously.

The librarian's thin lips compressed into a tight line, and big red blotches popped up like little red apples on her sharp cheekbones. A few students continued to talk, ignoring her.

"For those of you who do not consider this important, you are welcome to get back on the bus. The driver will take you back to school, where I'm sure Mr. Giles will deal with you."

At the mention of the principal, you could hear a pin drop, which was quite impressive as Bland Elementary had parked one of their buses next to ours, and a couple dozen grade-schoolers stood nearby.

I spotted Emily's dark, curly head and she sent me a huge grin as she tried not to hop from one foot to the other with excitement. I shook my head slightly, trying to send her a message to be still as I wasn't sure how far Mrs. Graham's sharp talons would reach.

"Now, the Wighcomocos were one of the tribes first encountered by John Smith in the year 1607," Mrs. Graham chirped in her bird voice. I remembered Brian's speech. So far he was dead on. A little brown head bobbed closer to us, making me focus on someone other than the birdlike Mrs. Graham. I tried to pay attention as I watched my little sister. The younger kids beside us had shifted over to form their own group, but Emily had stayed apart from them and had seemed to edge closer to us.

I shook my head harder at her, but she just grinned and hopped, looking back and forth between me and Mrs. Graham. Either she didn't get the message, or just couldn't help it, because she started bobbing up and down faster.

"Be still, Em," I whispered.

In that next instant, two things happened. First, Emily realized her group had moved, so she sent me a quick little wave and bounced back in the midst her friends. The second was that I seemed to have attracted way more attention than my energetic little sister.

Mrs. Graham stomped over in front of me and stood so close I could see the tiny dark hairs sticking out on her upper lip. In that instant, I realized I must be looking into the most drawn, scrunched-up face in the world. Her grey-streaked hair was pulled tight in a tiny bun, behind her head. Sharp, grey eyes seared straight into mine. I stared at her, mouth agape. Even the little crow's feet wrinkles around her eyes looked pinched.

"You're new. What is your name?" She demanded. I felt her hot breath on my face.

"Nikki Harmon," I said, not wanting to meet her gaze again, straight on. I settled for staring at the tight fitting collar of her dress, which should have strangled her.

"Well, Miss Harmon," she sneered, seeming to bite each syllable of my last name into pieces. "You do speak English, do you not? Or is it only that you want to take me up on my previous offer of the early ride back to school? Because that can be arranged."

"No, ma'am." I dropped my eyes to her sensible-looking black leather shoes. "I mean, I would like to stay. I'm sorry. It won't happen again."

She let out a long, noisy breath through her nose, and stayed silent just long enough that I found enough courage to dare to look back up. The steel grey of her eyes bore into mine, unblinking, as if she were trying to see into my soul. Or maybe she was just trying to see if I was the kind of kid who was going to give her more problems throughout the day. Either way, she had me spooked.

"See that it doesn't." She turned and walked back to her original spot before the group. As if nothing had happened, she started right back up on her speech where she had left off.

Someone behind me let out their breath in a whoosh, and I turned just enough to see a pair of bright, blue eyes and an amused smile. I jerked my elbow back, catching Brian in the ribs. A slight grunt escaped him. Thankfully, Mrs. Graham hadn't heard it, as she was thoroughly ensconced in the history of the early Native American tribes.

After a rather lengthy, although informative, ten minutes of background and birdlike chatter, we started down the dirt path past the small building that looked to be a gift shop. The path wound around the back of the building and into the woods. I was already familiar with part of the Res, as the guys called it, but had never been quite so far into their land.

At least not physically, anyway. But in my dream I had seen this place.

The campfire circle sat dead center, the same one I had dreamt of the first night we arrived. But today, there wasn't a fire and no one was sitting around the circle.

"C'mon, Nikki, unless you want to unleash her wrath again," Brian whispered. I must have stopped and had been standing there gaping, because all of a sudden, he grabbed my hand and gave it a quick tug and squeeze at the same time to get me walking again.

After a reminder to to meet back at the buses in two hours, Mrs. Graham took her leave.

At a small hut on the right, we began our tour. Sitting cross-legged at the door of the hut was a pretty girl with a buckskin dress. Her hair had been braided in a single plait with pretty blue beads weaved through it. A large, flat stone lay on the ground before her. Sun glinted on her dark hair, casting a blue hue on her bent head. She laid a few kernels of raw corn on the stone, and began grinding them with a smaller stone.

When she had finished, Penny looked up and smiled. "Anything that we would have eaten years ago, we would have had to make by hand. Something as simple as flour that you can buy in a store, was not so simple to get back then."

Hands flew up everywhere, and one-by-one she answered each question, everything from the different kinds of food they ate to how it was stored. The quiet, calm Penny had captivated the entire group and gave them the thirst for more knowledge. After answering each and every possible query, she stood and walked us over to the next hut.

As beautiful as Penny was, Hannah seemed exotic. Her hair swung wild and loose to her waist except for a single braid on one side. Surrounding her were piles of furs. Some stretched tight on sticks, others hung on poles. She held a large white pelt in her arms.

"Pelts were one of the main sources of trade," she stated, as if everyone already knew that particular bit of information.

"Trade for what?" A boy in the back prompted.

"Food, blankets, sometimes people," she smiled devilishly.

"People?" he gulped.

What rock did this kid come out from? I thought and snorted a little too loud. She looked over at me and lifted one perfectly arched brow. She shook her hair back over her shoulder and continued,

"Yes, sometimes a war party would steal women and children from a different tribe. If the hostages were lucky, they would be bought back with furs, beads, blankets, or whatever else their family had of worth. Of course, sometimes there were other instances one tribe would welcome trade from another tribe for their unmarried women if it meant the survival of their people." At this last statement, she had the whole group in the palm of her hand.

"So how many furs are you worth?" someone snickered in the back.

"Trust me, you'll never have enough," she retorted, a few of the guys laughed and elbowed each other in the ribs. She stood aloof, as if she dealt with this kind of idiocy on a daily basis. All the while, she stroked the glossy white fur in her hands.

I had noticed that she hadn't put it down it the entire time, which I thought was kind of weird. There were plenty of other smaller furs everywhere that would have been easier to handle. Curiosity got the best of me, and hoping I wasn't about to find out that it had been a personal pet, I lifted my hand.

"What kind of animal was that?" I asked, pointing.

"This," she said, her voice almost reverent, "this is wolf."

A split second of silence and the air seemed charged with energy. It was almost as if it would have seemed right to hear a wolf cry in the distance, or appear by her side as if summoned. Not this was wolf, this *is* wolf.

As if noticing, she broke the silence and recaptured the audience by pointing out the different species of animal that each pelt belonged, offering to let them touch and feel each. Deer, rabbit, fox, and bear, but never the wolf. It never left her arms.

After explaining the long, tedious steps of tanning hides, Hannah wrapped up her demonstration and relieved to be free of her duty, pointed us over to wait under the shade of a large tree and disappeared with her wolf pelt into the shadows of the hut.

"What do you think so far?" Brian asked, leaning against the trunk of the tree.

"It's neat. Penny was awesome, don't get me wrong, Hannah was good, too, but it just seemed like she was worried someone was going to touch that wolf pelt."

"Yeah, I don't know what the deal is with that. It was like that last year, too, only reversed. Hannah was the one grounding corn meal and Penny acted like she was about to jump out of her skin, so I think Hannah does better with it. Come to think of it, that pelt is always there. Somewhere, somehow, it's always worked into the history of their tribe. Maybe it's old and they're afraid they'll be in trouble if it gets messed up on their watch," he said, then looked down at his watch. "Adam had better hurry up, or we won't get to see everything."

"What is he...?" I got cut off with a loud whoop, and suddenly we were surrounded.

Five ferocious warriors, their faces painted black, circled us until we were bunched against the tree like sardines. Then they quit circling and the one who must have been the leader, stepped closer and spoke.

"A-da-wi u-la-gu. Ni-ga-da da-na-da-s-ka-gi. Tsu-sa-si," he said in a grave voice.

Penny appeared behind him, her face solemn. "He says he is U-la-gu. Leader of his people. You have invaded this land. You are not friend, but stranger, and therefore enemy. The blood of his people cries for revenge—so now you must die."

The warrior stalked closer to Beth, who was stuck on the edge of the crowd. Bernie was behind her taking pictures, one after the other. He crept closer, tomahawk poised to strike. The flash from Bernie's camera caught his eyes, and they sparkled amber.

A quiet oath behind Beth proved that Bernie had dropped his camera, but Beth hadn't noticed. Now she was backing up, squashing Bernie's glasses onto his face, in spite of his attempt to save them and his beloved camera.

Adam grinned, snow white teeth showing in a face black with paint. "Any questions?"

The four members of his war party burst out laughing and came to stand behind him. Each of them was bare-chested, with only a pair of pants and a loincloth around their waist. They were all armed with a bow and arrows on their backs and a tomahawk and a knife either on their side or in hand.

Bear grease was on each of them, though in different patterns. Seeing through the paint, I found each familiar face. Adam's eyes, nose and mouth were covered, while Ed had opted for a sideways smear going across his angular features. Tommy and Michael were very much alike with their entire face blacked, but Erik was the most memorable, as it looked like someone had smacked him with a giant black handprint in the middle of his round face.

The group around the tree loosened up a bit and spread out, splitting up into smaller groups, as each brave was being asked questions from everything about hunting to scalping.

I stayed back and listened. And watched Adam.

I backed up to lean against the trunk of the tree, when I whacked into something I hadn't expected. A foot dangled at my shoulder.

"Easy, now," Brian said, jumping down from his perch up in the tree.

I bit my lip, embarrassed that I hadn't missed him.

"I thought about grabbing you and taking you up with me, since they sometimes like to demonstrate how they would kidnap women and children, but since you'd never seen this before…"

I laughed, feeling rather relieved that he thought I was only observing a demonstration instead of Adam. For some reason I didn't want him jealous.

I changed the subject. "You should have pulled me up, although I faired better than Bernie did. Well, his camera, anyway."

Beth was still shooting questions at Ed, who had taken on an aura of patience worthy of the Pope himself. The star journalist of the school paper, however, was oblivious that her sole photographer was mourning the loss of his camera as he wiped his running nose, and picked up yet another piece up off the ground. As if he had reached his wit's end, Bernie dashed off toward the restroom, and disappeared.

"Poor ol' Bern, he never can seem to get a break," Brian shook his head, and his dark hair fell toward his eyes. "Listen, I'm going to go check on him. If they get finished up before I get back, I'll meet you at the bus, okay?"

"Yeah, sure," I nodded.

Our group started to disperse and wander back toward the gift shop and the buses. I was still at the back of the crowd when someone fell into step with me, and I turned, expecting to see Brian with Bernie in tow.

"What do you think?" Adam asked, his eyes flashing warm amber behind the black paint.

I think wow, I thought, staring at him. From a few feet away, he looked great, but as he stood right beside me, my brain had decided to go into overdrive and was trying to soak up every inch of him that my eyes could see.

"You didn't like it?"

I love it, my brain screamed as I kept staring and walking at the same time.

"Y-yes," I stammered a split second before I tripped over my own feet and somehow slammed sideways into him.

His arms came out and steadied me again as they had before and everything sizzled and popped around us again. Where his fingers touched my arms it felt as if tiny electric currents zinged between us, like a constant current of static electricity. Curious if there were actual sparks popping between us, I looked down at the exact second he turned loose.

"Are you okay?" he asked, very politely. I felt my cheeks flush red. Maybe he was still angry from earlier that day.

"Yes, thank you." I got the nerve to look up at him.

His eyes were locked on something or someone behind me, near the hut at the end of the row. I turned. Out of the corner of my eye, I thought I saw something. Just a quick flash of white skin, as translucent as an opal and a sheen of cool blue. It felt as if the very atmosphere had shifted.

"Who was it?" I asked, looking around. I was certain someone had been there.

"No one's there," Adam whispered, then took my arm to get me walking again and steer me toward the buses.

"No, you saw something, too," I argued, feeling a stir of anger since I knew that I was being lied to.

"Is there a problem here?" a familiar voice demanded on the other side of me.

"No, ma'am, not at all," Adam said, giving a warm smile to an irate-looking Mrs. Graham.

It was as if Adam's smile was the sun, and Mrs. Graham was an iceberg. She melted. She gave him a rather beaky, bristly-looking smile back and then turned to me and barked, "On the bus, girl."

Best not make her mad, she's not someone you want to mess with, a voice cautioned.

"Making enemies again, are we?" Brian hissed into my ear, while grabbing my arm, and jerking me on the bus. "Nikki, you don't want to screw around with that lady, she's not your typical quiet librarian type."

He herded me to the very back of the bus and into a corner and then sat down beside me, darting a quick look back out the window to make sure no attack was going to come our way. He let out a whoosh of breath that he must have been holding, and flopped against the back of the seat.

I dared to take a quick glance out the window, and saw Adam standing, hands clasped behind his back while he talked with Mrs. Graham, who seemed quite at ease. Students filed past and the buses filled. After a few more moments, she boarded the bus. After a quick head count, the bus driver started the engine.

I looked over once more to see Adam staring at me. His eyes locked with mine and he gave me a nod. Somehow feeling that he was trying to say goodbye, I pressed my hand to the glass. He stood in the same place and watched us until we were out of sight.

SEVEN

ADAM DIDN'T MAKE it to school at all the following week. Another hiker was missing, Erik informed me, as he dropped off the title to the Jeep one evening after school. They were helping search for her and he didn't know when they would be back.

Each day crawled by slower than the one before. Then Saturday came.

I started to dread the idea of the hike, and almost called Brian to tell him I didn't want to go, but the possibility of seeing Adam if he showed up, kept me from dialing the number.

I had gotten my driver's license after school that week. I stopped and picked him up at his house and we met the rest of the group at a wide spot down a gravel road. I counted more than a dozen people when I got out of the car and more kept coming.

"News travels," Brian looked at me, apologetically. "If you want to go back home, I'll understand."

My eyes lit on two boys that stood where the trail crossed. Their backs were turned to me, but I could see their black hair tied back in tight plaits that ran down their backs. "No, it's okay. Let's go."

"I'll be right there," Brian said, waving me on, as someone called out to him.

I walked towards the trail and the two boys turned. I tried not to look disappointed as the two youngest members of Adam's lunch group saw me and smiled, their dimples creasing their left cheek.

"Hey, Nikki," Tommy and Michael said in unison.

"Hey. Where have you guys been the last couple of days? Still searching for the lost hiker?"

"Yeah. We've been looking for her day and night. We haven't found anything, though. Adam, Erik and Ed are still out looking for her."

"Did you guys need a break?" I teased.

"No, not really." Tommy shifted around, not meeting my eyes.

"Adam sent us to keep an eye on everyone and to make sure everyone stayed safe," Michael said quickly, elbowing his cousin.

"You mean he sent you to keep an eye on me." I said, remembering the promise I had made to stay close to Brian.

"He was worried about you." Tommy met my gaze and ignored Michael's incessant jabs to his ribs. "Although he did say to keep an eye on everyone, he said specifically to keep you safe."

He turned to Michael, who had resorted to stomping on his foot. "Quit that. She'd figure it out anyway when she realized we were two steps behind her all afternoon."

I left the squabbling cousins and walked back to meet Brian.

"Sorry about that. I think everyone is ready to go," he said.

A large part of the group had started up the hillside. We fell in behind Beth and Ronnie as they started up the trail that seemed more of a path. It narrowed with some spots barely wide enough to accommodate a single person. Everyone's head was bent down; watching for roots that could trip them and send them toppling down the hill.

It was quiet, except for the sound of labored breathing as we trudged onward. I kept my eyes on Brian. As he took one step, a small rock came free from the dirt and went bouncing down the mountain. I stopped and watched it, catching my breath.

True to their word, Michael and Tommy must have been two steps behind me. No sooner had I stopped when I felt someone bump into my back.

"Sorry," Michael said sheepishly.

"It's okay," I huffed, and then looked back at him.

Neither of them seemed to be even winded. I looked down at the watch on my wrist. We had been hiking for an hour and most of it was uphill.

"You guys must be in good shape. I envy you."

"We do this a lot," Tommy voice came up from behind Michael's shoulder. "It will level out up around that curve up there. It will be wider, too, so it will be easier to walk for a little while."

I turned back around. Brian was a good ways ahead of me. He hadn't noticed I wasn't behind him any longer. I focused on putting one foot in front of the other until we reached the spot that Tommy had pointed out.

The trail widened and opened out into a big meadow. By unspoken consent, everyone decided that here was the place to take a break. Backpacks and walking sticks went flying as people searched for water bottles and energy drinks. I sat down on a tree stump, took a long drink of my lukewarm water, and looked at all the red, sweaty faces that sat sprawled in various places.

"So what do you think?" Brian grinned.

"I think I'm in bad shape," I said. He looked as if he had just gone for a stroll out in his yard. He hadn't even broken a sweat.

"Nah, you're just not used to it." Brian sat down next to me as Ronnie and John came over.

"I love hiking, but I don't like uphill. I think everyone has been too out of breath to even look for clues so far. I wouldn't have noticed the trail killer if he was covered in blood and brandishing knives, unless of course he was standing directly in front of my feet. I don't think I looked up past Ronnie's boots the whole way up." John grinned, plopping down on the ground across from us as he pulled Ronnie down with him. "I wonder if we'll see the wolves up here."

"Have you seen them before?" I asked.

He shook his head. "No, if I had, there is no way you'd catch me up here."

"He's just trying to scare you," Ronnie said. "He loves scaring people. There aren't any wolves anywhere near here, it's just stories."

"Oh, they're real. Just ask some of the hikers that have wandered off the trail. There are actual reports of wolves that have been seen by hikers that have been lost in this forest. According to urban legend around here, they are huge dog-like creatures that are four or five times the size of a wolf. Supposedly, they guard the forest from outsiders, hunting and killing anyone that wanders away from the trail. I think that's what has happened to the missing hikers. Not the legend, but the wolves. The idea of the trail killer is ludicrous, if you ask me. I mean, what guy is just going to hang out in the woods and wait for young women to happen by? He could be standing around forever, just waiting. But think, you guys, the forest has all sorts of wild animals living in it. They all eat something, right?" He shrugged. "I think the hikers just got lost, died, and then nature took its course."

"But they would still find bones," I pointed out. I wanted to defend the wolves, though I didn't know why.

"Maybe, maybe not. The forest is a big place." John grinned, as he watched Beth sneak up behind Ronnie and grab her. Ronnie squealed.

"Are you guys ready to go again?" Beth asked. "We'll just go as long as it stays level then we'll turn around so it will be downhill on the way back."

"Sounds good." I got up off my stump, and looked over at Brian.

His knuckles were white as they gripped the sides of the stump. The muscles in his jaw tightened. He was staring straight ahead, not looking at anyone.

"Are you okay?" I waved my hand in front of his fixed stare.

He blinked, then looked up at me. "Oh, sorry. Yeah, I'm fine. Let's go."

Everyone had gotten their breath and the woods echoed with the sounds of voices and laughter of the people ahead of us. Brian stayed quiet. I thought we were the last of the group since I hadn't heard any voices behind us, so I looked over my shoulder. Michael and Tommy were still behind us, moving soundlessly along the trail. Their brown eyes looked back at me, and I realized that it was the first time they hadn't smiled at me. Their faces were serious and they looked older without their dimples.

On the way back down, I noticed a small path cutting to one side of the trail, hidden by some low-lying bushes. Curiosity peaked, I left the trail. I looked over my shoulder to see if my two protectors had seen me wander off. So far they hadn't. I decided I would go just a bit farther to see where the path took me. A small bend behind a clump of bushes led me to a small clearing packed with raspberry bushes, the path ended there. The plump, red berries were ripe and ready to be picked.

I heard my name being called, and turned around to find Michael and Tommy coming up behind me.

"What's up? Did you find something? You know you could have said you were taking a detour," Michael said, frowning.

"I'm sorry, I just wanted to see where that little path led. I'm coming." I walked back to them, wishing I could stay and pick berries.

Everyone else had made it to the bottom, leaving the three of us to come down last. Beth was busy talking to Brian, as he waited for me by the car. She was talking animatedly, gesturing with her hands, then realized he hadn't heard a word she said. Irritated, she shrugged and walked off.

Strange, I thought, looking at his face.

I stopped in front of him, inches away from his face. His blue eyes stared through me as if I weren't there. I reached up and pushed a dark lock of hair out of his eyes, and he blinked.

"Hey, Brian. You're worrying me again."

I saw his eyes focus on me and he gave me a weak smile. "Sorry, let's go, eh? I mean, if you're ready."

"Sure."

I walked back around and got in the car and saw Tommy and Michael were standing just a few feet away. They were still solemn-looking and they seemed to have lost all interest in me now. They were staring at Brian with that very close, guarded look I had seen on Adam's face.

I dropped Brian back off at his house and offered to stay with him until he felt like himself again. He made me go, saying he was just going to lie down for awhile, though I made him promise that if he needed anything he would call me and then I left to go home.

The construction guys were finished, I could start painting. It wouldn't be dark for a few hours, I decided, as I pulled up in front of the house. Mom hadn't made it home yet and Emily was at a friend's house for a sleepover.

Looks like it's just you and me, I looked up at the big, rambling house as I went up the steps. I put on my old jeans and an old tank top and pulled my hair back in a messy ponytail. Then I scrounged around to find a big paintbrush and the paint.

I set the ladder up against the house, then I popped open the can and stirred the thick, white paint, watching the oil on the top disappear. Satisfied that both the paint and I were ready, I started up the ladder, paint can in one hand, ladder in the other, and the brush shoved in my back pocket.

I had never been afraid of heights. In fact, I loved them. The thrill of seeing how far up I could go constantly got me into trouble when I was younger. I was always getting grounded for going up the neighbor's apple trees, but I couldn't help it. They were the only trees around. I learned fast that palm trees would skin your knees and didn't have enough places to hold onto to climb. So Mr. Bugg's trees always tempted me. By the time I was seven, my parents decided the only way to stay in the neighbor's good graces was to put me in gymnastics class. There I could climb, flip, jump and tumble with a nice, safe padded floor to catch me as I learned. I never did get up into the apple trees anymore after that.

There isn't anyone here that teaches gymnastics. There are plenty of mountains, though. Maybe I could take a rock climbing class, I thought, climbing up near the top of the ladder, to set my paint in the upstairs windowsill.

I concentrated on filling the cracks in the old wood siding. I grinned, watching the old boards seem to transform with the new paint.

I hummed to myself. I should have put my stereo near the open window. It was too quiet. Normally, I heard the birds singing from the nearby woods. The only noise I heard was the wind as it blew through the trees and stirred the leaves in the yard.

Everything was quiet. That means there was something there earlier. There are things in there you wouldn't understand. Promise you won't go into the woods by yourself, Adam's words echoed in my mind as I listened to the silence.

I shook my head, there wasn't anything there. It was just my imagination at work. I looked over at the trees near Adam's path. A dark shadow flickered among the darkness. I blinked and then stared harder.

Nah, you're just nuts is all. Nothing is there, I thought, and began painting again.

Soon, I became engrossed in the task, and didn't pay attention to anything but the paint and my brush in my hand. Time flew by. I almost had the top part finished. I stretched to reach the last bare spot in the top corner of the house so I wouldn't have to get down and move my ladder over.

I can reach it. I stretched, willing my short arms to be longer. I was as high as I could go, but I needed an inch more. I slid my foot closer to the edge of the ladder. I could almost reach it, if I could just make it a little farther.

I felt the ladder shift to one side. I lost my grip and fell.

Oh, no, I thought as nothing but air brushed by me, this will kill me. I'm too far up.

I noticed a dark flash from out of the corner of my eye. I tensed, waiting for the ground to take me. I closed my eyes tight. I felt myself hit, and then the breath was knocked out of me.

The ground grunted with my impact. I gasped, trying to get my air back in my lungs. What felt like an air bubble, burst in my chest, and I gulped in the warm summer air. I lay there, looking at the sky. I was afraid to move when I realized the ground beneath me was moving up and down as it took short, shallow breaths.

It grunted again, and a muffled voice came from below me, "If you're okay, can you get off me? You're heavier than you look and I'd like to breathe again."

I rolled over to my side. I had landed on someone.

Brian took a deep breath and sat up. "Are you all right?"

"Yeah, I think so." I experimented in bending my arms and legs.

"You're nuts. Why did you hang off the ladder like that? Do you just like falling off of stuff? Why didn't you wait until someone got home and held it for you? You know you could have called and I would have come and helped." He sent questions flying at me one after another before I could say a word.

I sat calmly. When he finally took a breath, I answered, "I thought I could reach it. I normally don't fall off of anything, and I'm quite capable of going up a ladder by myself, thank you very much."

"It appears you're capable of coming down it, too."

"Yeah, I guess it appears that way. But I am glad you were at the bottom to break my fall. Other than getting squashed, are you feeling better?"

"I am, thanks. I thought I'd get some fresh air and walk up and see if you had heard the news," he said as a reluctant smile spread across his face.

"I haven't heard anything from anyone since I saw you last." I stood up to retrieve my paintbrush out of a rose bush and smacked it against my leg to knock the dirt out.

"Mom made it home a little while ago and told me. They think they've caught the trail killer."

"No way. Who was it?" I stopped and turned, giving him my full attention.

"They think it was Mr. Walters that lives in the rental house across town. The Appalachian Trail comes down pretty close there. Someone called in a tip and they went and checked it out. They found one of the girls' ID bracelets in his garage, so they took him in for questioning," Brian said, brushing the dirt off his jeans.

"That's great."

"Yeah, maybe he'll tell them where he put the bodies. But on the upside of things, at least there's one body they won't have to look for now. Adam and the other guys found the last hiker, right about the time we finished our hike. She had wandered off the path and stepped in a hole. She hit her head when she landed. They took her to the hospital. She has a mild concussion, but they think she's going to be fine."

"I bet Tommy and Michael aren't too happy they got left out of that adventure," I mumbled, turning my attention back to the house.

"You're not going back up there."

"I have to finish that spot, it won't paint itself. Besides, you're here now so you can hold the ladder and catch me if I fall again," I said as I set my ladder back up.

"You're not going back up there," he repeated, grabbing the brush out of my hand. "As much as I love to play hero, I nearly didn't catch you. *You* hold the ladder and I'll finish it."

He was halfway up before I could object, so I stood there holding the ladder and watched him finish what I started.

"I found raspberry bushes on the way back down the trail today," I said.

"I know where they are. You can get there from here. It isn't far. Mom and I used to visit Aunt Mae and we'd all go berry picking. It was fun. You just go through the trees over there and walk straight ahead for about fifteen minutes, it will lead you to the other side of the patch you found." He used the brush to point toward a clump of trees behind the shed.

"Since they've already caught the trail killer, maybe I'll go tomorrow and pick some. Do you want to come?"

"I would love to, but I can't. Tomorrow we have to go visit my grandparents over in Roanoke. We'll be over there all day. But thanks for the invite, maybe I can go some other time," he said as he came back down the ladder.

"It's a deal. Thanks for finishing that up. I hate to leave something half-done."

"No problem. Just do me a favor and don't do something that crazy again without someone else here," he said, stepping closer to me, his eyes serious. "You could have gotten hurt—or worse."

"Okay, I'll call you next time and see if you want to come and play catch again," I teased, trying to lighten his mood.

"Promise?" Brian stepped closer. He was only inches away from me now.

"Yes," I whispered.

He looked different to me now. The bones of his cheek and jaw were more pronounced. He looked stronger and more mature. The sun seemed to bring out the glossy black of his hair as it fell forward. His skin was darker, now a bronze that made his bright blue eyes stand out like two sparkling sapphires.

He reached up and traced his finger down the line of my cheek. I felt my heart start to race as he leaned in closer and closed the small gap between us. He kissed me, a bare whisper of lips as his brushed mine.

Over the pounding of the pulse in my ears, I thought I heard a snarling growl that came from the trees. A small smile played on Brian's lips and his eyes hardened as he turned and looked toward the edge of the woods as if he had heard it, too.

"I need to head back," he said, suddenly. "I'll call you tomorrow night?"

"Sure," I said, unable to stop the blush that rose in my cheeks. "I'll walk you around."

After making me promise not to paint anymore that day, he gave me a quick kiss on the cheek and started back down the road. I watched him walk, taking in the breadth of his shoulders as their muscles strained against the fabric of his black t-shirt. He seemed stronger all of a sudden. I shook my head. He had to have been like that all along, I just hadn't noticed.

Hero worship, I thought. I fell and he caught me. That's why I'm noticing all the muscles now.

I watched until he was out of sight, and then I turned and walked back to the porch. It still felt as if eyes were staring at me from the forest.

HE DIDN'T SEE what the big deal was. Hidden under a canopy of darkened trees, he sat watching her as she climbed up the ladder. He was curious. He couldn't understand what the whelp of a boy saw in her. She was short, with frizzy blonde curls, and eyes the color of mud. He couldn't figure out why the boy liked her and wanted her so much. It would be a lot easier if she wasn't in the picture to muddle things up. He did not want her here. Truth be told, he didn't want anyone here. This place was his. He worked very hard at keeping this particular house vacant. It had been his to look after.

It was their fault, all of it. This stupid girl and her family were to blame. He had lost his job because of them. If they would have just stayed away, none of it would have happened. He would still have the run of the place. He would be free to come and go as he pleased, but now he had to be careful. So careful.

He snorted, causing the dead leaves below him to ruffle and move. The girl turned from her perch near the top of the house, and peered back over at her shoulder. His breath caught as instinct kicked in. He crouched lower in the shadows. She seemed to be staring right at him. Had she heard him? No, that was impossible. She was only a girl, after all, and a dumb one at that. Still, he sighed in relief when she turned back and started humming and painting again.

The boy and his mother had lived by the woods for so long that they were used to the sounds that came from the forest. They didn't pay attention to what lay so close to them. He watched them occasionally, too, but he didn't mind them. In their own strange way, they felt as if they belonged there as much as he did. He enjoyed watching the pretty woman with brown hair plant her little flowers in the window boxes while the boy tinkered with his old, dilapidated truck. It was odd, but he felt protective of them, and did not like the boy coming to this house.

Then, the idea struck him. He could do it now. He could run up there and knock against the ladder and cause it to fall. It wasn't exactly the way he preferred to hunt, but she wouldn't survive such a great fall. No one would suspect. They would call it an accident. The mother and little girl would move away, the house would be vacant again and the boy would stay away. It was perfect. His lips moved up in an eerie grin that emphasized his sharp fangs. His muscled tensed with eagerness, and he felt almost giddy as he readied himself for the kill.

Ready to spring, he stopped and watched in awe as she took one foot off the ladder and stretched. He watched the ladder wobble as she continued to reach for the corner. He sat back down in his shadows, content to let fate do his dirty work. Eagerly, he waited for the second she would fall. Anticipation was the greatest part of the hunt, he reminded himself.

Then, it happened.

His glee turned into astonishment at what he saw next. The boy had run in to save the day. He fidgeted. He should have seen him coming. Or at least heard him. He had moved like a blur, and was just *there*. Just in time to ruin his perfect plan. Well, wasn't that just...perfect. Rage surged through him as the animal in him awakened, eager to hunt. Wasn't two better than one?

No, no. He took deep breaths to calm his beast. He couldn't hunt them both, he reasoned with himself. Her? Absolutely. That would be just fine. But not *the boy*. Shaking from the urges of the animal, he sat with tremors running up and down his body and watched.

It was far worse than he had feared. The boy was besotted with the little tramp. He watched as the paint made it on the corner of the house, and then watched in disgust and horror as the boy leaned over to kiss her. His control loosened just enough that a low growl rumbled out of his chest.

The boy turned and stared at him with cold, blue eyes. He had heard him. But how? He had never sensed him before. His animal in his control, he sat calm, yet astonished, and stared back at the boy. Then, he knew

EIGHT

THE NEXT MORNING I left to find the berry patch. The
small walk from the house through the woods was peaceful.
I found the path behind the shed as Brian said I would. It
was well-worn. The dirt was packed so well that there wasn't any hint
that grass had ever been there. I followed the path as it curled around
the base of the trees, swinging an empty basket in one hand, and a
water bottle in the other. The quiet sounds of nature were soothing, I
decided that must be the reason the path hadn't been overgrown

since my grandmother's death. She must have enjoyed a walk here often. Either that, or those raspberries were to die for.

After a few more minutes of walking, the forest didn't look quite as appealing. Everything had gone still, as if every animal in the forest had fled, or were in hiding. The trees even looked foreboding and half-dead with shriveled leaves and branches that stuck out like skeletal arms. The path was barely discernable from the rest of the ground now since there wasn't any grass or moss anywhere around, only dirt. I picked my way through the eerie place as fast as I could and came out on the other side, finding myself happy to hear the sounds of birds as they sang high above me in trees. The trees made me happy, too, since they were green and alive. It hadn't crossed my mind to turn back, only to get through that strange place. Now I wasn't so sure that I would want to return on this same path. Maybe I could make a wide circle and not have to go through it again. If I was careful I wouldn't get lost, I decided.

Lost in my musing, I was on top of the berry patch before I realized it. Then every thought left my mind as I started gathering berries.

I ate the first few handfuls, and then decided to fill my basket. I had it half full of berries and was just starting to reach for a juicy-looking clump over my head when I heard a snuffling sound coming from around the side of the bush. The sound was coming closer. I was stuck with one leg placed in between several thorny branches. I froze as I saw a large black shape appear out of the corner of my eye. I jerked my leg free, wincing as I felt the briars dig their tiny barbs into my jeans and down the length of my leg. I whirled around to face a large, angry-looking black bear that was watching me a few feet away.

"Be still, Nikki. And when I tell you to move, run back down the path," a voice said calmly from the other side of the bush.

I looked over and was as shocked by who was there as I had been by the bear's arrival.

"Adam," I whispered. "There's a bear..." I was cut off by a low, threatening growl.

"I know. Just do as I say. Now be quiet." Adam moved to my side.

The bear saw him and stood on its rear legs, as if daring him to come nearer. Adam took one step forward in front of me, shielded me with his body, and whispered, "Now, go."

I ran down the path a few steps and stopped. I couldn't leave him there. Everything I had ever read was telling my brain that bears didn't attack unless they were provoked, but this one was angry about something. Adam was speaking in a low, soothing voice, in a language I didn't understand. He murmured, his voice a gentle lull, as if comforting a child. It seemed to be calming the bear down. I took a deep breath. This had been a close call with disaster. The bear looked like it was going to back down, then it roared and swung a giant claw down and struck Adam on the chest. He went airborne, barely missing a huge branch on a nearby tree.

The bear ambled over to where he lay, and nudged his face with its large muzzle. After what seemed forever, Adam raised one arm up and laid his hand on the bear's massive, furry head. As if it were happy with the current state of events, it turned and disappeared into the forest in three great bounds.

I ran over and fell down on my knees to where Adam was lying on his bare back. I leaned over his face. His eyes were open and looked at me with a mixture of relief and anger as he sat up. A huge, bloody mass of deep claw marks stretched from the top of his shoulder down the front of his chest. Small rivulets of blood ran down onto his bare stomach.

"Are you okay? Are you crazy? Are you hurt? She could have killed you!" He took me by the shoulders and shook me once hard, and then one hand came up to cup my chin and turn my head from side to side, as if to reassure himself that I was in one piece. He seemed oblivious that he was the one in pieces.

"Adam, you're hurt. We have to get you to a hospital." I ripped the bottom part of my t-shirt off and pushed it into the wound to try to get it to stop bleeding. He grunted as I pushed against his chest.

"You didn't run when I told you to." His golden eyes shot arrows at me and once again the air around us popped and sizzled.

"You were about to get eaten by a bear. I wasn't going to let it kill you."

"No, *you* were the one about to get eaten. I was just explaining it to her. You were the one who shouldn't have been there in the first place. Don't you know you shouldn't go wandering around in the forest alone?"

"I thought I was fine, thank you. I was just picking berries, that's all." I lowered my eyes to the ground, suddenly ashamed. "What were you *explaining* to her?"

He smirked, "That you didn't mean any harm to her cub, and…"

"A cub. I didn't see it, I swear," I watched as the blood seeped through the thin shirt and covered my fingers, "I don't think she believed you. We need to get you to a doctor, Adam. It isn't far to the house. Let me help you get up."

"You didn't let me finish," he said.

"Sorry."

"I told her you didn't mean any harm to her cub, and that you were mine. I wouldn't let any harm come to you. She did give me a swat, but it was just to let me know that she wasn't happy about it. She did apologize, though." His eyes sparkled with mischief.

I was shocked. He had just claimed me as *his*. He acted as if an apology from a bear was a regular occurrence and was bleeding and looking as if he didn't feel a thing. He was in shock and delirious, I decided. Under normal circumstances, he never would have said something like that. I had known him for a few weeks, which could hardly make me *belong* to anyone.

I reached up and ripped a sleeve off my shirt, getting ready to switch it with the blood-soaked one that was stuck to his chest, when his hands caught mine and held them between his.

"Nikki, stop. I'm fine," he said.

I looked at my hands streaked with his blood. I felt my eyes fill with tears.

"No, you're not. I think you're in shock and I need to get you out of these woods. You aren't feeling pain, so that must mean it is deep. We need to get you help, I have to get you to a doctor, so please help me and stand up," I pled.

"Wait, Nikki. I need to show you something," he said, letting go of my hands. "It's not as bad as you think."

He pulled the sticky piece of shirt off his chest, "I saw a water bottle in the side of your basket over there, if you don't mind, go grab it and bring it here."

I handed it to him and watched as he poured water at the top of his shoulder and let it run down his chest. He wasn't bleeding anymore. Some of the smaller, shallow marks had already closed and the larger ones just looked raw. I reached over and touched his chest in wonder. My brimming eyes spilled over.

"Don't cry, Nikki, please. I'm okay. It doesn't hurt much at all. I'm fine." He pulled me toward him in a big hug. One hand petted my hair while the other held me close.

I pulled back and looked up at him, one last tear slid free and slid down my cheek. He brushed it away with his thumb, then slid his hand behind my neck. Leaning forward, he kissed my cheek.

"No one has ever worried that much about me before," he whispered. His eyes looked troubled.

I'm the one who watches out and worries for everyone else. No one does it for me, a voice whispered in my mind. *I am a Keeper.*

I realized my hand was still against his chest, I slowly moved it away. His wound had closed itself under my hand. It looked like it had been healing for weeks, instead of a few short minutes. Faint, pink scars in an outline of a huge claw, were all that was left.

"What are you?" I whispered, looking up into his eyes. The word *Keeper* kept echoing in my head.

"You don't want to know," he stood up and turned his back to me.

You'll be afraid of me if I show you, and you'll run as far from me as you can get. I can't stand being away from you, the voice whispered.

"I'm not afraid of you, and I'm not running. Why should you stay away from me?" I asked, frowning. "What the heck is a Keeper?"

His eyes narrowed. "You heard me."

"I guess I did," I shrugged, giving into the fact that I must indeed be nuts to admit to the voices in my head. Oh well, at least I wasn't the only insane one here. "Show me."

He looked at me uncertainly, and then seemed to make up his mind as he nodded.

The air stirred again, snapping and popping as if it were charged by a thousand tiny currents. The amber in his eyes shimmered. The little onyx specks in his irises pulsated and circled his pupils.

I am a Keeper. I am U-la-gu of my tribe, the leader of the Six.

A soft black mist materialized out of thin air. It flowed down his shoulders and across his chest, creeping towards his hands as it left a soft black fur in its wake. Where the fur reached, the muscles tensed and changed.

Our tribe is one of the oldest in the land. When white men came to this land, we were a mighty and fierce people. We were many. When they came, they took everything they wanted. Our land, our food, our lives.

He was covered in the black fur. He dropped down to his knees and doubled in size. His hands and feet clawed into the soft moss, his head bowed down.

A few of my people survived. They took refuge in the mountains. The wolf had been watching the white men, and went to the mountains to speak to the elders of the tribe. He said, "They do not respect our Mother Earth. They take and they do not give. They are men of no honor. Your people must survive to teach your children the old ways, so that the land may heal. I will give you a gift to protect you." The wolf dug up a large stone and scratched it with his foot, and then gave it to the elders. "In the morning, they shall come," he said, and disappeared into the fog.

His spine straightened, and he raised his head.

When dawn came, the firstborn sons of the elders, their best warriors and hunters—the only six that had survived—transformed into wolves. They were the first of the Keepers, the protectors of the wood.

I stared into the beautiful amber eyes of a giant black wolf. I walked closer to him as he sat back on his haunches. He never moved when I walked around him. He stared straight ahead, as if I weren't there.

I reached out and put my hand between his shoulders and ran my fingers down his back. His fur felt like silk. The muscles in his back quivered where my hand touched. I came back in front of him and looked back up into his eyes.

I smiled and reached out to touch his soft, furry cheek, "You're still just Adam. Your eyes haven't changed. They're still beautiful."

Yeah, I'm still me. But there's still a lot you don't know.

"Then tell me."

The air sparked again for what seemed like a split second, and then the fur melted away in a black fog. I was staring into his human face. Nothing he had done had seemed unusual. He could change into a wolf—a really big wolf—but it didn't matter. He was Adam.

I ran my hand across his perfect chest. The scars were completely gone. I rose up on my toes and kissed him. The air around us sparked, seeming to take on a life of its own. He froze for a second and then kissed me back. He buried his hand in the tangle of curls at the base of my neck. His other arm wrapped around my waist. He lifted me off the ground and closer to him. The kiss deepened.

I wrapped my arms around his neck and filled my hands with his long, silky hair. I felt like I could kiss him forever. The air shimmered around us, as if it were charged by magic. Adam broke the kiss, but still held me in a hug against him.

"There's still so much you need to know. I've wanted to tell you since I first saw you. You need to know it all," he whispered. His breath was warm against my neck.

"It doesn't matter," I said, clinging tighter to him.

"Yes, it does. It matters a great deal." He set me back down on the ground and looked down at me, his eyes serious. "We need to go to the Res."

He walked over and picked up the basket of berries that I had forgotten, and came back to take my hand.

"Does your mother expect you home soon?" he asked.

"No, she's working late today, and Emily's been at friend's house for a sleepover all weekend. There's no one home."

He nodded and led me down the path.

"There is someone we need to talk. That way you can be sure," he said.

That way I can be sure, too, of what you are. Of who you are, his thoughts came into my mind unbidden.

I didn't say anything in response. I was pretty sure these were thoughts he wasn't trying to send to me, but somehow I heard them as clearly as if he had spoken aloud.

The Seer. She isn't tribe, but how does she have it? Does it matter? The clans have never mixed, so the elders won't like it. It still doesn't matter, though. I will fight for her if it comes to that, his thoughts clouded my mind and my vision blurred, then a flash blinded me.

I sat around the campfire, laughing with my brothers, when I saw her coming toward me. The girl I watched was me. I watched myself reach out toward his eyes.

Another flash...*Panic. There was a bear. I had to save her.*

Flash! *Warmth, heat sizzling in the air. She's mine. I think I love her.*

My vision blurred again, and then I saw Adam's hand waving frantically in front of my face.

"What's wrong? You just stopped walking and stared. You wouldn't answer me. Are you okay?" He looked as if he were getting ready to throw me over his shoulder and go running to find help.

"I'm fine. Just have a little bit of a headache, but I'm okay," I tried to sound reassuring as I looked at his worried face and took a deep breath.

"You're a terrible liar," he said. "What did you see?"

So much for pretending. "How do you know I saw anything?"

"I know. Now tell me." He crossed his arms across his chest and waited.

"I saw you at the campfire, at my house, and in the woods. I felt your fear, then warmth, and then I heard you think something was wrong," I concluded, leaving out the "love" part, in case maybe he didn't want to know I had heard or felt that particular word.

"You can see, hear *and* feel what I'm thinking?" His mouth dropped open.

"It appears so, yeah," I said.

"None of the others could do all three."

"What others? There are other people that do this?"

"They are called the Seers. For every generation of Keepers, there is one Seer. So far, they have had either the gift of sight, sound, or touch. Never all three. Jenna White Hawk is the Seer for my father's generation. She has Sight. She is who I want you to meet today." He laced his fingers into mine and we started walking again.

"Jenna. Erik's mom?" I asked. The petite, happy, little waif of a woman that I had met earlier didn't seem the type to be dubbed something as ominous sounding as *the Seer*.

"Yeah, Erik's mom. She told us that the Seer for our generation would not be from our tribe. The elders were not happy about that, being as the powwow starts in a couple months, and there will be at least one other tribe in town then. They aren't thrilled with the idea of the clans mixing, but I don't think they have anything to worry about with them," he said, looking over at me. "I think it's you. You are our Seer."

"Me?" I squeaked, tripping over a root in my astonishment. I caught myself before I fell. "But I'm not Indian. Well, not entirely. My great-grandmother was Cherokee. All that's in me is from her. There's nothing of the Wighcomocos tribe in me at all."

Adam nodded. "I know that. I don't know how you have The Sight, but I do know you have it. I haven't told anyone else, since I wanted to make sure. I knew something was going on the day I felt your pull when I came to your house. I didn't know who you were; I just knew you were there, and that I had to see you. That's a trait of tribe, buy it's never happened before with outsiders. I thought maybe I was just going crazy, and then I saw you that night at the campfire. Your spirit was hovering around the flames. I still didn't tell anyone, but Erik knew I had seen something. Today, I knew where you were and I knew you needed me. You've heard, felt and saw my every thought, which is something that I've never even heard of. We need to tell Jenna, though she probably knows. I think she was going to say more until the elders got upset thinking about the other tribes. She didn't say anything else about her Sight after that. She's waiting."

We reached the edge of the reservation, when I saw that Jenna really did seem to be waiting. She was sitting on her front porch. She smiled at us as we walked up. Erik came out of the house, letting the screen door slap shut behind him as he walked over and sat next to his mother. When he saw me with my t-shirt torn and blood on my hands, his usual happy-go-lucky grin left and something animal came into his eyes. He jumped from his chair and over the porch railing to land mere inches from us in a crouch. His nostrils flared as if he smelled the blood.

"Yours?" he asked Adam, his dark brown eyes wide.

"Yeah," Adam replied.

"So, she knows." Erik stood up to his full height and looked down at me in wonder.

"Yeah, she knows," I repeated, grinning at him.

His smile returned and he threw an arm around my shoulder, giving me a quick squeeze. "It's about time. Now maybe he'll quit bellyaching and ask you out. The rest of us are getting tired of listening to him. He gets cranky when he can't figure something out."

Adam gave him a cold stare. Erik dropped his arm from my shoulders, but kept his grin in place.

"Enough, boys. Erik, take Adam and show him the new parts you got for your bike," Jenna said, getting up from her chair on the porch. "Nikki, come on in, we'll get you cleaned up and get you a fresh shirt."

As she herded me toward the door, I looked back over my shoulder, to see Erik punch Adam in the arm as they walked towards the little garage.

"Okay, old man, tell me everything. What did she say? What happened? Did she bloody you? And if she did, what did you do to make her so mad? That was a lot of blood. You know, if you needed help, you should have called. I was just kidding about the cranky part," I heard him chatter non-stop as they walked away.

"Boys, especially my two," Jenny shook her head as she opened the screen door for me to step inside.

She led me through the little house to a small bedroom with a small bathroom that set over to the side. "You'll find what you need in there. I had Erik leave you a shirt on the bed. You're a bit bigger than me, so there's one of his in there. It may be a bit big, but it should work. Go clean up, and then we'll answer your questions. I know you must have quite a few of them."

I went in the bathroom and found a washcloth with a fresh bar of soap lying by the sink, as if it were there just for me. I looked into the mirror. My shirt was half hanging off me. I had torn it in a way that had bared my stomach. It kind of looked like what Jane wore on Tarzan, I thought, amused. I scrubbed my hands. They were streaked a brownish red with dried blood. I watched as the water turned bright and scarlet as it swirled in the sink. After scrubbing all the way up to my elbows, I got it all off and splashed water on my face. I pulled the shirt over my head and threw it into the trash bin beside the sink. I found the shirt on the bed right where Jenna had said I would. I picked it up and smiled. In bold print across the front it said, *Sure you can trust the government, just ask an Indian.* The solemn picture of Sitting Bull stared back at me.

How did she know we would be coming today? And how did she know I was going to need a shirt? I wondered as I pulled the fresh shirt over my head. It came halfway down my thighs. I tugged my hair out of the collar, untangling the curls with my fingers.

I found Jenna sitting at the kitchen table, sipping a Coke. Looking at me in the huge shirt, she rolled her eyes. "Erik and his sense of humor. Did you find everything else you needed?"

I sat down across from her and she slid me a can of soda. "Yes. How did you know?" I asked, popping the top and taking a drink. I hadn't realized I was thirsty until then.

"I saw you before you moved back. The Seer of the current generation will find the Seer for the next when they have their first vision. I saw you moments before the police came to your house. I watched your eyes lose their innocence and then I knew you had seen your first vision. I am sorry for your loss, Nikki. I knew your father. He was a good man." Her eyes filled with sympathy and her hand came over to squeeze mine.

My mind flashed back to moments before the doorbell rang. I saw my father, driving in our black SUV as he headed toward home. He wasn't far away, only a couple miles from home, when a gravel truck ran a red light. I felt his panic and heard the tires squeal as the brakes tried to stop in vain. I saw the blood on the windshield; my father slumped over the wheel. I heard his last thought, *I haven't told my girls I love them today. Who will take care of my girls?* I had known before I heard the doorbell. The doorbell still haunted my worst nightmares. I had stood motionless, while my mother screamed and fell sobbing to the floor. But I already knew. I stood stripped of all emotion. I knew he would never come home again.

I looked back into Jenna's face as tears filled her eyes. "You poor baby," she whispered.

"Did you just see all of that?" I asked, uneasily. That experience wasn't something I had ever planned on sharing with anyone.

"Yes. Sometimes the Keepers or the Seer will project their emotions so vividly that you can't help seeing them. If they feel strongly enough, you will be forced to see. I think your father loved you so much and his feelings for you were so strong that it forced you to see. I am sorry that your first sight was something so hard."

"What was the first thing you saw?" I asked, ready to change the subject.

"I saw my husband, although he wasn't my husband then. When we were about your age, a group of us would go out to the lake to fish. Before we left, I had a vision of him tripping, and landing in the lake. I knew he couldn't swim. All day I watched him, I followed him barefoot wherever he walked, ready to jump in and save him. He didn't understand why I was so close to him all day and turned around to tell me to leave him alone. When he did that, he tripped and in the water he went." She grinned, "Of course, I was ready to save him and dove in and drug him back to the bank. He still likes to blame me for his landing in the water. It wasn't long after that, he became a Keeper, one of the Six. I saw that before it happened, but I didn't tell him. By then, I knew what I was and was afraid to tell anyone. Eventually, the Seer before me explained everything to me, as I'm explaining it now to you."

I frowned. "The only other person I have seen or heard has been Adam and I think the other boys while they were wolves. I can hear Adam's thoughts, but I don't think he wants me in his head. Why can I hear him so clearly? It's as if he's speaking out loud most of the time."

"He's feeling something very strongly and projecting it to you. Knowing Adam, he's trying to figure things out. He's thinking hard. That's why you're picking it up. Plus, you're new at this. Before long, you'll be getting everything from the Six until you learn to control it. I'll teach you how to channel, so it doesn't catch you off guard. There are times that you won't be able to control it. You'll be locked in if the other person's emotions are not under control," she explained.

"Adam told me I was the only one that could see, hear and feel. Am I the only one who can do all three?" Questions kept popping up in my head as I tried to figure it all out. My brain was on overload.

"The first Seer of our tribe, who lived hundreds of years ago, was said to have all three gifts. She wasn't from our tribe. She appeared one day in the mountains, in the form of a wolf -the color of untouched snow. The Keepers thought it was a message from the Wolf that had given them the stone. When they came up to where they had spotted the wolf, there stood a young girl with white skin and hair, and eyes the color of a pale, blue sky. They named her White Wolf and took her into the tribe. They raised her as their own. It is said she could predict anything from drought to war with another tribe. She lived to be over a hundred years old and her sight stayed with her to the end. Her last vision came to her on her deathbed. She saw a young girl, one like herself, who would come into the tribe without the blood of the tribe running through her veins. When she died, our people saw the white wolf at the edge of the village again. When they returned later, her body was gone and the white pelt of a wolf lay in its place.

When one Seer sees the other for the next generation, her sight starts to fade. She won't see as clearly. White Wolf was the only one who kept her gift her whole life. My sight has faded, and I cannot see what reaction the elders will have now. I am hoping that they will remember White Wolf when they learn of you. I hope they remember her prophecy."

Voices drifted in from the front porch, announcing the boys had finished inspecting their motorcycle parts. Jenna smiled and stood up. "They've stayed away as long as they could, I suppose. Adam is worried about you. Let's go see what they are into."

We went back out onto the porch to find that Ed, Tommy and Michael had shown up as well. They all moved, leaving me a spot on the steps next to Adam. I smiled as I dropped down and sat beside him.

"Well, Mom?" Erik asked, looking over at Jenna, "Is she?"

"You guys are looking at your new Seer."

"Ha. I knew it. I knew it when I saw her drawing Ed's wolf in art class," he said, grinning from ear to ear. Then he looked down at me. "Nice shirt, by the way."

I stuck my tongue out at him and his grin stretched even farther.

"Hannah is going to be very upset," Ed said, in his usual philosophical manner.

"Hannah?" I asked, perplexed, "Why would she be upset?"

"She thought she was going to be the next Seer, since she is the only other girl our age other than Penny," Erik explained.

"What about Penny?" I asked.

"Penny doesn't have it, I would know," Erik shrugged.

"How would you know?" I asked. This was getting more confusing by the second.

"A trait of tribe," Ed said, going into his teacher mode. "When one of the Six finds his other half that will complete him, he just knows. Or so I've heard. Erik, what is Penny doing right now?"

"She's in her room, close to the phone, I think. She was in the garden with her mother, but she's moved inside. She might have seen you guys come," Erik replied.

He had just finished speaking, when the phone rang inside the house and we listened as Jenna went back inside and answered it, "Hi, Penny. Yes, they're all out here. Yes, just visiting. Nikki's here with Adam. Sure, tell your mother I would love some tomatoes."

We all listened to the conversation and my mouth dropped as I realized what it all meant. I glanced over at Adam. His sneakers hadn't even gotten tied in his hurry to find me, the laces were still dangling. He turned and looked me full in the face, watching my expression. He always knew where I was. The air sparked around us. His eyes softened as he stared at me.

Erik laughed, looking at us. "Yeah, Hannah's going to be pissed."

"She'll have to get over it," Adam whispered.

"Adam, I hate to run you and Nikki off. If you're planning on walking her home through the woods, you'll have to get started soon to get her back before dark. She won't be as fast as you, you know," Jenna said, coming back out of the house. "Come back anytime you're free, Nikki, and we'll work on channeling so you can choose when and what you want to see."

Adam stood up and reached down for my hand to help me up. His hand was warm and solid when I took it and stood. Erik whistled. The cousins grinned, their dimples showing deep in their cheeks. I turned and thanked Jenna, who gave me a big hug.

We walked back into the woods the way we had come earlier. My mind was still reeling from everything I learned. There was still so much that I didn't know.

"Why does everyone keep calling the Keepers, 'the Six'? There are only five of you," I pointed out.

"There are only five of us, one is missing. There have always been six Keepers. We think maybe one of the other guys, Darren, may be our sixth. His dad, Reuben, is the only one of the elders that still is a Keeper. Reuben rarely runs with us anymore. He isn't as strong as he used to be, which means he hasn't passed on his gift yet, but it won't be long. So far, the wolf's gift has always been passed from father to son during a full moon. If Jenna told you about how the Seers sight fades as the one comes to take her place, it works the same way with the Six. Reuben's wolf is getting weaker. He's starting to fade," he explained.

"Oh, there was just a full moon last week. I saw it when you were searching for the lost hiker. I guess you guys will have to wait for the next one." I said, then stopped as I felt the tiny splats of ghost-like raindrops that hadn't fell. "We'd better hurry. It's going to rain soon."

"How do you know that? Never mind. Dumb question. I already know the answer." He grinned when he saw the large, dark clouds overhead moments later.

"We're going to get wet," I said staring up at the sky.

"Maybe not," he looked down at me, "I could carry you. I'd have you home in a matter of minutes."

"Carry me?"

The black mist had already rolled down him and he sat there staring at me. The wolfish smile on his face showed off his razor sharp teeth.

Sure, carry you. I've never done it before, but if you hold on tight, I don't see how it would be a problem. His shoulders did a small twitch that resembled a shrug. *Just get on my back. We'll go slowly at first to see if it works. Worse case scenario, it doesn't work, and we get wet.*

Well, it sounded logical, I thought, as I crawled up onto his silky back. My feet dangled several inches from the ground. Unsure where to hold on, I wound my fingers into the soft fur between his shoulders, where the collar of his shirt should have been had he been wearing one.

"I have a question," I said as he began an experimental walk, "I don't mean to sound crude, but where do your clothes go when you shift? Your shorts were there when you shifted back earlier, so where did they go just now?"

They're still there, I guess. It works better when you shift with no clothes, though sometimes that's not possible. As long as you wear clothes close to the same color as your wolf, they tend to blend in. That's why I wear black most of the time. You can wear other stuff, but your fur ends up looking kinda weird when you shift in them, he snorted, amused.

Erik, for example, he continued, *loves tie-die stuff. We were called up to help look for a lost hiker on the trail last year. We split up to cover more territory. Erik was wearing a tie-die Mickey Mouse shirt and forgot to change. He found the hiker, who had fallen over a small embankment. He switched back when he realized his mistake, and managed to jerk off his shirt and hide it in a hollow tree, but not before the hiker had seen his wolf. When Erik reached him, the hiker told him he thought he may have hit his head and that he was going to need medical treatment. He said he had just seen a huge gray wolf with a neon colored chest in the shape of Mickey Mouse ears.*

I laughed, imagining the hiker staring dumbfounded at a tie-die colored wolf. A loud clap of thunder made me look up at the sky. The clouds rumbled over us. It was getting darker.

We'd better try going a little faster, he said, picking up speed.

I gripped his fur tighter as the trees flew past us. I leaned forward and buried my face in his neck, trying not to look down at the ground that passed beneath me in a blur. I breathed in the earthy, wooded smell of him and closed my eyes. His muscles worked beneath me in strong fluid motions. We were slowing down, I realized, as I turned my head to look and saw the trees with their outstretched limbs that seemed to move out of our way as if by magic. I saw my house up ahead as Adam stopped and waited for me to get off. I slid off him, and came around to wrap my arms around his furry neck in a big hug. I felt him lift me off the ground as he shifted, then his arms came around my waist to hold me close to him. The air sparked around us as a clap of lightening streaked across the sky.

"You need to go now before you get wet," he said as he set me back down.

I leaned back and looked up into his eyes. He brushed my hair back and kissed my forehead, then turned toward the forest. I grabbed his arm and turned him back to me. I kissed him hard, and watched as his eyes widened, then closed. He kissed me back, holding my face between his hands.

"Goodnight, Nikki," he whispered as he shifted back into the black wolf, and then turned to disappear in the trees.

"Goodnight," I whispered to the empty spot where he had been.

A giant splat landed on my head, forcing me to turn and make a mad dash toward the house before the torrent of rain soaked me. I reached the front step a second before it poured.

NINE

GOOGLE WAS AN unstoppable force. There were over 800,000 links that promised information on werewolves, but nothing on the Wighcomocos legend. I sat there for hours in my room, trying to find the right source for information. It was exasperating. Everything I saw wanted me to watch this movie, or read that horror book. All the pictures were of horrific creatures that promised certain doom with beady eyes, sharp, blood-covered fangs and long claws. The only chance for my survival? A silver bullet. It was all wrong. I sat, disgusted, and stared at the monitor where a grotesque figure with long, scary claws stood on its back feet and glared back at me. Adam wasn't this monster at all. As a human, he was a gorgeous guy. But as his wolf, he was graceful, powerful, sleek and astounding. He was beautiful, plain and simple, as a guy and as a wolf.

I clicked on another link that informed me of the saving power of silver ammunition. I wondered if even that would slow Adam down. I wound one blonde curl around my finger as I looked at the screen. If he could tangle with a bear and come out untouched, a bullet wouldn't stop him either. As long as he was a Keeper, he had to be safe. I hoped he would always be safe.

"Nikki, phone."

I ran down the stairs and caught the phone as Mom tossed it to me from the kitchen.

"Hello?"

"Hey. It's me," an unidentified girl gushed on the other end of the line. "You're never going to believe this."

"Ronnie?" I asked, perplexed, as I curled up on the sofa and tucked my legs under me.

"Oh, yeah, sorry. It's me. Listen, you know how Bernie and Beth were at cheer practice the other day? Well, guess what?"

"I..." one word was all that made it out.

"Never mind, you'll never guess. Who would? I mean, it's like, just amazing that's all." She sounded giddy.

"Ok, Ronnie. What on earth are you talking about?"

"I just talked to Beth. You're the main story for the school paper tomorrow. Bernie took lots of shots of the pyramids at cheerleading practice last week. He took *tons* of close-ups, and they just developed them today. They saw where Tiffany's leg was moved when you fell." She sounded like a chipmunk chattering away.

"I'm the main story for the paper," I groaned. Just great, as if I didn't have enough going on in my life right now.

"Didn't you hear me?" she asked, "It means that the crazy Barbie doll may have to answer for what she did. They could kick her off the squad. It's proof in black and white. We could get a new captain. Maybe we could vote you in. You are better than she is, anyway."

"No," I bellowed into the receiver in alarm.

"Oh." She sounded as if her feelings were hurt. I took a deep breath and made a mental note to grab aspirin for the migraine that had started to throb in my temple.

"Sorry, Ronnie," I sighed. "What I meant was that I don't think I could handle being captain, but thanks for the vote of confidence. Please don't vote me in. I'm not cut out to be a leader, and there are other girls with way more experience than I have. We need someone who has been in the squad awhile that would know how to help the new girls. I think you would be the one that would be perfect as captain." I needed that aspirin. I got up and made my way up the steps towards the bathroom.

"You think so?" she asked.

"Absolutely. In fact, if they ask for suggestions, I'm going to tell them you should do it," I spoke with as much conviction as I could muster. My head felt as if it were going to explode. Small pulses of pain throbbed and my vision was starting to blur.

"I wouldn't be against it. Listen, I need to make a couple more phone calls. Do you want me to call you back?"

"No, no, that's ok," I said, secretly rejoicing as I found the little bottle and popped the cap open. "I'll see you at school."

"Okay. Bye, Nikki." The phone clicked and she was gone.

I had just swallowed two of the little white pills when it rang again. So much for a quiet evening. I snatched up the phone again.

"I'll talk to you tomorrow at school." I couldn't keep the anger from seeping into the words.

"I hope so," Brian said, laughing in my ear. "Or even on the way to school would be nice, too."

"Sorry, I thought you were someone else," I said, embarrassed.

"It's okay. Beth just called me a little while ago, so I know what's going on and how news travels. I was just calling to check on you," his voice softened, "Are you okay?"

"Yes, I just don't like being the center of attention. Maybe I shouldn't go to school tomorrow," I mumbled as I went into my bedroom and sat in my chair. I watched the rain come down, making tiny rivulets that ran down the window.

"You know it won't help if you skip tomorrow. The whole school is going to be up in the air about it for awhile. You're going to have to face it."

"I know, but I still don't want to go."

"If it helps any, Tiffany will be getting way more attention than you will," he pointed out the obvious in an attempt to help me.

"I know," I said, "so how were your grandparents? Did you have fun in Roanoke? Was it a good weekend?"

"Yeah, change the subject, won't you? But to answer you, they were fine and I didn't have as much fun as I used to have going up there, but it was still okay. It would have been a better weekend if I could have spent it here. Did you get your berries?"

"Yes." And a whole lot more, I thought. I hated lying to him, but what was I going to say? Well, I found out that I'm some kind of telepath/empath that can hear the thoughts of werewolves. Nothing major, just your usual weekend. Yeah, right. No way was I telling him this stuff, he wouldn't understand. "Just berry picking and you missed the rain."

"I didn't miss the rain. I think we got home just in time for it. I wish I could have gone with you. Next time you go if you'll let me know, I'll come and help. Four hands are better than two."

"Deal," I said, glad not to have been questioned anymore on the state of events of the last two days. "Am I picking you up tomorrow?"

"If you'd like. I shall be honored to ride in your rag-topped chariot."

"You should be. I don't do that for just anyone."

"Okay, so I'll see you in the morning. Bye, Nikki."

"Bye, Brian," I listened to the faint click as he broke the connection.

Adam and the guys must have gotten a heads up about the paper. The next morning, they surrounded us as if they were secret service agents. As soon as I parked, Adam opened my door and waited for me to get out. Brian looked past me and gave him some kind of drop dead look that I had never seen on his face before. Adam ignored him and stood holding the door like a seasoned, professional doorman. I just stared from one to the other, wondering what I was supposed to do. It kind of felt like one of those western movies my dad used to watch, where the two guys come out of the saloon and challenge each other to a duel. I was stuck in the middle and I was wondering who was going to draw first. I picked my books up and held them in front of me, ready to smack the first hand that reached across.

Brian snorted and rolled his eyes. "Well, Nikki, the cavalry has shown up. I don't think you have as much to worry about as you thought or maybe you have more, I don't know. Either way, I'll see you in class." He got out of the car and shut the door a little harder than I approved of, then headed toward the school.

I looked at Adam, who still held the door. "Hi, what's up?"

His solemn façade broke and he grinned at me, his amber eyes sparkling. "Power in numbers. Everyone leaves us alone, so now they'll leave you alone, too, since you're with us. We would have protected Brian, too, if he hung around," he joked as he held out his hand for me.

"Yeah, I don't see that happening—ever. I've never seen that look on his face before. He's mad at you." I took the offered hand and got out of the car.

"Yeah, I encroached on his territory. Or so he thinks. If you want to get technical about it, he's on mine. It doesn't matter, he'll get over it," he shrugged as if Brian was the last thing he was worried about.

I felt my cheeks burn hot with anger, causing the air to spark and sizzle around us. I jerked my hand free of his. "He is my friend, my best friend actually, and I don't like the way you're treating him."

"That's not the way he thinks of you. He wants a lot more than just friendship," Adam replied in a steely voice.

"As if you can read his mind." I glared at him and turned to jerk my books from the dash of the truck.

"I don't have to. It's obvious what he wants. He wants *you*—and not just as a friend.". He crossed his arms over his chest and scowled.

Erik cleared his throat beside us. We both turned and shouted, "What!" Causing him to flinch and take a cautious step back.

"Um, I hate to interrupt you. But in like two minutes, we're all going to be late for class, and then everyone's going to notice us more than before." He pointed at the empty steps. Everyone was already inside the school.

"You're right, let's go," Adam said, waiting as the four boys took off in front of us. He turned back to me. "I'm sorry, it's just that I don't like sharing. I'll try to take his feelings into consideration, for your sake."

"Thank you, I'm sorry, too. My nerves are on edge today, I shouldn't have snapped at you." I managed a half-smile and reached over to take his hand as we walked behind the human shield of the four guys in front of us.

At the door, he leaned over and kissed me. "Ed and Erik are in most of your classes. If you need them, let them know. I was going to ask if you wanted me to walk you to classes, but I'll let Brian do it. It may help calm him down if he thinks he's protecting you and I back off a little. I'll see you in English."

The entire day consisted of people asking me if I knew that Tiffany made me fall. It was a dumb question, but I still shrugged and said that I hadn't been looking down at the time, which wasn't a lie. I had felt her move, but I hadn't seen it. No need to add fuel to the fire, by the way I figured it. She was going to be answering a lot of her own questions, so I didn't say much to anyone. I tried to look as boring and uninteresting as I could. I doodled on papers, stared off into space and even tried pretending to be asleep in one class, although that didn't last long. The last thing I needed were teachers getting angry with me.

In English class, no one bothered me as Adam stayed close, guarding me as if I were the Queen of England. By lunch, my plan had worked, and everyone decided that I was pretty dull and not very forthcoming, so instead of pestering me, they settled for Ronnie, since she had been my escort to the nurse's station. The fact that she loved to talk was a bonus and they had flocked to her, bombarding her with questions. All the while, she smiled and talked some more. I looked at our little table that was packed with people. Ronnie was surrounded, and was chattering nonstop. Brian was immersed in some conversation with some other boy. His dark hair fell down to his eyes as he shook his head in answer to some question he had been asked. He looked up as if he felt me watching him, took a quick look around the table and lifted one shoulder in a small, helpless shrug.

Come sit with us, a voice suggested and I looked over to see Adam watching me.

He pulled out the chair beside him in invitation. I sat my tray down on the table and slid in next to him. I stared down at my food, which was looking less appetizing by the second. I looked over at Michael who seemed to be shoveling more food down than the others. His plate emptied in seconds, and I pushed mine, still untouched, over in front of him.

"Are you sure?" he asked, politely. His fork was poised above the plate in midair.

"Yeah, have at it," I replied, a second before he dug in.

"Thanks," he murmured through a mouthful.

I looked over at Adam. "What have you been doing to him that he's eating so much more than the rest of you?"

"We've been splitting up shifts at night, keeping an eye on everything. Michael was the last wolf out. He didn't have time for breakfast this morning. So, he's hungrier," he shrugged, tossing a cookie that was leftover on his plate at Michael's bent head.

Michael's eyes snapped up as if he had heard the movement and he snagged the cookie a millisecond before it whacked him in the head. In two bites, it was gone, and the rest of my plate was cleared. He sighed, contented. "Thanks. I feel better."

"So if everything is okay and the trail killer has been caught, why are you still patrolling at night so much?"

"They've arrested Mr. Walters, but we aren't so convinced he's the trail killer," Ed replied.

"Yeah, something just doesn't feel right about that. Have you *seen* Mr. Walters?" Erik chimed in. "He doesn't look like the serial killer type, if you know what I mean. He's all sweaters and loafers. He works in the library." The frown on his face suggested that one would never find a killer in such a setting.

"Yeah, but those are the types that are the serial killers. They are always the ones you least suspect," I said, thinking of some of the forensic shows I had watched.

"Still, something just doesn't feel right. It's not anything we can explain. It's a gut feeling. We walk through the forest and something just feels wrong, as if there is evil just lurking there, just waiting," Ed said in a hushed voice.

"Speaking of evil lurking," Tommy lifted his chin, pointing towards the far corner of the room, where Tiffany sat alone, glaring at me as if I were Satan himself.

I bit my lip and looked down at the table. Her eyes were boring holes into me. Adam's hand came under the table to squeeze mine. I heard movement and snuck a peek in her direction. She slid back from the table, her chair scraped against the floor. The entire room went quiet as she stood up, threw me some more *I could kill you* glances, and stalked out of the room. Her Ugg boots made padded thumps against the tile floor as she stomped out, her long blonde ponytail bouncing back and forth on her back as if it were as angry as she was.

I took a big gulp from my bottled water with my free hand, and plopped it back down on the table. My hand shook just the tiniest bit. I thought it was barely noticeable. I was wrong. Adam's hand squeezed mine tighter and automatically I was bombarded.

Are you okay, Nikki? Nothing to worry about, she's scum. We're here for you; we won't let anything bad happen. Did you see the way she walked out of here? Everything's gonna be just fine, you'll see. Anger, protectiveness, worry, and a faint bit of panic coursed through my brain all at once.

"Whoa," I yelped. "Everybody, stop."

Most of the heads in the room that had seconds before been watching Tiffany's retreating back, were now turned and watching me curiously. I cringed. Great, just what I needed. More attention.

"Would everyone please stop thinking so loudly? I'm fine," I hissed through my clenched teeth.

Several apologies were whispered to me from across the table. After a rather uncomfortable moment, everyone else turned back around and stopped staring at us. I breathed a sigh of relief and managed a halfhearted smile at the worried faces that sat with me.

"Do you need me to sit in the bleachers and watch out for you at practice?" Adam asked. "With the way she's looking at you, I wouldn't put anything past her."

"No, you have class too. They're not going to let you skip just so you can ogle the girls' cheerleading team. I appreciate the concern, though."

"I can get out of it. I think I may have pulled a muscle. You can't work out if you're hurt." He managed a fake, unconvincing grimace and rubbed his shoulder.

I stifled the spastic giggle. Adam hurt? Yeah, right. He was the picture of health with all his taut, lean muscles. He looked like the kind of guy that would be on the posters for milk advertisements. The guy radiated strength and power as if it were all ordinary for him. Even if they didn't know about Adam's healing capabilities, no teacher in his right mind was going to just let him skip class. He looked too healthy.

He skipped class.

He sat in the lower bleachers, nearer the guy's basketball team than to us, watching us as we came in and walked over to our side of the gym. I looked over at him and raised an eyebrow. In return, he lifted one shoulder and gave me a sheepish grin. It seemed he was a better actor than I realized. I smiled to myself and turned back, making sure that I stayed somewhat close to Ronnie and as far as I could get from Tiffany while we stretched and waited for Ms. Perkins to arrive.

"Everyone quiet now, please." A very determined-looking Ms. Perkins strode out onto the hardwood floor. Her face was grim and serious. "I'm sure you have all seen the school paper today. Per the suggestions made from the principal, we have come to a decision. This year, for the first time, we will be putting the position of captain up for a vote."

Excitement rippled through the line of green-and-white pom-pommed girls. Nervous giggles and small exclamations of surprise echoed up and down the line.

"Quiet, please." Ms. Perkins smiled at the eager faces in front of her. "I am going to give you each one slip of paper. Write the name of the person you think should be captain on it, only one name, and then fold it and give it back to me. Whoever has the most votes, will be the new captain if they choose to accept the position."

The pom-poms fell into a heap on the floor as everyone began searching in earnest for an ink pen to jot down their choice. Tiffany stood over to one side, ashen-faced, her mouth open in shock. Whatever she had expected it hadn't been this. That much was obvious. Her mouth worked closed and open a couple times like a fish that was out of water as she stared at the back of the teacher. Then she saw me watching her and her face changed color to that of a boiled tomato, which at least looked more natural for her.

I snuck a look over at Ronnie and was pleased when I realized that others were looking at her as well. It was looking better all the time. Somehow, a pen found its way into my hand and I wrote down Ronnie's name, folded the slip of paper, and handed it back to the teacher. I handed the pen to the next girl I passed and stood waiting, while the last few finished up and came back into the line.

Her hands full of folded bits of paper, Miss Perkins sat down on the nearest bleacher and started sorting out the names. She ended up with four different piles. The pile farthest from her started stacking up higher than the other three. It was pretty obvious, whoever's name was in that pile, was going to end up being our fearless leader. I sucked in a breath as she finished, looked once more at the name in the biggest pile and stood back up in front of us.

"Your new captain is," she paused for dramatic flair, "Ronnie Stevenson."

Ronnie threw hands over her mouth in surprise and started jumping up and down, while I blew out the breath that I had been holding and went limp with relief. I looked over at Adam, who was grinning from ear to ear across the gym. The entire group seemed elated with their new captain. Well, nearly the entire group. Tiffany, hearing the wondrous news, had gone from her tomato color to a pretty fuchsia and magenta color. It was a color I had only ever seen in tie-dyed clothes, never on the human face. It was quite lovely, and the expression on her face was priceless.

"Being as I believe our new captain will accept her position, we should be getting started now." Miss Perkins clapped her hands to get everyone's attention.

Everyone calmed down and we got back to work. Although she stayed in the group, Tiffany may as well have been on a different planet, though she still managed to shoot me murderous glances whenever the opportunity presented itself. I joined the rest of the group and pretended to ignore her. Thankfully, we didn't work on pyramids again and everyone kept their feet on the floor.

TEN

E RIK SOUNDED ALMOST gleeful as I slid into the chair
between him and Adam. "Turkey nipple soup!"

"Huh?" I asked, perplexed, as I plopped down my tray
on the table.

"You didn't notice that the line over there is like nonexistent
where you went through?"

"Yeah, so? I thought it would be quicker."

"Quicker, yes. Better? No way, you'll see." Erik pointed at my tray,
then over at his in comparison.

"Here, Nikki, take mine," Adam tried handing his plate over to me, which held a cheeseburger.

"No, it's okay," I looked down at my tray to see what the big fuss was about.

In the bowl, a round slice of what looked like turkey sandwich meat lay floating on top of a congealed, yellow substance that was as thick as concrete. I guess it was supposed to be gravy. Small white noodles resembling maggots popped up here and there, surrounded by what I supposed were tiny chicken bits. In the exact center of the meat, a small peak poked upwards, giving the term turkey breast a whole new meaning.

I crinkled up my nose at the weird lunch tray and before I could object, Adam had switched trays with me, placing his in front of me.

"Seriously, eat mine. I've had enough and you shouldn't be subjected to that. If I'd known you were going through that line over there, I would have warned you."

"It seemed like the better choice at the time," I explained, picking up the burger. "I went the long way around school trying to avoid Tiffany. I don't like her, and she knows it. I figure that I'll be telling her so."

"That shouldn't be news to her, nobody likes her," Erik mumbled through his burger.

"So where are you headed after lunch?" Adam switched the subject, eyeing my excuse tucked in a textbook.

"The library. I've got to do research on the history of Bland for an essay, and since I'm new, Mr. Blake gave me a pass to look up some books."

"I can help with that if you'd like after school," Adam offered.

"I bet," Erik teased. "I should place bets on how much homework is going to be done tonight. History. Sure."

Adam grinned. "You're lucky I can't reach you right this second."

"I can," I said, whacking my elbow between Erik's ribs.

The air whooshed out of him, and his tan cheeks took on a gray pallor. "Not cool, Nikki, definitely not cool."

"You'll live," Adam laughed. "Although if you don't watch your mouth around Nikki, you may not live much longer."

Erik rubbed his side, and shook his head at me. "You hit hard for a girl. Don't teach Penny any of that."

"Teach Penny what?" Penny asked, arriving at our table late.

"Here, take my seat," I offered, getting up. "I'm going to go ahead and head to the library."

"See you after school," Adam smiled, making everything inside me go warm and fuzzy.

"Okay," I returned the smile, and started toward the library, never realizing the trouble I had avoided all day had anticipated my next move and lay in wait.

"YOU'D BETTER BACK off." My archenemy had been waiting to ambush me the second I stepped into the library.

"I'm not backing anywhere." Tiffany came the two steps closer it took her to shove me so that my back smacked into the library's solid, wooden door.

"Whatever your problem is, you're going to have a bigger one if you do that again," I seethed, trying to keep from punching her in the face.

"I do what I want and I'll have what I want, too. You'd better remember that," she threatened in what I was guessing was her most menacing voice.

At this exact inopportune moment, I decided to glance over Tiffany's shoulder. I don't know if I had sensed movement over there or what. But whatever it was, it got my attention and left me half-ignoring the threat in front of me.

"Yeah, everybody knows you're a psycho," I murmured, still looking over her shoulder, but registered that the muscles in her shoulder were working.

She punched me.

It was hard enough that I snapped back into reality and landed in the floor at the same time. I brushed my mouth with the back of my hand and it came back sticky and red. The blonde Barbie had managed to split my lip.

I jumped up out of the floor ready to inflict whatever pain that I could. Somehow I managed to grab two handfuls of long glossy hair and was in the process of yanking with every bit of strength that I had when a rather high, nasal voice interrupted me.

"You will stop that this instant. There is no fighting in *my* library."

A sidelong glance proved that Mrs. Graham was on her way to break us apart. Tiffany managed to dig her well manicured claws down the length of my arm before Mrs. Graham grabbed her and pushed her back. Since one of my hands was still tangled in her beautiful hair, I managed to net lots of long, pretty strands between my fingers.

I smiled, bloody and triumphant, feeling as if I had just managed to scalp the enemy.

"You," Mrs. Graham barked at Tiffany, "go to the principal's office. Now."

Tiffany went out the door, making sure to send me one final glare on the way out. Her hair looked less than perfect.

I grinned.

"Don't get excited, you're going there, too, but I'm getting you a tissue first. You're bleeding all over my clean floor." She turned and started walking towards her desk.

As she turned and started walking, her image began to shift and almost disappear. It flickered back and forth, like a light bulb that was about to go out, but was trying to hold on for a little longer.

She came back, holding out a tissue. My fingers accidentally touched hers for a split second and it felt as if I had been jarred with electricity. My first thought was that she must have been shuffling those sensible looking shoes really hard to have shocked me that bad.

I glanced at her feet.

There weren't any shoes on them. Pale, iridescent skin glowed and sparkled on bare feet.

I looked up.

The creature in front of me was tall. Really tall. Even taller than Adam. Her face was oval shaped and her eyes were huge, fathomless blue voids surrounded by long black lashes. There weren't any pupils, they were just blue. She had a lithe, feminine body, with subtle curves. Neon blue hair fell in a straight silky curtain to the back of her knees. Her skin looked like opals, translucent white with blues and reds brushed through. As if all this wasn't strange enough, I found myself fascinated with her clothes. It was as if there were thousands of tiny books, no bigger than the tip of your little finger, sewn together, making a dress of sorts. Tiny pages and covers flitted and fluttered in a beautiful array of browns and whites. I stood there agape. I wondered if I was the only person seeing her, but was afraid that if I quit looking straight at her, this beautiful, magical creature would disappear.

"What are you?" she demanded in a voice that sounded like rainfall.

What are *you*? I thought. And what happened to Mrs. Graham?

"I'm Nikki Harmon," I stammered.

"Not who. I asked you *what* you are." Her blue eyes swirled as her voice took on a sound like thunder.

"Um, human?" I pondered if perhaps I shouldn't be welcoming her to Earth.

"Human, yes, but something more," she spoke as if to herself, her voice changing musically to that of single raindrops falling, soft and lilting, as if the storm had slowed.

The form of Mrs. Graham tried to fit over her again, but failed and fizzed like a bulb that had finally burnt out.

"What do you know of me?" she sounded angrier this time, as if it were all my fault.

"I don't know anything of you. I mean about you. Who are you?" I said in as calm a voice as I could muster.

"It is doubtful, yet you have magic because it recognized my own. If it is meant for you to know of me, then you shall in due time," she sounded resigned.

"Mrs. Graham?" I asked.

She gave me a sad sort of smile. And then I stared into the pinched face of the grouchy librarian.

"Get on to class, and the next time you stir up trouble, it's the principal's office for you," she sniffed, and went back to sit at her desk.

I ran back through the library door, with just enough time to glance and see the opal-skinned woman watching me go. No one else in the room had seen anything but the body of Mrs. Graham where she sat dutifully at the front desk, watching them with a pinched, sour scowl.

"Whoa. Easy, now," Adam exclaimed as I ran smack into him. "I could hear your heart hammering all the way on the other side of the school. What's happened?"

I looked up at him. It took a minute to register that he was the one I had collided into.

"Your lip's bleeding," he frowned, tilting my chin back with his fingertips. "Nikki, tell me what's going on."

"What is Mrs. Graham?" I demanded, ignoring the tickle of blood that oozed down my face.

"Mrs. Graham did that to you?" The frown deepened, causing a tiny line to pop up between his brows.

What did you do to make the Spriteblood angry? The voice in my head sounded cautious.

"Huh? Oh." I wiped the blood off with the tissue in my hand. "No, that was Tiffany. But I got her worse." I lifted my other hand that somehow still clutched my enemy's pride and joy.

Relieved, Adam grinned. "Well, that's worth detention, I guess."

"Who's in detention?"

"Me, more than likely, for standing up and walking out of anatomy class without permission so I could come and check on you. Unless Ed has thought up some kind of excuse to get me out of it," Adam said, peering over his shoulder at the boy who came into sight.

"You've had a stomach ache since lunch, and had to run to the restroom. They've sent me to check on you," Ed relayed the excuse as he walked to us. He eyed my blonde trophy. "Nikki, the next time you decide to scalp someone, ask me the correct way to do it. You keep the individual strands together better if it's still attached to skin."

"Ew." I crinkled my nose at him, noticing though he appeared serious, his dark eyes twinkled.

"What were you trying to ask me about Mrs. Graham?" Adam prodded, taking the tissue from me to wipe off a bloody smear on my chin.

"What is she?" I asked, watching as both he and Ed went very still at my question.

"Not here," Ed mumbled behind Adam's shoulder.

Adam nodded, then took my hand and ducked into a small room off to the right that stored extra equipment. He turned on a small fan as Ed closed the door behind us. The whir of the fan was low and steady.

"She shouldn't be able to hear over that." Ed nodded his approval.

"Okay, tell me what you saw." Adam pulled out a plastic seat from a desk and sat down across from me.

"Well, Mrs. Graham came over to break Tiffany and me apart. Then she went to give me a tissue for my lip and I accidentally touched her. Then she ended up being something else, tall with blue hair."

"She's a Spriteblood," Adam said quietly. "And not one that you should ever make angry—not that you should make any of them angry."

Ed rolled his eyes and cut in, "Spriteblood aren't your typical fairies that you have in myths and legends is what he is trying to say, Nikki. Unlike what you might be thinking, they aren't like cartoon Sprites, all cute and cuddly. Spriteblood are the nighttime stories that are told to children to scare them into making them behave. You know, do what you are supposed to do or the scary, mythical creatures will come and eat you."

"I've not eaten a child in many a-years," a sad voice said, "and I've tried hard not to for such a very long time."

All three of us (the non-fairy people) jumped at the sound of her musical voice.

"Although, sometimes I do miss the taste of them so." The fairy's red lips stretched back to show sharp, pointed teeth. Her liquid, blue eyes flashed.

In a blink, sour Mrs. Graham stood in her place in front of the door. She snapped off the fan and looked at us with a dour expression. "I do believe you are all expected to be in class. Unless there are any questions you wish to ask of me?"

"No ma'am," both Ed and Adam murmured in unison under their ducked heads as they headed toward the open door, herding me between them. I stopped, trying not to pay attention to their pulling and tugging, as I looked back at her.

"Why do you pretend to be someone you aren't?" I asked, nonplussed at her show of viciousness. I figured that if she wanted to eat us, she would have already done it.

As if surprised at my courage, her lips twisted in a slight smile. "Because I'm not who I want to be."

She held out a book to me. "I think you may need this."

I took it, careful not to touch her, and read the title, *A History of the County of Bland*. Wow. How had she known that was what I had come into the library to find? Apparently, Spriteblood must be psychic, too. I smiled at her.

"Tha--" I got cut off by Adam who gave me a hard shove through the door.

Do not say anything else! His voice warned, bouncing and echoing through my head.

Somehow we managed to get all the way down the hall and around the corner in record speed before he spoke.

"Never say 'thank you' to a fae of any kind," he warned me, squeezing my hand in his. "They think that you will be implying that you are grateful to them, and that you will owe them a favor in turn one day. Their favors never tend to be small, either, so never owe them anything. Understand?"

"Sure," I said, finding myself at the door of my next class.

"We've got to go," Ed warned, heading down the hall towards a bald, frowning teacher who stood with his hands on his hips.

Adam ducked his head down and gave me a quick kiss before following Ed. I took a breath and opened the door, hoping that my next class was taught by someone as ordinary as me.

"As far as I know, her real name is Wynter," Adam said, safe in the confines of my Jeep after school. "She's old. Really old.

Hundreds of years at least, although no one knows how many. Like we said before, her race is Spriteblood, and normally you would never run into one anywhere during your entire lifetime. Generally, they hate humankind, unless of course, they get a taste of human flesh and want more. My people have stories of entire tribes that have been wiped out by a single Spriteblood. Wynter's different, though, and likes humans. She even envies us, I think. That's why she takes on the form she does, to try to fit into our world."

"*Mrs.* Graham," I said weakly. "She's married?"

"Was married, and no she didn't eat him," he laughed. "This husband died of old age. She's been married several times. When she falls in love, the man sees her how she is, in her true form, not the grouchy old woman. They say she was heartbroken over her first husband when he died, so that the next few after him, she tried to change into Spriteblood so that they wouldn't die. It never worked and they ended up dying long, excruciating deaths. Mortified by the pain she had caused, she gave up trying and now she just lets them go when their time comes."

"That's why she seems so sad," I murmured. "I wonder why she works at the school? Seeing people grow up and get older must be hard for her to do."

"She loves history and books. That's why she works in the school. And like I said, there's something that she likes in humans. You know, you could always ask her for some books on Spriteblood the next time you're in there. I doubt there is such a thing, but the school has an awesome library you should check out one day when you're not out trying to scalp people, my fearless war squaw," he smiled, and his eyes sparkled amber, as he leaned forward and kissed me.

"Fearless war squaw," I laughed. "I like it."

HE WATCHED HIM from his safe position behind the counter at Kwik Parts. He had been lucky to get this job. Real lucky. The tables were turning in his favor and things were beginning to look up. He still missed his old job, though. Everything had been great when he worked at the real estate agency. He had been able to keep everyone away from the big, rambling house at the edge of the forest. As the caretaker, he kept it barely livable and in near shambles to ward off any potential renters who could interfere with his plans. It worked until the blonde girl with her family moved in, complained about the upkeep of the place, and got him canned from his job. They threatened everything he held dear and were so close to learning his secrets. To finding the truth.

And the truth was the only thing that truly scared him.

As if it weren't bad enough to be on edge every time one of them wandered into the woods, now it was even harder to keep an eye on the boy and his mother. He had taken it for granted with all those years of being so close, to be able to drive by their little house without any fear of being recognized as anyone who shouldn't be there. Now he missed it.

Missed them.

It was so much harder to watch them. Sure it could be done. He could watch from the safety of the trees, but it wasn't the same. He couldn't just stop by and say "hello" without some reason to be out that way. There were no reasons now, not that he could admit to them. Well, not that he could admit to the boy's mother, anyway. After all, what could he say to her? "Sorry to drop by so much, but I'm drawn to you both, and can't seem to stay away. I feel the need to protect you from everything and everyone, and I have no idea why." Yeah, right, like that would work. Even thinking such a thing was taking a chance. She was a deputy at the sheriff's office, and chances like that could not be taken.

The boy, though, he thought. He needed to be told. He owed him that much, he supposed. He watched him pick out a set of wiper blades for his old rickety truck. The boy had grown strong and sure, just in the few days since he had last seen him. His chest was wider, shoulders stronger, skin darker...yes, there wasn't any question to what he was now. He sighed. Yes, he decided. Truth would be told to this boy. Maybe not all of it, but enough to help him. Besides, maybe he would believe him and then he could share more with him, tell him more about who he was, and maybe, just maybe, he would tell him his secret. *The* secret.

The boy flopped the blades on the counter, reaching into the back pocket of his jeans for his wallet, his hair falling thick and dark toward his blue eyes.

He smiled from his perch behind the register. "Can I help you with anything else, son?"

ELEVEN

J ENNA SAT ACROSS from me at her kitchen table, watching
me with sharp eyes. "The key to blocking everyone else out is to
focus. Turn all your attention inward, far into yourself, and
concentrate. Now, close your eyes and take a deep breath and focus."

I closed my eyes and took a deep breath. Ever since I had learned
about *my gift* and about the Keepers, my mind had been running a
mile a minute with thoughts, most of them not my own. Everything
from school, to girls, to football games ran amuck in my brain.
Anything and everything which occupied a guy's teenage mind. It was

like hearing a television that someone was changing the channel on. No sooner than one thought would bounce in my brain, another crowded right behind it. It was enough to make one dizzy. I couldn't concentrate on anything else around me and had been getting strange looks from people at school, from teachers and students alike. I thought I was doing ok, until Brian started avoiding me and found strange excuses to stay away. He suggested that I start taking myself to school and always gave me some vague excuse about having to leave early for some reason or the other. It felt as if someone had punched me right in the stomach. It left me to wonder what on earth I was to do. What can you do when even your best friend won't have anything to do with you? Brian was the straw that broke the camel's back.

Being avoided made me feel like a freak, which was saying something.

I never fit in before and it had never bothered me. In fact, I loved being the outsider and I thrived in my individuality. Funny, now that I had this so-called *gift* and all I wanted was *not* to be noticed. I wanted to crawl under a rock and hide from everyone. The Keepers started acting different around me. More than once I had caught their faces flush after I had *heard* something that they had never meant for me to know. I had noticed the averted eyes, as they stared at anything to keep their minds occupied, which only made them think more. Ant the more they thought, the busier and more crowded my brain got.

I was going insane.

Adam had found me on the verge of tears, sitting on the bleachers, as far as I could get from them, which hadn't helped. He didn't say anything, but sat down beside me. Adam gathered me up close to him and patted my back when my tears spilled over, soaking through his shirt.

He thought about a waterfall, while he sat and rocked me as if I were a baby. I felt cool, little water droplets against my skin, and saw the lush green ferns and grass around the pool at the bottom of the fall. I wondered if it was just a figment of his imagination, or if it existed somewhere. I felt relaxed, and sat up, sniffling. I wiped my eyes and smiled at him. I wasn't certain that I was feeling him being relaxed or if it was my own sensation of calmness.

The voices were back again and were rioting through my head as soon as I got up from the bleachers. After school, Adam came to my house He had come to take me to get help. Even in the forest, their thoughts jumbled and swirled in my mind the whole way to the reservation.

"Focus, Nikki, think of something that would act as a barrier in your mind," Jenna urged again, reaching over to clasp my hands. I relaxed and took another deep breath as I willed my mind to concentrate on nothing. I focused on the blackness. Deep, dark walls of nothingness. I stretched it into every corner of my mind and pushed out everyone else, leaving myself alone behind my walls.

Everything quieted to a dull, jumbled whisper, and then went silent. I was more alone than I had been in months. I was ecstatic.

"Good job," Jenna's voice brought me back and I opened my eyes and grinned at her. She grinned back, a flash of neat, white, even teeth against her bronze skin. "Now, the next trick is to hear only what you want to hear, and who you want to hear. Are you ready to give it a try?"

I nodded. "Sure, I'll try. Just tell me what to do. Do I have to take my walls back down to hear them again?"

"No, not exactly. Don't think of it as taking your walls down. Concentrate on one person, as if you're just letting them in, and no one else. If the others try to come back in, focus back on your walls again and push them all out."

"Okay." I nodded again and closed my eyes. I concentrated on Adam, letting him seep through the darkness. Other voices muttered, and I stretched my black walls back up higher. They hushed back to a whisper, then left. I concentrated on Adam again, and heard his deep, sultry voice as if he had been standing next to me.

I'm worried about her. I wish Erik would either go apologize to Penny or shut up. He's getting on my nerves. If he'd just say he was sorry, then everything would be fine. I'm worried about Nikki.

I opened my eyes again, and grinned my big jack-o-lantern smile—all teeth. "It worked. I heard him. Adam's worried about me and Erik is getting on his nerves. He and Penny must be fighting."

"That sounds about right. Penny can handle anything, but my son can be very trying at times. He gets it from his father. It's hard to tell what the problem is. Erik's mouth opens before his brain kicks in. That's what gets him in trouble. They'll work it out, they always do," she said in a matter-of-fact tone, and then turned back to the subject at hand. "Now, Nikki, sometimes your walls won't work. Sometimes they'll project their emotions. They'll come busting through your walls and there won't be anything you can do about it. Don't fight it. Focus in on that person and nothing else. It may give you some kind of control."

All five of the guys were on the porch waiting for us when we came out. Several pairs of wary eyes watched me as I crossed over to Adam. Reaching his side, I turned and stared back at them.

"What?" I asked, nonchalant, as I laced my fingers through Adam's.

The cousins turned to look at each other, while Erik gaped at me openmouthed as if I had just accomplished some strange feat of magic. Ed watched me with his arms crossed over his chest.

"I don't know what's wrong with them," I turned to look at Adam and tried not to smile. "Maybe they're getting sick or something. I can't hear a thing."

Whoops of laughter circled around as Michael and Tommy doubled over at my look of innocence. Erik gave his usual grin, then threw his arm around my shoulder and gave me a quick squeeze.

"I'm glad you got it fixed, Nikki, you were starting to worry all of us. Some things are better left unsaid, unheard, whatever," he joked.

I gave him an evil smile. "You'd better go apologize to Penny."

"Um, yeah," he said as he dropped his arm from my shoulder and shoved his hands in the back pockets of his jeans. "Actually, I need to go see her. I'll catch you guys later." He sauntered off in the direction of Penny's house, which for some unseen reason made the cousins roll around on the ground and laugh even harder.

Ed smirked at his friend's retreating back. "One day he'll learn that he has a brain and then maybe he'll learn how to use it."

"Doubtful," Adam grinned, then looked over at me and something changed in his eyes. "Come on, Nikki. I'll walk you home." We said our goodbyes to Jenna and the boys, and then he took my hand and led me towards the woods.

"I'm glad you're okay now, I was worried." he said as we made our way through the forest.

"I'm glad, too. Thanks for taking me to Jenna." I smiled my thanks at the broad, muscled shoulders in front of me that led the way. His hair was caught at the nape of his neck and swayed in a silky rope that swayed back and forth between his shoulder blades with each step he took. I had the urge to reach out and run my hands through it. I had started to reach out, when he turned to face me.

His eyes flashed gold. "You have nothing to thank me for. It is us who should thank you or apologize to you, or, or something," he shrugged in agitation. "We're the reason this happened to you and, well, just don't thank me, *please.*" He blew out a loud breath and scrubbed his face with his palms in exasperation.

"Okay." I wondered what I was supposed to say. I decided to just stand there feeling like a moron. I shifted from one foot to the other and clasped my hands tightly behind my back.

He took a step closer and leaned his head down so that his forehead touched mine. "We hurt you, and I couldn't stop it. I can't stand to see you cry." His eyes blazed down into mine as his palms rubbed up and down my arms so lightly it was as if he thought I would break.

"Adam," I whispered as I felt his warm breath against my skin.

His hands came up to either side of my face and his head bent down that extra inch to kiss me so quick I didn't have a chance to finish what I was going to say. I couldn't even finish what I was going to think. My hands came out to rest on his arms, and I could feel the tension that seemed to radiate off him. As gentle as he was touching me with his hands and his kiss, the rest of his body seemed ready to snap.

Shaken back into reality again, I broke the kiss and leaned my head back just a little to look in his eyes. "Adam?"

"Forgive me," his voice came out low, and choked as he stared down, not meeting my eyes. "I couldn't keep us from hurting you. We made you *cry*, Nikki, and I've never wanted to do that, ever. I should have taken you to Jenna sooner. Please forgive me." His voice was still low, but he raised his amber eyes to look at me through his thick, dark lashes.

"Oh, it's okay. You didn't make me cry, I was just, frustrated, I guess is the word I'm looking for. But you did take me to Jenna, and I'm okay now," I reassured him and patted him awkwardly on the shoulder. I gave myself a mental kick in the butt. A gorgeous guy stands in front of you and begs your forgiveness because you cried and that's the best you can come up with? A pat on the shoulder? I wondered what Adam would do if I threw myself at him and swooned in his arms like Scarlett O'Hara.

"You're sure you're okay?" he asked again.

I nodded a little too quickly, my blonde curls bobbing in rhythm with my head. Exit Scarlett, enter Bobble-Head Nikki. "I guess we'd better start heading to the house. I didn't leave Mom a note."

"Right," Adam watched me for a moment, then nodded, straightened and turned to start walking again.

So much for romance. Maybe next time. I stifled a sigh. I decided that I was going to practice swooning on the bed. It might come in handy later on. We walked in silence for a few more minutes, Adam treaded as stealthy as a ghost, and I followed behind him like a thrashing machine, tripping over roots and vines that seemed to grow wherever I put my feet. I kept a few feet behind him and wondered what was the most romantic way to suggest that I would like to be carried. I smiled at the thought of Adam holding me tight to him like he would never let me go as we walked through the green, beautiful forest, as if we had all the time in the world.

Well, nice thought, but what I wanted was a piggyback ride on his wolf.

I gave up the notion of how to ask politely. I was just going to say I needed to get home soon. That would work. I opened my mouth to make my request and got a rather unpleasant surprise instead.

Where there hadn't been a limb two seconds before, one appeared and swung into place just in time to slap me across the face. It left my whole face stinging.

"Okay, that was not there," I complained, wiping at my watering eyes.

Adam turned around so quick he was just a blur. "You okay?"

"Yeah, but I swear it seems like everything moves for you, and just snaps back into place just as I follow behind you. It's like that tree didn't like me. It did move, didn't it? Or am I just imagining things?" I stayed motionless watching the offending limb.

He opened his mouth and started to speak, then turned his head as if listening. Then he smiled.

"Come here," he whispered, taking my hand and pulling me to his side. "Now look at that tree over there, with the fallen log next to it. Do you see that?"

"No. What am I supposed to see?" I squinted at what looked like an ordinary tree and a rotting one lying beside it.

"Concentrate and keep looking. Focus on it, but be still. Don't speak," he urged.

I shrugged and turned to look back at the fallen log. I resisted the urge to just walk over to it and see what the big deal was, instead I just stared at it, waiting for whatever it was I was supposed to see to jump out at me.

It looked like any other tree that we had walked past, long limbs and branches splayed out from the log, reaching like long arms, the leaves long since dead. My eyes roamed up to where it seemed to meet up with the other tree. There was a big dark shadow where the two trees met. I focused on it, thinking it an odd place to be so darkened, even with the canopy of the other trees.

Something moved in it, just the slightest bit, and my heart sped up. It felt as if it were about to beat out of my chest as I stared at the big shadow. It moved more now, and at first I thought it was one of the guys in wolf form, out to scare us, but it stood on its back legs. Long arms dangled by its sides, as it stared back at us with small, beady eyes. It looked human. I gulped, looking at the biggest, hairiest thing I had ever seen and the good Lord knew I had seen lots of big hairy things as of late. It had to be eight feet tall if it was an inch.

I remembered watching an episode of *Unexplained Mysteries*. At the time, I thought that the entire episode was kind of kooky, but kind of cool, too. It was one of those shows that made you wonder if stuff did exist that you didn't know about. I thought it should have been on the Sci-Fi channel. If I had remembered it right, the title of the episode was *Myths and Legends*. At the time I had wondered who the tall guy was that they got to wear the hairy suit and if he was wearing stilts. I thought now that their re-creation wasn't off by much at all. The guy in the car had seen one of these things walk across the road in front of him. He had explained what it looked like well. He claimed it only took three huge steps to get across the entire road. I looked down at the thing's long, hairy legs and humongous feet.

Yep, it wouldn't take many steps at all.

"Bigfoot," I said weakly, gripping Adam's hand. I wondered what the odds were that I would be holding the hand of a werewolf while I stared at Bigfoot. They had to be slim if nonexistent. Still, here I was doing it.

The huge, hairy mass that hadn't moved an inch since it had stood up and made its presence known.

"Sasquatch. Hello, friend," Adam's voice was soft and lulling as he switched into his native tongue. I relaxed just a little, knowing Adam would know what to do. But then, I remembered the episode with the bear. He had gotten his chest clawed open that time. What would Bigfoot do to him? I bit my lip, and got nervous all over again.

A low humming sound answered him that sounded almost like a purr intermixed with periodic clicking sounds. The Sasquatch straightened, standing to its full height. It was bigger than eight foot now. I fidgeted next to Adam. It stared at us a moment longer, still humming and clicking. It looked at us one final time and snorted, as if thinking we were the oddity instead of itself, then turned and walked off through the trees. Its enormous steps not making a single sound as it made its way through the dried, dead leaves like an enormous, hairy ghost.

"They don't come this close. They usually avoid human contact. But this one was curious, he wanted to see what you were since you were with me," Adam smiled. "Are you alright?"

"Yes, I'm fine," I said, turning his hand loose. I watched as he flexed his hand to get the circulation moving again. "I thought they were only myths."

"Every myth has some basis in truth," he explained, "and you as you can see, he was very real. They are very shy creatures. He never would have come so close to you if he hadn't known you were with me. That's one reason they are thought only a myth or a legend, very few people ever see them."

"You told me before that there were things in the forest I wouldn't understand. Is he dangerous?"

"No, they have never attacked anyone and are strictly vegetarian. They're docile creatures and don't like conflict of any kind. Like I said, they tend to avoid all contact, even with us. They know we are the Keepers and that we would never hurt them, but they still keep their distance. I'm surprised that he came that close."

"So the library has a Spriteblood. What else does this forest have? Just werewolves and Bigfoot?"

"Wherever there is life, there is magic. So many people just don't see it. They look, but they don't see. Every tree and every animal are full of life and magic. It's not just in this forest, but in everything, everywhere. The trick is to teach yourself to see, like you did with the Sasquatch. When you learn to see, you'll find things you would have thought were only in your dreams." His amber eyes were warm, their onyx specks pulsed lightly as his wolf came just below their surface to stare out at me and prove that he, too, knew of the world's magic.

"Show me something else," I said, excited with my new-found knowledge.

Adam laughed. "We have to get going. We're going to be late, and I don't want to explain to your mother the reason why I kept you out was to show you how to see wood nymphs and fairies. She might think I'm on something and not let me come back to you."

"It doesn't matter, no one can keep me from you," I whispered, "I'm yours, remember?"

"I know," he whispered, leaning his head down to brush a chaste kiss against my brow, "and I belong to you. But it's time for us to go." A dark fog flowed down his body and the black wolf watched me with big golden eyes.

Sitting atop his back, I stared at the trees and the underbrush and tried to learn how to see something I hadn't seen before. Adam seemed to pick up on what I was trying to do, and kept his thoughts silent as he padded along the forest floor. I closed my eyes for a few seconds and breathed in slow, deep breaths, willing myself to relax.

I opened my eyes and focused on different things, a leaf here, a flower there. I took in deep breaths of the forest. I saw a slight flicker on a branch as we went by and turned my attention to it.

It was just a butterfly, I thought, as I got ready to turn my head back. But then I stopped, and looked again. A pair of powder blue wings fluttered next to a clump of leaves. A tiny pair of hands clasped the edge of a large, round leaf while a small head with curly brown hair watched us with big, curious eyes.

TWELVE

ADAM TOOK MY hand and half-dragged me down the dirt road. "It won't be bad, Jenna has already told them you are the new Seer, so they already know. Trust me, everything is going to be fine."

I cringed. "That didn't help. Are you sure we have to do this today? Can't we do this later? Like next year, maybe?"

"No," he laughed, "If we get this over now, then there isn't anything to worry about later, right?"

"I guess," I grumbled.

The last thing I wanted was to go meet the elders of the tribe. Now or ever. These guys were the ones in charge. The Keepers watched over the forest, but the elders watched over the Keepers. Everybody had a boss. And if Adam and the others had given me more than my mind could fathom at the time, what were the elders going to do to me?

I had one last try.

"If they already know about me, then what's the use of going? We're just wasting their time." I gave him my most convincing smile.

"We're not wasting time. This is very important. You have a test to pass to prove you are the new Seer. The entire tribe will be there for this. It affects us all."

I stopped dead in my tracks, while Adam kept pulling on my arm.

"A test in front of the whole tribe?" my voice came out in a squeak.

He stopped and took my face in his hands. "Do you trust me?"

I managed a slight nod.

"Then believe when I say everything will be okay. You are mine. I won't let anything bad happen to you. They are people the same way that you and I are, and soon they will be your people, too. You have nothing to prove, you are the new Seer. It's nothing that you can fake, so there is nothing to fear. Just be yourself."

"Okay," I closed my eyes as he leaned forward to kiss my forehead.

The sounds of laughter came from the circle around the campfire. Erik appeared to be trying to start a fire. His tanned face was scrunched in concentration as he blew on the kindling, trying to coax a flame to life.

"How long has he been at it this time?" Adam asked Ed as we came to the edge of the circle.

"Awhile. It's a good thing he doesn't show the school kids how our ancestors built a fire. They would have to bring sleeping bags and spend the week with him." Ed grinned.

"I've almost got it. Honestly. I swear there's a little flame in there just waiting to come out." Erik looked at the little pile of sticks.

"I'll show you a secret," Ed offered.

"Sure. What is it? I'm open for suggestions." Erik flopped down on the ground.

"Secret white man trick," Ed said as he took out a lighter, and set the little pile of sticks ablaze.

"But this is a tribal meeting. Shouldn't we be building the fire in the old way?" Erik protested as he got up from the ground.

"Only if Nikki wants to spend all night here and wait for you to improve your fire building skills. Trust me, son, the lighter is fine." A tall man with Erik's big grin walked up and clapped him on the shoulder.

Jenna came up behind the man and linked her arm through his. "Hello, Nikki. How are you this evening?"

"Well, okay. No, I don't think I'm okay at all." Panic flared up in me again.

"You're going to be just fine, you'll see. Nothing to worry about at all," she smiled.

"I promise we won't eat you or anything." The man's eyes sparkled with humor as he put out his hand. "I'm Luke White Hawk, Erik's dad."

I shook the offered hand. "Nice to meet you."

"So how is the Wrangler working out for you?" he asked, switching tactfully to another subject.

"It's great. I love it," I smiled.

More people drifted in. I squeezed closer to Adam's side as I watched them come in and take their places around the campfire. Everyone was at ease, talking and chatting with one another. Tommy and Michael came in with their parents and I saw why they looked so similar. Tommy's mom and Michael's dad were twins.

"I've found where they got their dimples."

"Yeah, Debbie and Donnie Tallman are twins. Tommy's dad, Thomas, is standing behind him, everyone seems to get named after each other around here."

"That's cool," I murmured watching more people come in.

"There comes Dad and Grandpa." He nodded toward two tall figures on the far side of the crowd.

"Evan and Evan Black Water," I said, remembering my search of the phone book.

He laughed, "Yeah, I'm glad they didn't name me Evan Black Water, the third. I would be like Ed, trying to figure out when to change my name."

An old man took his place at the circle. His long salt and pepper hair was pulled back in a tight braid that ran a thick rope down his back. His lined face was serious and contemplative as he sat staring into the flames. As if he felt me watching, his sharp, dark eyes pierced into mine through the fire. I jumped when someone on the other side of me cleared his throat.

"Hello, Miss Harmon," Adam's father smiled down at me.

I nodded. "Hello."

"I'm Sheriff Black Water, Adam's dad," he said, still smiling.

"Yes, sir, it's nice to meet you." I put out my hand.

A warm, sure grip enveloped my hand. "Likewise. I hear you are the one to thank for Adam's progress in English class, so I thought I would come over and say thank you."

Not to mention that I have been very curious to see who my son has been keeping such close tabs on.

Focus, Nikki, I chided myself, this is not the time to pry into any Keeper or former Keeper's thoughts. Pull yourself together.

"You're welcome, but he did most of it by himself. I didn't help that much." I shrugged and smiled up at him.

"Thank you just the same." He nodded at me and turned to Ed who had wandered closer to us. "Where are Barry and Marianne?"

"Mom should be here any second. She was cleaning up some paintbrushes when I left the house. She said Dad called. He had some loose ends at the office he had to tie up, but he's on his way."

"Everyone will be here once they arrive. I'll let him know." The sheriff nodded towards the serious face of the old man at the fire. He had never stopped watching me. "He'll want to get started soon."

He crossed over to the other side of the fire to kneel at the older man's side. A car door shut a few seconds later, and a man in a business suit appeared and walked toward us.

"They're all here now. It's time." Adam took my hand and drew me to two empty seats near the fire.

I tried to keep my face looking as calm as I could in spite of my heart that tried to beat its way out of my chest. There were so many people. No one had paid any attention as we took our seats. For a few seconds, I was expecting someone to offer marshmallows and hot dogs to roast. It was as if they had these kinds of meetings all the time. I started to relax, when the old man raised his right hand and the group hushed.

"We are the children of the wolf. Generation after generation we have come, one following the next. So it has been for many years. We have been the Keepers of the forest, the protectors of Mother Earth," his voice was calm and sure, strong in spite of age. "Elders of the people join me."

Luke White Hawk, Barry Young Eagle, Donnie Tallman, Thomas Greene, and another man I hadn't met, took their places on either side of him. Everyone seemed to be at ease except the last man. Something just didn't feel right with that one, I thought, watching him.

"Since the first of the Keepers came, there has always been one to See. Just as the Keepers watch over the forest, so the Seer would watch over us, to warn and protect us. Will the Seer join us?"

Wondering if this was my cue to stand, I looked over at Adam. He set his hand on my leg as if telling me not to move. Apparently, this wasn't my turn. I bit my lip and looked back over to the old man. Jenna White Hawk came to stand opposite the elders.

She spoke in a clear, soft voice, "Seer I have been, but one comes to take my place. I have seen her visions and she is true. Her sight is stronger than my own. My sight fades as hers grows clearer. I ask the elders to let her join them now in my stead."

Voices muttered around us. This must not have been common knowledge. My stomach started turning cartwheels as I saw several heads turn to look in Hannah's direction. Hannah stared at me with some kind of look that was a cross between contempt and someone who just sucked on an entire lemon. Well, no help was coming from that direction. I wanted to find a way to melt into Adam and become invisible.

"Please bring forth the one who is to take your place," the old man said.

Jenna walked over to me and put out her hand. "Come on, Nikki."

Adam patted my leg as I took her hand and stood. Sure that I was going to fall or trip since my knees seemed to be knocking together, I gripped Jenna's hand like a lifeline as she led me towards them. Everyone seemed to be talking at once now, and I felt as if I was being led through a gauntlet, waiting for the first blow. Each step seemed to take longer, as if I were moving through a huge bowl of Jell-o. I didn't think we'd ever make it to the other side of the fire.

Somehow we made it and the old man raised his hand again. Everyone quieted.

"Who are you, child?" The question caught me off-guard.

I caught myself before I just said my name. "I am she who Sees."

His dark, sharp eyes twinkled, as if he was pleased with my answer, and I loosened my death grip on Jenna.

"It is time for you to prove your gift if you are she. We must all be in agreement for you to be accepted into our people. To each elder, you must prove your sight. Show us that you are whom you say," he nodded to those on his right.

Feeling more certain of myself, I walked to the closest elder, who was Luke White Hawk. He smiled and I took a deep breath and concentrated on him. I let my breath out and tuned out the rest of the group, focusing as Jenna had taught me to do.

I sat in the recliner watching the football game, hoping the 49ers would score the winning touchdown. They did. The phone rang. My assistant from the shop was on the other end. He sounded out of breath and frantic. His wife had gone into labor.

"Greg's wife went into labor and the 49ers won the game. You have to call and check on Greg later. You're thinking he will be the one needing the hospital more than his wife," I smiled. This was going to be simpler than I had thought.

He grinned at me. "You're in, Nikki."

I sidestepped over to Barry Young Eagle, who looked preoccupied. I took another deep breath. He noticed me and smiled politely, "Hello."

"Hello," I nodded, and focused in on him.

This case is impossible. I can't focus on something for her to see. I can't focus on anything. Edmund Rodriguez is as guilty as hell. His wife just won't admit that he beats her. Too bad they aren't in this tribe, we'd take care of him ourselves. Oh well, I'll just have to keep trying. Shoot. I forgot to get milk. Marianne is going to kill me.

I grinned at him. "Edmund Rodriguez beats his wife and she won't admit it. You think it's an impossible case—and you forgot the milk."

"He always forgets it." A woman with paint splatters on her t-shirt shook her head in Ed's familiar, sophisticated way.

Barry Young Eagle gave his wife a sheepish grin. "Sorry, Marianne. I'll go back out later."

Two down, four to go, I stepped over to Michael's dad.

Hmm, I need to think of something better than Barry did. Let's see. Debbie has the most beautiful smile in the world. It's as if the sun shines just for her when she laughs. She is the only woman I will ever love.

"You thought of your wife. You think she has the most beautiful smile in the world and you wonder if you ever told her that before."

"I should have thought of something else so I could have told her myself. Good job, Nikki," Donnie Greene smiled.

His brother-in-law sat next to him. He smiled and a familiar dimple dented his cheek. "It's too bad he didn't tell me about my smile, I could have reminded him to tell Debbie."

Let's see if you can remember this, Nikki…

"You harvested five bushels of corn today, two of cucumbers, four of peppers. Tomorrow you plan on starting tomatoes, radishes and carrots," I recited.

"Good sight and good memory. Welcome to the tribe."

I stepped in front of Adam's grandfather, and looked into his wrinkled face. Poker face, I thought. He wasn't going to let me see anything easily. I was going to have to work for it. He had put his hand in his pocket and held something I couldn't see as he sat watching me, waiting with that careful, blank stare it seemed the whole tribe had.

The Wolf stood before the elders, making his covenant with them, promising them protection as he clawed a small stone. The stone had been handed down for generations, from one down to the next. Used ceremony after ceremony, its presence had been expected and revered. To be the Keeper of the stone was a privilege, an honor. It was a reminder of the past…a promise for the future.

"Wa-ya nv-yu. The Wolf's Stone," I whispered.

An eternity passed, then the old man moved to take his hand out of the pocket. A round stone, smooth from generations of handling, lay in his palm. Giant slashes were scraped across it, a testament to what had been, and the Wolf of long ago. Low murmurs ran through the crowd as everyone stared at the stone and then at me.

"You are she," he nodded.

I let go of the breath I had been holding. I knew that they all had to agree, but for some reason, this man's acknowledgement meant more than the others. There was only one more to go. I stepped in front the last man and froze. The uneasy feeling I had earlier was back and it was stronger than ever. Panic surged through every nerve ending in my body.

There was a small shock of silver hair at his left temple, though the rest was dark. As I watched, he gathered his hair back and tied it in a ponytail at the base of his neck. It was a quick, efficient manner of one who had done it for years. His eyes locked into mine and I froze. Something animal lurked behind those black eyes. It watched me as if I was prey and he was waiting for me to run so he could give chase. I struggled to take deep breaths. So this was the final of the six Keepers, the only one who hadn't passed his gift on. He was staring at me as if I were food. I fought an irresistible urge to shake all over.

I wanted to go back to Adam, but I still had one more to go, which meant I had to get into the mind of this man in front of me. I took one deep breath in and found my resolve. I focused on him.

The football game was ending. We won, but I couldn't care less. I wasn't there for the game. I was there for her. I was always drawn to her. I always knew how to find her. She was with her friends. They were laughing and making plans for the graduation party. The wind blew her long, brown hair around her shoulders, sending her scent to me on a soft breeze. I inhaled. The wolf inside me stirred. I had to be closer to her. There was no way to ignore her now. Her friends were saying their goodbyes, now was my chance. If I could just go over and talk to her, ask her to the prom, maybe…

I shook my head trying to get out of his, I'd had enough.

"You were thinking about your wife when you asked her to the prom after a football game," I said, relieved to be finished.

"No. I never had asked my wife to a prom. I'm sorry, but you're mistaken."

I took several steps back and shook my head in disbelief. "But..."

He stood and smiled. "I'm sorry, but that isn't at all what I had thought. I don't agree with the others. I don't believe in your Sight."

Adam came to stand beside me and linked his hand in mine. He faced the smaller man, who looked away. The motion didn't go unnoticed. I felt Adam tense and a black mist edged him as if his wolf had come to see what was happening.

The silence went unbroken until the old man sighed and spoke, "I am sorry, child, but without the agreement of all elders, we cannot permit you to be one of the tribe. You are welcome to stay. We just can't acknowledge you as our Seer yet." He stood, "We shall give it time. Maybe your Sight needs to be stronger and you simply misunderstood. Time will be the answer. It always is." He turned and disappeared from the circle.

A low growl emanated from Adam as he watched Reuben's retreating back.

"Easy, son." The sheriff came over to us as the crowd began to disperse. "Losing your temper and letting your wolf try to solve the problem won't help anything right now. Just calm down. I'll talk to Reuben later and try to find out what happened. You should take Nikki home. Her mother will be worrying about her." He turned to me. "It was nice to meet you, Nikki. I'm sorry you had a rough evening. I'm sure it was just a misunderstanding and we'll get it worked out soon. Please don't think too badly of us."

"No, sir," I smiled, but it was weak. "I don't."

Black mist edging around his body, Adam grabbed my hand. "Come on, lets go. I need to get away from here."

I saw Jenna start to come toward us as he pulled me to the edge of the forest. She stopped and smiled at me and gave a little nod as if to say we would talk later and that she understood Adam's need to leave.

Safe inside the canopy of trees, Adam slowed down enough that he wasn't pulling me like an unwilling puppy on a leash. He walked, moving through the forest as quiet as a ghost, while I followed beside him, sounding like a bulldozer in a construction zone. Anger radiated from him, but this thoughts remained quiet, which was a blessing and a curse within itself. It was nice for a change to hear nothing but my own footsteps, even if the whole forest could hear me coming. I took a deep breath and let out a huge sigh, breaking the silence.

"What's wrong?" Adam asked as a frown deepened the little wrinkle between his brows.

"Nothing."

"I've told you before. You're a terrible liar." He tilted my face to make me look at him. "Are you okay?"

"Yeah, I will be, although I don't think my going back to the Res would be such a good idea," I murmured.

"Why not? Everyone knows you belong there, and everyone knows you belong to me. There won't be any problem." The air picked up and sparked around us.

"But Reuben..."

"You will always be welcomed there, no matter what."

You are part of me now, so wherever I am, you are welcome.

It's too bad this works one way, I thought, staring back up into his amber eyes, I wish you could hear my thoughts, too.

The black mist dissipated, and Adam's eyes were clear, their onyx specks no longer pulsed and swirled. I knew the wolf was back under his control. He had been ready to fight for me, I realized. He would have defied the elders, and had been ready to break tribal tradition, had it been necessary. At that moment, I knew I could go back to the reservation when I needed to. Where he would go, I would go. It no longer mattered where.

The air warmed around us as he traced along my jaw with his fingertip. He looked like a cross between an avenging angel and an ancient Indian warrior, beautiful and lethal. His hair draped around his shoulders in a thick, silky curtain of glossy black. The muscles in his arms and shoulders were still taut, every curve announced the power he was capable of.

"You're beautiful," I whispered, looking up at him.

"Umm, no," a small smile tugged at the side of his mouth, "that would be you."

He took a step closer to me and the air snapped around us and got warmer. His hands went down to my waist to draw me closer to him, so that my body brushed his. Something vulnerable lingered in his eyes for a second, and then vanished as resolve took its place.

"Nikki."

"Yes?" My heart beat quicker, as my sides tingled from the warmth of his hands.

He leaned his head down towards mine. His lips were inches away, parted. He looked into my eyes. My hands went to the hard muscles of his chest, where I could feel his heartbeat. He drew in a sharp breath and his hands tightened on me.

Nikki, I have something to tell you.

"Yes," I whispered, somehow feeling as if my entire life would change in this moment. I stared deep into his eyes, losing myself in their depths.

"Nikki, I…"

"Click, click, click, snort, click, huff," said an impatient voice in front of us.

I found myself airborne and set down behind Adam with a small thump. I tried to peek around his shoulder through the black mist that had appeared.

"Click, click, grumble, click."

Adam straightened back up, and the mist left as quickly as it had appeared. I looked at the huge Sasquatch that stood a few feet away from us. It took a hesitant step closer and kept up its clicking repertoire, then stopped and looked behind itself.

"Is he the same one we saw before?" I asked from behind my sanctuary of Adam's shoulder.

"Yes."

"He isn't acting the same as he did before. He looks worried." I stated the obvious, watching it turn around and look again.

"No, something is wrong. He's asking for help." He switched over into his own lulling language and took a step closer.

Thinking that we understood the dilemma, the creature turned and took a step back the way he had come, looking back over his shoulder as if to say "Are you coming?"

"Get on," Adam spoke a mere second before his wolf waited where he had stood.

He will be quick. This is the only way we'll be able to keep up with him.

I knotted my hands up in his soft fur as Adam leapt up and started a run to catch up. The creature took large, hurried steps as Adam trotted us along a few feet behind him. Every few seconds, it would huff as if worried, and quicken its step a little more.

A few seconds later, I heard soft keening sounds. The Sasquatch made a low, grumbling moan. Over a small embankment, lay a form curled into a ball. The high keening only got higher-pitched as we got closer. The Sasquatch clicked a couple times, and the balled up form sat up. Two beady eyes looked at us.

"Chewy's got a baby," I said, awestruck, as I watched the miniature version scoot back in fear.

Chewy? Adam asked, *You named him Chewy?*

"Yeah," I grinned. "I think it fits him."

Adam's laugh echoed in my head as I slid off his back and his wolf melted away.

The baby, if you could call it that, had tried in vain to scoot back farther and caused a metal chain at its foot to rattle. It cried out as all the slack left the chain. A metal, tooth lined trap was clamped shut around its little hairy ankle. Blood had matted the dark brown fur and stained the ground beneath. The teeth from the trap had broken the bones and small bits of white peeked through the flesh.

"Oh, you poor baby," I moved to get closer to help. The baby started its keening again, higher-pitched in fright. The other one gave a loud, aggravated snort.

"Better wait, Nikki," Adam said. "I don't know if they trust you. Let me go to her. Just stay right here."

He walked over as Chewy stayed close behind him, as if guarding its little one from any more harm. Adam knelt beside her, speaking in his soothing tongue. The keening stopped and the baby stared at him. Her worried parent seemed less anxious when the cries stopped and he sighed and came to stand opposite Adam, though he still kept watch.

Adam's hands ran from the ground up the length of the chain to the trap, a frown of concentration etched on his face as he searched and prodded for the springs. He bit down on his lower lip as his fingers ran feather-light around the little foot.

"There, there, now," he soothed when the baby gave a small start. "Just a minute more, little one. Everything's alright now, just another minute."

His fingers found the springs and he stood, setting his feet on either side of the trap as he pulled the jaws of the trap apart. Her little leg now free, the baby, which was nearly half as tall as I was, jumped up and limped over to her parent, clicking her joy. She was picked up and held close.

I stared at her leg that was hanging in the air. From the time she was released to the time she was picked up, the wound had started healing. The small, raw bits of flesh moved and repositioned themselves. The white, boney parts had disappeared and fur started growing back over the skinned, bare places.

It was magic. I stood in awe, watching them as they backed away. The one still carrying the other, they melted back into the forest as if they had never been there.

Adam was still kneeling in the same spot. He was looking down at the opened trap. He stood up and picked up a dead branch that lay on the ground a few feet away. He poked the end down into the middle of the trap.

It clamped shut with a loud clang that made me jump as the metal teeth smashed the wood to bits. Adam stood still, still holding the end of the branch, which was now much shorter. It swung free in his hand, dangling back and forth. He dropped it on the ground, and bent over to pick up the trap.

"Trappers," he muttered with a contained rage that seemed to pulse through his body. He jerked to the side, snapping the chain as if it had only been a small piece of string.

He took a step closer to the water, as if ready to send the metal-jawed prison to a watery grave, then stopped and tucked it under his arm. Turning on his heel, he came back to me, took my hand, and laced his fingers between mine.

"What are we going to do with it?" I asked.

"We're not leaving it here, that's for sure. Whoever left it will be looking for it. These traps are hard to come by. They are also illegal," he murmured, gripping my hand tighter.

"What were they hoping to trap?"

"I don't know, but if I had to guess, probably bear. I'll give it to Dad and let him look into it. He hasn't said anything about trappers, but at least now he'll know to start looking. I'll get the guys to watch this part of the forest. Hopefully between us, we'll find whoever it is." He looked up at the darkening sky. "Nikki, I'm sorry. I'm probably going to be getting you into trouble with your mom. I didn't realize it was this late. It's going to be dark soon."

"She knows I was at the Res. As long as she doesn't call over there to check on us and they tell her we left a good while ago, we should be okay," I said, hoping that I was right, and that she hadn't called. After all, what was I going to tell her? Sorry Mom, can't come home just yet, I'm busy with Adam. We're saving Baby Bigfoot. Yeah, I didn't think that was going to make for a good conversation. I would end up being grounded until I was eighty for lying.

Please, don't let her have called, I thought. If I was grounded, it would mean no more Adam. And that was not a happy thought. Being away from him was not an option. It would kill me. Well, okay, maybe not literally, but it wouldn't be pleasant.

"If I can find a place to leave this trap so I can come back and get it, then I can shift and get you home quicker," Adam said.

He pushed the bulky metal trap under a scrubby, little bush, and then shoved some dead leaves over the gleaming metal to camouflage it. A second later, his wolf was padding over to me and then I was clinging to his fur as the trees raced by us in greenish blurs as he hurried to get me home.

I closed my eyes and buried my face in his warm fur in an effort to keep from getting sick. We had never went this fast before, and while he still ran fluidly, the sensation of the air whipping against my skin, confirmed the fact that we were going fast.

I remembered the motorcycle ride that my cousin had given me a few years before, the way the air had stung as it hit my face, and how my nose didn't seem to be getting enough air. Just as I had opened my mouth to take a big breath, a huge bug of unknown origin had flown into my mouth. I had swallowed. My stomach lurched and I found myself praying for the second time in minutes—with my mouth clamped shut.

Please, oh please, don't let me puke.

I didn't think Adam would appreciate vomit in his fur, not to mention that it would be embarrassing, gross and unromantic. I tried to think of something other than racing through the trees, while my stomach groaned in protest. At the very second that I didn't think I could take anymore, Adam slowed down to a walk. I breathed a sigh of relief as my house came into view and he stopped. I slid off him in a heap and gulped in the warm, summer air.

Uh-oh, Nikki. I'm sorry. I didn't know I made you sick. You should have said something. He walked over and head-butted me in the shoulder.

"I'm okay." I got to my feet, pushing against his head for support.

Are you sure? You look a little green.

"I'm fine," I said firmly.

He gave me a wolfish grin, sat back on his haunches and watched as I turned and walked toward the house. Once at the porch, I turned in time to see him turn and dart back through the trees as a big, black blur. I hoped we hadn't been going that fast. My stomach revolted, sending me doubled over in my attempt to back as far as I could get away from the house.

I made it as far as the nearest rhododendron bush before I retched.

THE SEER. HER? They must be joking. He hoped it was all just a big joke, but he had a sense of dread that weighed heavy in his belly. She could undo everything, if she had the gift. He had a hard enough time keeping everything from Jenna White Hawk. Sometimes she would give him an odd look, as if she suspected something wasn't right. But she never knew.

The girl was a bigger threat than she'd been before. It would be so much harder to get rid of her now. It was bad enough with the boy sniffing after her all the time, but now there were *two* of them vying for her attention. How was he ever to get her alone? He didn't know the boy that well, but he did know the wolf. He wouldn't stay away from her. He was unrelenting in anything he set his mind to, just as his father and grandfather before him. And one thing was certain; Adam had no doubts as to who she was. He had been ready to fight for her, against the entire tribe if it came down to it.

No, the boy wouldn't be a threat, and the girl would be easy to kill if she was alone. His challenge lay in Adam. In a way, he admired him. He had such rigid control, only letting his wolf out to hunt when humans were away. If he had been able to control his animal when he was his age, everything could have been so different.

No sense in looking back, he chided himself. After all, animals weren't meant to be controlled. They were wild things, meant to run loose and free. It wasn't his fault that he was always stronger than his prey. And after all was said and done, when the animal inside him was sated and content, so was he.

"YOU KNOW, I wish you guys wouldn't think so loudly," I grumbled, sitting down beside of Adam with my tray. I gave Erik a cold look. "I know you're worried about that Biology exam, but you're projecting it so hard that I can't concentrate. Mr. Webb doesn't think I'm paying attention, and I'm not. I'm too worried about you passing your classes instead of my own."

"Sorry, Nikki, I can't help it. They want me to cut up that pig heart." Erik grimaced, his face looking as gray as his shirt. "I know it's dead already, but butchering the poor thing for no reason other than satisfying someone's morbid curiosity just seems wrong to me." He shrugged, gave me a weak smile, and then started into his first plate of food.

"I don't know, Erik, but you've got to deal with it somehow. I'm not trying to sound unsympathetic or anything, but how can you eat right after you came out of Biology class? Especially if you've been messing with pig guts."

"Pig hearts. It's not that I want to eat, it's because I have to. And yes, I realize that biology shouldn't bother me, but it does. I'm sensitive," he mumbled through a mouthful of hot dog, leaving me to wonder if he had lost his mind. He kept chewing and swallowing more food, without any other explanation.

"What he's trying to say, Nikki, is that we use massive amounts of energy anytime we shift into wolf, and energy requires fuel. We patrol at night as a pack; it uses a lot of energy. It helps if we hunt in wolf form, but often we can't, so we have to eat two or three times more than a regular person would soon after we shift back," Ed explained, squirting more ketchup onto his fries.

"Hunt. In wolf form," I whispered.

"Mostly deer," Erik volunteered before swallowing another bite of hot dog. "Sometimes elk, since they are migrating up this way."

I felt Adam move and glanced over to see him looking at me.

Let me show you, his voice whispered before a sudden flash blinded me.

I was hunting with my brothers. A musky animal scent crept up my nostrils and awakened the animal inside me. I could hear it grazing on the grass a few yards away. It didn't know we were even there. The wolf in me wanted to startle it and make it run. It was eager for the chase. I knew the others felt the same as I, but they would only follow me. We are pack, and I am the leader. I'm the alpha. I gave in to the wolf and lunged in front of the deer, startling it. I saw the large doe's eyes widen in fear for a split second, and then it turned and bounded through the trees. The adrenaline rushed through me, there was nothing human in me now. I only wanted to hunt. To kill.

It was over in a matter of seconds. It always was. After all, when you are the greatest predator in the world, nothing can hide. I could hear her heart beating, fear emanated off her in a wave. I lunged over a fallen log and took her down. I sat down on my haunches with my muzzle still clamped on her throat and felt the last pulse of life as it filled my mouth with the tang of coppery blood. The pack ate until all of us were satisfied. Then the wolves left us and went back down into their shadowy depths, leaving us only in their form, with more strength than we had and our appetites sated.

I blinked, and swallowed, trying to rid my mouth of the sickly sweet taste as I focused back at the solemn, dark faces that stared back at me across the table.

"Like Ed said, it helps to hunt in wolf form. It eases the animal in us," Adam whispered as he stared straight ahead. "No gift comes without a curse."

THIRTEEN

SLEEK, LITHE FORMS *moved through the dark shadows of the forest. These animals were big, but were too long to be the wolves. I strained to see them more clearly. I was busy trying to count how many* there were, when one that I hadn't seen jumped in front of me. A low, feral growl rumbled deep out of its chest.

Mountain lion, I thought, calmly, knowing that it didn't see me. There were definite advantages to knowing you were seeing a vision.

The cat's big yellow eyes watched an unsuspecting deer. It settled in a crouch. Its long, tawny tail twitched with anticipation. Muscles tensed, it was ready to spring.

"Nikki, Adam's here," my mother's voice rang out through the trees.

Startled, the doe looked up and ran.

"Nikki?"

The forest vanished. I blinked and found myself looking at the homework spread on the bed in front of me.

"I'm coming," I yelled and started for the door.

Adam stood waiting at the bottom of the stairs. His hands were clasped behind his back. A small frown furrowed a crease between his brows. I stopped halfway down the stairs, trying to sense any feelings from him. Nothing. Worried that I had somehow turned off my sight, I came down the stairs and stopped in front of him. I returned his frown and concentrated. We stood there, frowning at each other.

"I'm going to go pick Em up. It looks like you two need to talk," Mom said as she squeezed past me and headed out the door.

I glanced over in time to see the door shut.

"Hi," Adam said when I looked back up to him.

"Hi."

"Are you okay?"

"Yes, but I can't hear you at all. Not a single sound. Am I broke? Did I somehow return my gift? No, wait, I know it's still there, because I just saw those big cats. So why can't I hear you? I've always been able to do it before." I stopped and took a breath, trying to think of what to do next. I needed help and there was only one place to get it.

"Nikki."

"I need to go to Jenna. Are you coming?" I shoved my feet into my sneakers, not bothering with tying the shoelaces.

"Nikki."

"Where are my car keys? I know I left them on that table. Maybe they are in the kitchen," I mumbled as I stumbled around him.

Stop and listen to me, his voice rang sharp through my head and stopped me dead in my tracks.

"Oh." I blinked and turned to look up at him.

"There is nothing wrong with you. You are fine, and we aren't going to see Jenna. I asked her if there was some way to keep you out of my thoughts for awhile since I didn't want you in my head. I guess it worked. I'm sorry if that worried you," he spit out the words rapid-fire before taking a quick breath.

"You don't want me?" my voice came out in a choked whisper.

"No, that isn't what I meant." He reached over and rubbed his palms lightly down my arms, and then leaned down and touched his forehead to mine. "No, I always want you, just not in my head for a few minutes, that's all."

"You looked worried, what was wrong? Was it those big cats I saw?" I stayed unmoving, whispering the words, as still as a statue.

He smiled and shook his head. "No, the Sioux are coming. They aren't the trouble and I'm glad you saw them. Those big cats are the mountain lions. They are to the Sioux what the wolves are to us. The last I had heard, Rune hadn't decided if they were going to make it to the powwow, so they must be coming. I'll let my grandfather know you saw them."

"So what are you worried about?"

"I have something to ask you." He straightened up and took a step back from me.

This is all Erik's fault, his voice bounced accusingly in my head as his eyes narrowed, and then looked vulnerable.

I chose to ignore it. "Okay, go ahead. Ask me."

"I was wondering if…well, I mean if you wanted to, of course," he said, swallowing hard. I bobbed my head at him in encouragement. He took a breath and tried again, closing his eyes tight. "I-was-wondering-if-you-wanted-to-go-see-a-movie-or-something,-or-we-could-go-get-something-to-eat-if-you-wanted-to-but-if-you-don't-that-is-okay-too."

I let out the deep breath I had been holding. One golden eye slit open and peeked at me. I grinned at him like the Cheshire cat. So that was why it was all Erik's fault. He had been pestering Adam ever since I had found out about the wolves. "You're asking me out."

To that, he opened both eyes and blinked. "Yes."

I stood there and grinned like an idiot.

"Well?" he asked, impatient.

"Well, okay," I shrugged and kept my thousand watt grin.

"Okay, as in yes?"

"Yes, that's a yes."

He let out a whoosh of breath and grinned down at me. "That's great. So what shall we do?"

"What? Right now?" I asked a second before I realized that he was not wearing his customary black tank top or t-shirt. Instead, he wore long-sleeved, black silk shirt. His hair was pulled back in a tight braid. It left his face open and his eyes sparkling like gold.

"If you would like," he said softly. I broke my gaze from his, and turned to look out the window. His Jeep sat in the yard next to my car as proof that he hadn't come through the forest.

"I know a nice place where we could go eat," he said cautiously, as if he wasn't sure that I wasn't going to back out.

I looked down at my faded blue jeans and stained t-shirt.

He smiled. "Your mom said that if you said yes, you should go and look in her closet on the left side. She left you a surprise. I will wait here if you want to go look."

I gave him a suspicious look, and then ran up the stairs. In my mother's room, I took out a bag hanging in the closet. A pretty, powder blue dress made of a super soft material spilled out in my hands. A note was pinned to one of the thin straps.

"Surprise, Nikki," I read, "Adam stopped by the other day and asked my permission to ask you on a date. I never would have thought of him as the old-fashioned sort to stop and ask, but I am most impressed. I thought you would like a new dress, and found this one at an outlet next to the sheriff's office. Your shoes are in the bottom of the closet. Hope you have a wonderful time. Don't forget to be home by eleven. Love, Mom"

I sat down on the bed and stared at the note in my hands. I heard Adam at the bottom of the steps, as if he wasn't sure if he should come to check on me or not.

Are you okay?

"Yes, just go get comfy on the couch. The remote is down there somewhere. I'll be down in a little bit," I called down.

I laid the dress on the bed and sat at my mom's dressing table. I saw that she put out what makeup I normally would have borrowed. I raked my fingers through my hair and pulled it up in an experimental knot on top of my head. Wild corkscrews popped out everywhere.

Nah, I thought, letting it drop down my back before I tamed it down with a few drops of water and some hair gel. I think he likes it better down.

I shot a quick look at the clock on the wall. More than twenty minutes had passed since I had come upstairs, and although he was shielding his thoughts well from me, I could tell he was anxious from the telltale squeaks from the springs in the couch. I didn't want to keep him waiting much longer.

I looked back in the mirror and smiled. The girl in the reflection looked as if she belonged with the boy downstairs. The blue dress clung from the thin spaghetti straps to my waist like a second skin, and then flared out at my hips in wispy, light layers that fell just above my knees. The light blue showed off my tanned legs and my Cinderella shoes, as Emily called them, finished off the look. I looked as if I had transformed into a magical princess, complete with glass slippers.

I took a deep breath, and tried to relax. "Okay. Let's do this."

I came down the steps quietly, even though I knew he would hear me. I walked to the door of the living room to see him standing and waiting for me. He took a quick breath in and the air between us began to spark and sizzle as it swirled around us in a warm hug.

I walked up to him and stopped merely a few inches away and looked up into his eyes. His eyes blazed down into mine, but he never moved. Nervously, I bit my lip and ducked my head. "Is this okay?"

"You're beautiful," his voice came out deep and gravelly as he reached out and slowly traced one finger down the line of my cheek to my chin and lifted my head to meet his gaze again.

Beautiful isn't the word, but it's the closest thing I know. I don't trust myself to find a better word or to hardly touch you for fear you're just a dream.

"Kiss me," I whispered so low that I wasn't sure even he would hear me.

He kissed me, a tentative brush of lips at first, and then his hands found their way around me and brought me closer. The kiss grew stronger, sending a searing heat through every inch of my body. Just at the moment when I thought I would either melt or burst into flame, he broke the kiss and stepped back.

"We should go out now, I think," my breath came out raggedy and uneven. Much more of that, and I would suggest staying home and making out on the couch all evening.

I started to open my mouth to suggest precisely that, when he took a quick look at his watch. He smiled and took my hand. "I've got a surprise for you. Are you up for it?"

"Sure."

He laughed. "You don't sound so sure, Nikki. I promise it's nothing bad. C'mon."

"So, where are we headed?" I asked, after we made our way out onto the interstate.

"North," he grinned.

Watching the I-77 North sign go past us at that particular second, I rolled my eyes. "You don't say."

"It's a surprise, Nikki. Trust me. You'll see soon enough." He reached over and entwined his fingers through mine.

"Okay," I conceded. I was content to sit and hold his hand for however long it took.

It didn't take long at all, and moments later we exited the interstate and made our way through downtown Beckley, West Virginia.

"Sorry," Adam said as he took his hand from mine to concentrate on the traffic around us.

A couple of moments later, he had pulled us into a parking spot in front of an expensive-looking restaurant. *Dmitri's* a sign said in simple, elegant cursive on a plaque near the door.

"Reservation?" An austere-looking man wearing a starched, white shirt and black pants asked us when we entered.

Adam nodded. "Black Water."

"Of course, sir. This way."

Our table sat in the back. It was a small, private place for two, illuminated by soft candlelight. Menus were handed to each of us as we sat down. I glanced over mine, then peeked over the top to look at Adam.

He looked up from his own menu and smiled. "What do you think?"

"It's beautiful. How did you find this place?"

"Erik told me about it. He likes to surprise Penny sometimes. He said he highly recommends the steak." Adam grinned. His eyes glowed in the flickering light.

The waiter came to take our order. We both ordered steaks. Adam ordered his rare. A band set up and started to play a song that was soft and seductive. The lead singer leaned into the microphone and began crooning soft lyrics.

Adam stood and held out his hand. "Would you like to dance?"

"Yes," I smiled, taking his hand while the air around us warmed and sparked.

The atmosphere seemed to sparkle in the candlelight as we danced slowly, and I leaned my head on his chest, listening to his heart beat in rhythm to the music.

He leaned his head towards mine and sang softly, "You're beautiful, you're beautiful... it's true..."

It was this moment, I knew I loved Adam.

ALL TOO SOON, we were back at my house and Adam was saying good night on the front porch. It started to rain.

"Thank you for a great night," I said, still clinging to his hand.

"Thank you for coming," His voice was low and deep.

I leaned forward and kissed him. I didn't want this night to end.

He broke the kiss, leaned back the tiniest bit, and traced my chin with his thumb. "I love you, Nikki."

"I love you," I whispered before closing the gap between us. I kissed him again as the air sparked and swirled, and the rain pattered like music.

HE WAS SO alone. There was no one to help him, no one left who cared. She would never love him. Not the monster he was.

He watched her as she went inside and the Jeep drove away. She looked so happy and so complete. She closed the front door, and a moment later, he saw the upstairs light come on.

He stood outside her window and wished. He wished for a different world. One where she wouldn't belong to someone else. He watched as she passed the window. She looked like an angel in powder blue with her hair surrounding her in a golden, curly halo.

Tears ran down his face and mingled with the rain. Thunder cracked overhead, echoing that of his broken heart.

FOURTEEN

I HAD SOLVED the mystery. I was sure of it. "We should ask Wynter."

"Ask her what?" Adam asked, perplexed, as we sat waiting for English class to start.

"She may know who the trail killer is."

"The elders thought of that a long time ago. She won't interfere in anything that may alter the history of humankind. So, yes, it is a good idea, but it's been done already."

I wondered how hard the elders had tried. Somehow the fact that this particular Spriteblood was a reformed fairy, and one that used to feast on human flesh, had me questioning how hard they had asked for help. There was the fact that they didn't want to ask her for any favors, too.

She hasn't exactly been ruled out as a suspect, just so you know, his voice whispered through my mind.

"Ah," I nodded, deciding not to argue with him as the teacher took her place in front of the class.

But after school, I headed to the library. Something told me that I would find answers there if I asked the right questions.

Just before I stepped through the door, I stopped and took a deep breath. The last time I came through this door, Tiffany had ambushed me on the other side. I peeked through the crack. The coast was clear. I opened the door. The image of Mrs. Graham was leaned over a student at a far desk and pointing at a computer screen. She looked busy, so I took the opportunity to look around.

It was astounding.

Enormous oak bookcases with intricate carvings were set up in a complex, semi-circular maze around the room. This room didn't look like it belonged in a high school. It was too intricate, too antique. A black metal staircase stood in the center of the room and spiraled upward to another level that you could partially see from the bottom. Straight back from the staircase sat the librarian's desk, against the wall.

It was the wall behind her desk that caught my attention. The same wooden carvings covered it as the bookcases around me, but as I focused on it the wood rearranged itself, shifting and realigning as if it had a spirit of its own.

Each section moved, clicking into place to form a door that was only accessible by going behind the desk.

I looked over at the computer section as I walked around the staircase. There wasn't anyone there now. A quick look the other way proved that I was alone in the bottom of the library, so I walked over to the desk and focused on the door again.

The carvings moved across the door and formed a sentence. The words written made no sense to me. I stared at them harder, thinking maybe they would shift again if I focused more.

"Wise am I and ancient in all things," I murmured.

"Restricted section," a cold voice said behind me.

I jumped and turned around to face Wynter, who looked at the door angrily, baring her pointed teeth.

"Show yourself to no one," she commanded, her voice cracking like thunder. Afraid to turn around and watch, I listened as the wood of the door behind me snap sharply at her request, slamming itself back into its original form. The ancient oak wood splintered in protest.

Wynter turned the full effect of her ice blue eyes on me, demanding, "What is it you require?"

"Um, I came to return my book." I held out the book she had given me. "It was very useful." I stopped before I said "thank you."

She noticed and a slight smile curved her lips as she took the book from me. She held it up in the air by its spine.

"Find your place," she told the book. I watched in fascination as *A History of the County of Bland* picked itself out of her hand and went floating to one of the bookshelves, squeezing between two other volumes that shifted over to make room.

As if in approval, Wynter gave a slight nod. It left me wondering if her books ever misbehaved. The books that were her clothes fluttered softly and caught my attention. The pages flipped and I could see tiny, elaborate writing on the small squares of paper.

"Is there something else you need?" Wynter asked. Her voice hadn't warmed even the slightest bit.

"Mrs...?" What did I call her? I wondered. She didn't look like sour, old Mrs. Graham, so it didn't seem right to call her that.

"I am Spriteblood. Those who know of me call me by name, and those who do not, shall never hear it. They will only hear the name of the woman whose image they see. I am known as Wynter," she said, with a slight incline of her head.

Taking it as an introduction of sorts, I smiled at her. It felt as though I were making some small progress in the strange world of the supernatural.

"The others do not know you have come." She bared her razor-sharp teeth in a way that did not imply friendliness.

Nope, no progress. She may eat me. I took a deep breath and decided to try anyway.

"No, ma'am. They don't know I'm here, but they won't ask you what they need to know, so I came alone."

"Their old ones asked many years ago," she corrected, looking thoughtful as her teeth were hidden again.

"Would you tell me what the truth is? Do you know who the monster is?" I asked.

"What you name monster lives in us all," she said sadly, and turned to walk away from me.

I was afraid that she wasn't going to tell me anything else, so I didn't stop to think. I just acted. "Please, I'll do anything."

She stopped in mid-stride. I wasn't the only one who realized my mistake, but now it was too late to take it back.

"They should walk their Deadlands," Wynter said in a sorrowful voice. "Slowly."

I ran out of the library with my heart racing. I had asked for help and gotten it, but I had also promised to help her, with anything.

The entire drive to the Res, I kept thinking of the bedtime story of the fairies that live under the hill, and wondered what payment I would have to give her when the time came.

I don't know if they had heard my heart hammering that loud, or if it was the way I slid sideways into the driveway and parked, but Adam and Erik walked out to meet me before I could jump out of the car.

"What's going on? Are you all right?" Adam opened the door of the Jeep and I jumped out.

"I just talked to Wynter," I said in a puff, feeling as if I had run the entire way instead of driven.

"That explains the hurry." Erik rolled his eyes. "What did ye ol' fairy queen have to say?"

Please tell me that you didn't thank her, Adam's voice begged through my mind.

I looked over at him and shook my head, "Well, no, I didn't do that. She says you should walk through your cemetery, slowly."

"Huh?" Erik's face was utter confusion.

"Are you sure that's what she said?" Adam asked. "Tell us word for word."

"She said, *They should walk through their Deadlands. Slowly.*" I repeated.

"Ah, okay. That makes somewhat better sense," Erik said with a nod.

What did you have to promise to get her help?

"I'd rather not say," I said quietly.

Will you tell me everything later?

I nodded, and Adam turned to Erik. "Call the others. We'll search."

Erik ran around the corner of the house. A second later, an ear-splitting howl pierced the air. Within moments, Ed, Tommy and Michael arrived and the group shifted to wolves. Adam had been the only wolf I had seen, but the others looked exactly like those in my dreams. Five sleek, beautiful wolves turned to run into the woods.

"Can I go, too?" I asked.

Sure, come on, Adam waited as I hopped up on his back.

"What are the Deadlands?" I asked as he started to run.

Magical places. I know with the name, that's not the way it sounds. There are places in the forest where there was so much magic, it soaked into the earth. Anything that breathes stays away from the Deadlands since they have a foreboding feeling. It's as if these places don't want anyone or anything around. We can't even scent anything there. The magic blocks us. I'm guessing that's why Wynter said to walk slowly. I felt his shoulders twitch in a shrug.

In a few moments, the atmosphere changed and the wolves slowed to a walk. The wind blew in a sudden gust that threw dead leaves into our faces as if it wanted us to stay away. The next instant, there was dead calm. There were no birds chirping high up in the trees, no bugs buzzing around us, no snakes slithering through the underbrush. The complete silence was unnerving and spooky. Tall, dark trees bent in strange angles. This place looked a lot like the one I had walked through to get berries. The hair on the back of my neck stood on end.

Tommy let out a low whine and tucked his tail between his legs.

I hate this place, his voice shook uneasily in my head.

Not finding my voice, I nodded my head in agreement. I didn't like it either.

We walked slowly through the trees. I had gotten used to the branches moving out of the way anytime that Adam and I walked through the woods. They always moved, as if trying to accommodate us. But here, briars reached out, clawing and twining into the wolves' fur. I heard a sharp yip, and looked back to see Ed limping, holding up his front paw.

He shifted back to human form and inspected his hand, "I stepped on a frigging briar."

I jumped off Adam's back and went over to help. What he had called a briar looked to be an inch long chunk of wood that was stuck deep in his palm. He sucked in his breath, grabbed the end of it, and gave it a quick jerk.

Blood welled up from the wound. I reached into my pocket and handed him a tissue. A few droplets fell to the dry dirt before he managed to squash the tissue in his fist. The ground shook, and seemed to suck the blood in. A loud moan erupted from the earth and the clouds blocked out the sun for what seemed an eternity. We all stayed frozen in place, afraid to move. Then, the sky cleared.

Okay, so that was weird, Erik announced, letting out his breath in a snort.

"It's a Deadland." Ed shrugged, squeezing the tissue tight. "It thrives on magic. And blood, too, it seems."

"I wouldn't call it thriving," I mumbled. The dead-looking trees looked even more imposing with their energy boost from Ed's blood.

I felt Adam behind us. He came over and took my hand, then told the others, "Split up, but always stay within sight of someone. We'll cover more territory that way. Walk slowly and use your eyes. Your nose won't do you any good here," He looked over at Ed, who still clutched the tissue trying to staunch the blood. "How's the hand?"

"Not healing yet," Ed said, opening his hand for Adam's inspection. Free of the tissue, blood welled back up and covered his palm a bright red. Adam reached over and closed Ed's hand around the soggy tissue.

"Keep it tight. Try not to let anymore blood drop. We don't want to feed this Deadland any more magic. It doesn't want us here and your blood will make it stronger. Nikki, have you got anymore tissues?"

"No, that's all I had," I said as I searched my pockets to be sure.

"If it doesn't heal up soon, you go back and wait for us. If you need to head back to the Res, get my grandpa to look at it. He may know how to counter the magic," Adam told Ed, who gave him a silent nod.

Adam squeezed my hand. "Let's look around. Stay close and don't let go of me, okay?"

"You've got it," I said, holding his hand in a death grip. This place was spooking me out. It seemed to be watching every move we made.

A dried up creek lay in front of us with a scraggly tree on the other side. The tree's roots were splayed, as if it were trying to find water. It was here Ed went to investigate. The rocks under his feet clattered as he walked across them.

"Oh, great," I heard him say, and looked over to see his hand spurting blood. A dark stream fell to the ground. The rocks surrounding Ed, clanked. I watched in horror as a root freed itself and crawled its way toward Ed, who for some reason, was engrossed in watching the blood fall from his hand.

"Look out!" I screamed. A split second before the root reached out to snare him, Adam slammed into Ed, rolling them both to the edge of the Deadland.

Avoiding the root that was now rolling itself in Ed's blood, Adam came back out to get me. Running to the safety of the trees with me in tow, he threw back his head and let out an ear-splitting howl to call the others back.

Within seconds, Erik, Tommy and Michael stood with us at the edge of the Deadland. Ed sat in the exact spot where Adam had left him, shaking his head as if trying to clear it.

"I think I'd better go back," he said in a shaky voice. "I don't feel right."

"We'll all go." Adam nodded, as he took in everyone's scrapes and scratches. "We've fueled it too much to search. It's alive and bloodthirsty."

"I'm sorry," Ed said dejectedly. "It was as if nothing mattered. I just stood there and watched myself bleed. It didn't hurt. I think I would have stood there as long as it wanted until it was satisfied."

"It's not your fault." Adam reached out and put a hand on Ed's shoulder. "Don't worry about it. We'll come back once it's calmed down. Let's go get you fixed up."

The way back took quite a bit longer being as both Ed and I walked. Erik offered to let Ed ride on his back, the same way that I did with Adam. Ed hadn't even bothered with a reply, he just gave Erik a steely look, and marched through the trees ahead of us.

Oh well, I tried, Erik shrugged, trudging after his friend.

It was nearing nightfall when we made it to Adam's grandfather's house. As if he heard us approach, the old man opened his door and motioned us in. He took note of Ed cradling his hand.

"You sit over here," he said, pointing the boy over to a chair by the window, and then turned to Adam, saying, "What dark magic have you brought with you?"

"It was one of the Deadlands, Grandpa," Adam said, not looking the old man in the eye. "We were told to search there."

His grandfather watched him through keen, sharp eyes, and then turned and looked at me. "Who told them to search there?"

"The Spriteblood," I said meekly.

The old man muttered under his breath, and from the way Adam's face flushed, I was guessing that he wasn't very impressed with Wynter. He started gathering various things from cupboards, setting them down on a small table in front of Ed.

After a few moments of crushing things in a wooden bowl, he scooped them onto a flat shell and lit the ingredients on fire, chanting as a small plume of smoke wafted up in front of Ed's face.

Singing a low, lulling chant, he fanned smoke over Ed for a few moments, and then stood and covered the rest of us in the same manner.

It was as if a dark haze lifted off us as the old man went back to sit across from Ed. He took a small bundle from his pocket, and began to unwrap it. The same stone I had seen when I had met the elders, the Wolf Stone, glowed in an eerie, bluish light. He took Ed's injured hand and laid the Stone directly on the wound.

The Stone held magic. An eerie, ghostlike howl echoed through the room. Ed's cream colored mist surrounded him, and his wolf came to peer at us from behind his brown eyes. The blood that had leaked from the hole in his hand, suddenly changed direction and bubbled around the stone as it made its way back into his body.

Once every trace of blood had gone, the old man took the Stone from Ed's hand. The skin was new, as if nothing had happened. As he wrapped the Stone and slid it back into the safety of his pocket, the old man looked sharply at Adam.

"I suppose you'll take greater care next time." It sounded more like a statement than a request.

"Yes, sir," Adam said, a smile quirking at his lips as if he had seen the twinkle in the old man's eyes.

"Off with you, then," he said, shooing us toward the door as he picked up his remote, "*Jeopardy* will be on soon, and you have places to be." He pointed at me. "Her mother will be looking for her. If she gets angry with you, that's something I can't fix."

"He's right, you know," Adam said as the door shut behind us. "If I don't get you home soon, your mom is going to kill us." He looked over at Ed, "Everything okay, now?"

Ed nodded. "Never better."

"Alright, let's go," Adam said as he shifted into his wolf.

"Huh-uh," I said, looking at the woods, then over at his driveway where a safe-looking Jeep sat. "You're driving me."

"How many Deadlands are there?" I asked, once in the sanctity of the Jeep. I buckled my seatbelt.

"Quite a few. We'll search them one at a time. I've never seen them take on a personality of their own like that before." The small frown between his eyes furrowed into a deep line.

"Promise you'll be careful," I said as I took his hand in mine.

He smiled, leaning over to kiss me, and then promised, "Always."

THE NEXT WEEK the Keepers searched day and night. They didn't even make it to school. What time they were home, they slept. I didn't see Adam at all that week, though he called a few times. It was also during this week that Tiffany went missing. One day she was at cheerleading practice, the next she vanished. And, once again, she made the front page of the school newspaper. This time, the headline read, "Have you seen Tiffany?"

But it seemed no one had.

The lack of seeing Adam, coupled with the strange disappearance of my arch nemesis, had unease seeping through every pore of my being.

Adam picked up on it, and surprised me by showing up for a quick visit before he left on another search. It was the first football game of the season that night, so I couldn't have been happier to see him.

"I don't want to leave you," he whispered, brushing his lips against my forehead. "Something is telling me I shouldn't go, that I shouldn't let you out of my sight tonight."

"I don't want you to go, but you'll have to." I snuggled next to him on the front porch swing.

"I know," he said as he wrapped me close in his arms. "But I really don't want to go this time. I've missed you, but this is different. It's a weird feeling that I've got."

"I've missed you too, but everything is fine." I tilted back my head to look up at him.

A cool wind picked up, rocking the swing. A few strands of silky hair blew loose from the thick plait at his back. Worry etched lines around his golden eyes as he looked back down at me.

If it weren't so dangerous for the others to search alone, his voice whispered, *I'd stay right here with you tonight.*

"Ooh." I grinned. "That would be nice."

"You know what I mean. Besides, your little sister is inside so we have to behave," he chided as he reached around and tugged my scrunchie loose, setting my curls free. "It *would* be nice to stay with you, but something is making me want to stay so I can protect you. It started as soon as I stepped on the porch. I can't explain it."

"What's going to happen is that I will be cheering my little heart out with the rest of the squad in a little while as you and the pack go search another Deadland. Hopefully, our evil blonde Barbie will bring her skanky butt back and grace us with her presence," I said, blowing a blonde corkscrew out of my eyes.

"Dad says they are still keeping an eye on Brian. He was the last one to see her," Adam said, avoiding my eyes.

"He didn't do anything to her, Adam. You know that," I said suddenly, feeling warmth creep up into my cheeks. "She could have just ran off to get attention. You know how Tiffany is. Besides, your dad already took him in and questioned him."

"How did you know that? Did Brian decide to answer your calls? As far as I know, his own mother doesn't even know they questioned him, Dad made sure she was patrolling the other side of town when they brought him in."

"No, he didn't call me," I whispered, my eyes filling with tears. "Mom saw him there and she told me."

"I'm sorry, Nikki." His voice softened as he took my hand in his. "You're probably right. Tiffany probably ran off to get everyone in an uproar, it's something that she would do. I didn't mean to upset you. I know you care about him, but I don't want you to get hurt."

"Brian didn't have anything to do with it, Adam, you've got to believe that."

"He probably didn't. I've known Brian for a long time, and he's always seemed like a good guy," he conceded. "But something has changed in him. Everyone is noticing it. He's not the same guy you met a couple months ago. Promise me you'll be careful, really careful, okay?"

"Okay," I whispered. "I promise."

A sudden howl, not-so-deep from the forest, made me jump and sent the chains on the swing clinking.

"They're waiting for me," Adam said wryly. "Erik's not known for his patience, and his timing usually sucks."

I laughed and got up from the swing with him. He hugged me close, squeezing me as tight as he dared, and then set me down. "I'll be back as soon as I can." He leaned forward and kissed me as the air swirled and sparked around us. The rest of the world melted away.

As he broke the kiss, he whispered, "I love you."

Then he was gone.

I went back to the swing and sat down. I wanted to soak up a few moments of silence before I went inside and got ready for the game. I ran my hand absently down the wooden armrest.

"Ow!" I exclaimed as a chunk of wood came off in my palm. I pulled the splinter free and looked at it. A tiny bit of blood stained one end, but it wasn't sharp enough to pierce anyone again, so I threw it down on the porch to inspect my hand.

I felt a weird jolt under my feet as if the boards of the porch had come alive and rolled like a wave, though I didn't see a thing.

I sat there for another minute, and when nothing else happened, I got up from the swing.

Suddenly, I dreaded going to the game. It was a feeling that washed over me quickly, and made me want to go find Adam.

Nah, I thought, I'm just imagining things. Nothing is wrong, I just have to cheer at the game. Everything is fine.

FIFTEEN

EMILY RAN STRAIGHT into me. She wrapped her arms around me as soon as I cleared the front door. "Nikki," she wailed.

"What? What is it?" I asked as I tried to dislodge her from my legs.

"Fred, it's Fred. I've lost him, Nikki." Tears streamed from her eyes, and she started to hiccup, "I can't find him anywhere." At the last word, she bawled, shrieking octaves that only a distraught toddler could reach.

"It's okay. We'll find him. C'mon, I'll help you," I coaxed. I patted her brown curls until she calmed down. A few errant tears squeezed out of her eyes. She took a deep breath, wiped her running nose on the back of her hand, and then nodded.

Ick, I thought. I grabbed her other hand and took her upstairs to search her room. I dove into the toy chest, shook out the covers on the bed, and searched the closet, but couldn't find a clue as to the stuffed bear's whereabouts.

"He's not there," Emily said, watching me got ready to crawl under the bed. "I done looked."

"You mean 'you've already looked,'" I corrected, bending over to search through a mountain of dolls.

"That's what I said," she sniffled and wiped her nose again. "And I done looked there, too."

"Okay." I puffed out a breath and straightened back up. "Where haven't you looked?"

She took a long look around the room. "I've looked everywhere." Her bottom lip quivered, and the tears started up again, I bent over and picked her up.

She wrapped her arms and legs around me, then buried her face in my hair, and whispered, "I'll never find my Fred, Nikki. Not never."

I patted her back as I carried her back downstairs. "He'll show up. He's not lost, just misplaced is all."

"Who's lost?" A muffled voice came from the other side of the screen door.

Catching the door with her foot, our mother came in with her arms full of grocery bags. She made her way to the kitchen to set them on the counter.

Emily wriggled in my arms. As I set her down, she ran over and locked her arms around our mother's legs.

"Easy, honey." Mom wobbled with the sudden force, nearly dropping a carton of eggs. She peered down into her youngest child's face. "What's going on, baby?"

"I've lost my Fred, Momma," Emily said solemnly, as if to make certain she had relayed the seriousness of the predicament.

"Okay, let me finish this up," Mom said as she tossed salad mix into the refrigerator.

Emily stood patiently, and beamed a smile at me as if she was sure of her mother's ability to fix any problem, regardless of magnitude. Apparently, big sisters just didn't cut it sometimes.

"Go ahead and get ready, Nikki. You don't need to be late. I'm dropping Em off at a friend's house later, so we may not be here when you get home."

"Are you sure?" I asked. I would have loved to have the excuse to stay and watch my little sister instead of going to the game.

"Absolutely. We're fine, and we'll find Fred, no worries," she said. "Have fun tonight, honey."

"Okay," I gave her my fake-smile and went upstairs to get my cheerleader outfit on.

"Since you've checked everywhere else, I'm betting you've left Fred in the car earlier today." I heard Mom's voice carry up the steps before the front door closed.

As the house went silent, I eyeballed the green and white outfit lying on my bed. "May as well get it over with," I mumbled, grabbing the top and pulling it over my head. I hoped the Keepers would find Tiffany, and bring her skanky butt back. Then maybe everything would quiet down, and I could find a way to quit the cheerleader squad. For some reason, Tiffany stayed on my mind the whole way to school until I reached the football field.

The evening was cool. I shivered, wondering whose idea it was to start football season on what was the coldest night I could remember. I stood on the side of the field with the rest of the squad and rubbed my bare arms, hopping lightly from one foot to the other. I took a deep breath, watching as it condensed and floated in front of me like mist the second it left my lips.

The game would start soon, and then hopefully I would warm up. A quick glance to either side of me proved that I was in the minority of the group freezing to death. Most of the girls had jackets or hoodies, and were standing patiently as they waited for the game to begin. I only counted three of us that stood with our teeth chattering.

After what seemed an eternity, the doors on the side of the school burst open and a sea of green and white helmets ran out to the field. The Bland Wolves, playing on their own field, were welcomed with a cheering crowd and a few, chattering cheerleaders. The opposing team, the Valley Bears, rallied on the opposite side of the field.

The pompoms swished up and down, as we began our routine and started to warm up.

I felt anxious and I didn't know why. My heart started racing and my palms started to sweat. One pompom slipped out of my hands and I had to bend over to pick it up. When I straightened up, I swooned and took a step backward, smacking into the girl behind me.

"Watch it," she warned under her breath.

"Sorry," I mumbled, I tried to catch up with the rhythm of the routine. I felt clumsy, as if the moves we had practiced for weeks were new to me. I did my best, but still was out of time with the others.

I caught Ronnie giving me a strange looks, as if she were trying to figure out what planet I was from and how she could send me back there.

I tried harder and did a little better, but was still off by a second from the others. I shook my head, trying to focus. I felt terrible, as if something were looming in the shadows to swallow me. Dread choked out my voice, and I gave up chanting with the others and tried to keep moving to the beats of the music. I felt like a robot, moving in short, choppy motions that should have flowed.

I took a wrong step and collided into the girl beside me. Avoiding the disaster of the whole squad, she barely kept from whacking into the girl next to her and setting off a domino effect.

I jumped out of the line, apologized to her, and then started toward a nearby bench.

"Are you okay?" Ronnie asked over the music as I walked by.

I nodded. "Dizzy," I mouthed and pointed to the bench.

She gave me a quick nod and I plopped rather ungracefully onto the hard wooden bench, backed by the speakers. I breathed in long gulps of cool air. My heart was still hammering, so I focused on the field, and the school band that marched across.

Suddenly, I was staring into my little sister's huge, terrified brown eyes. I glanced down to a big hand covering her mouth as her own small hands tried to pry it free. Terror seeped inside me as I watched her fight.

"Emily," I screamed, and suddenly was back again at the football field, standing near the bench. With all the noise, no one had heard me. The cheerleaders kept with their routine while the music blared beside me.

A flash of opal-white skin caught my eye across the field in the bleachers. She sat at the edge, and her blue, fathomless eyes were fixed on me.

Wynter had heard me scream.

She looked at me with such a sorrowful expression, that I felt as if my own heart were breaking. She lifted her hand towards me and said a single word, and then disappeared as if she had never been there. I blinked.

Emily's brown head popped up in my vision again. The tight corkscrews of her hair bounced as she was carried around a set of bleachers, toward the dark edge of the forest.

She was here at the game. Those bleachers were on the far side, where no one sat on account of the poor view. I ran around the side parking lot, to the far side of the grounds and the trees came into view.

Beware...Beware! Wynter's warning whispered in my mind.

All sense of caution left at what I saw lying on the ground. Near the trees, Fred, Emily's cherished bear, lay sprawled in the dirt. I started sobbing and bent to pick him up. I was too late. Someone had taken Emily. Hysterical, I turned to run for help.

I sensed him behind me a second before pain exploded in my head. Everything went black.

SIXTEEN

I WAS COLD. Shards of ice seemed to be running along my bones, chilling my blood. I stretched, trying to feel my legs. One thing was certain, I wasn't dead. It hurt too much. But where was I?

I lay still, trying to get my eyes to focus in the darkness. My eyes adjusted on a small crack of light that was shining down from high above. My head was laying against something hard and slick, propping me up at a weird angle as if I were a marionette with no strings. Uncomfortable, I lay still and tried to take a mental inventory of my body. Everything from my chest down ached in a surreal way, as if it wasn't really my body, but someone else's. The back of my head, by far, felt the worst. It felt as if my heart had decided to move there and work at thumping its way out of my skull.

Calm down, I thought, take deep breaths.

Getting my wits about me, I tried flexing my feet. Nothing broke there, just numb. A small current lapped up, splashing cool and wet against my neck.

It's okay, it's just water.

Forgetting any attempt at being calm, I sat up. The dark, murky water reached my waist, baring my chest to cold, stale air. I sucked in a startled breath. I sat motionless, resisting the urge to sink back into the water, which seemed a few degrees warmer.

It's okay, I told myself. Adam will come for me soon.

Heartened by this idea, I focused all my energy on finding him. Surely, he would know I needed him. He always knew where I was.

Adam, please. I need you.

I couldn't hear him, I stretched my thoughts out farther, seeking any link I could find. Everything was quiet. Getting worried, I tried to send out feelers for the others and took down all my mental blocks that had been keeping everyone out.

Erik. Ed. Michael, Tommy?

The darkness answered me in silence. Where were they? My mind hadn't been so alone in months. *I* hadn't been so alone in months. And I didn't like it. Wherever I was, something had to be blocking me, or maybe I was just too far away to hear them.

Silently, I prayed I wasn't in a Deadland. But even if I were, I knew that I had to do something. That meant I was going to have to get moving and find a way out of there.

When I moved, something other than water brushed my hand. A faint sparkle glimmered eerily a few inches from the surface. Moving more out of fear than curiosity, I pulled up the small disc shaped charm out of the water between my thumb and forefinger.

The small golden chain was hung on something. I took a better grip and gave a quick tug.

A bloated, white hand popped up to the surface, palm up. I shrieked and jumped to my feet, sending water flying in every direction. The hand floated back down, the charm bracelet sparkling like a homing beacon. I backed up against a wall, the sudden contact with cold stone knocked my breath out in a quick whoosh. That lack of air was the only thing that kept me from screaming when I saw the rest of her.

She lay on her side, her lifeless eyes stared at me. She looked like a broken, discarded doll. Long, blonde tendrils floated like snakes as her head swayed gently back and forth in the water, as if her neck were broken. A gaping hole was all that remained of her throat. I shuddered as I remembered the doe Adam had hunted, as his jaws clamped around the slender, delicate neck and tasted the gush of warm blood and the crunch of bone.

I gulped.

All at once the air was putrid and vile, thick with the scent of death. My stomach heaved and I ended up throwing up everything I had eaten for the past decade. Finally, with nothing left to lose, I looked back over at her.

The familiar green and white outfit, identical to the one I wore, was shredded, leaving her shoulder and chest bare. The short skirt was pushed up around her waist. One strong, once graceful, leg was lying at an odd angle behind her. Her feet were bare. Long, shallow cuts in the shape of a giant claw furrowed her pale flesh from shoulder to breast to stomach. Her killer had not left her pretty. My eyes welled and spilled over as I looked at her waxen face.

"Tiffany. I'm so sorry. Whatever you had done, you didn't deserve this," my voice came out hoarse and whispery.

I lay my head against the cool, stone wall behind me and cried while my thoughts ran rampant. My subconscious kept warning me, *You may be in a Deadland. This will happen to you and they'll never find you here.*

"It won't happen to me. I won't let it," I argued with Tiffany's still body as if she were the one who had thought the words instead of me.

My eyes fully adjusted, I stayed close to the wall of the small underground chamber, keeping one hand on the wall to steady me. The water, once at my knees, went up to my hips in some places, as I made my way around the small room. I ignored the small bumps of floating things in the water, since I was certain that I didn't want to know what they were, and concentrated on keeping my footing.

I realized there was no other exit as I came full circle to where I had started. The only way out was the way I had come in, which had to have been from above. I squinted up at the little crack of light. I had to find a way up. I made another circle, this time keeping both hands on the wall, feeling for any handhold I could get. I slid my hands against the cold rock until they sank into mud.

Ecstatic that I had found a way up, I made my way slowly up towards the light. For every inch I went up, I seemed to slide back two.

"You can do it, you can do it," I chanted, ignoring the scrapes of small rocks that dug into my stomach as I pushed upwards with my legs and grabbed for any hand hold I could find.

After what seemed hours, I made it to the top and probed the small crack with my fingers. It was only a couple inches wide and solid rock was all around it. I took my fingers back out and pushed as hard as I dared against the roof. It didn't give at all. I shoved harder, adrenaline coursed through my body as panic set in. I couldn't die here, I had to get out. This rock had to move. Forgetting that I sat precariously on a steep mud wall, I shoved with all my strength, hitting the rock as hard as I could with my hands. The shock reverberated back down my arms a millisecond before I lost my footing and went half-sliding, half-bouncing back down the wall and landed in the water on my butt.

I threw my head back and screamed as loud as I could in frustration. I curled my knees up to my chest, and hid my face in my hands. Hot, angry tears seeped between my fingers. I would never get out of here, I would be like the others, just another missing girl. The Keepers would look for me and never find me. Mom would never know what happened to me. What if they never found Emily, either? Mom would be all alone, with no one to help her if both of her girls were gone. I eyed the dark, putrid water as something pale and bloated bobbed inches from me. Some part of my brain reasoned that my little sister may very well be down here with me as well. I looked down at Tiffany's blonde tendrils and imagined Emily's dark curls floating in the water.

I stifled the urge to scream and forced myself to take deep breaths. The air filled my nostrils with the stench of rotting flesh. My stomach, having found some small particle of food deep down, surrendered, and sent me vomiting against slick, wet wall. Drained once again, I leaned my forehead against the cold rock and forced myself to concentrate on Adam.

I wondered if he could sense at all where I was. If he couldn't, would he think me dead? Would he stop looking if he knew all he would find would be my bones? Would he mourn me forever or would he find another? Would it be Hannah? That thought of Hannah had me back on my feet, more determined and frustrated than ever.

I was suddenly overcome with a feeling of absolute satisfaction. It felt as if everything was right with the world, I was on top, and nothing would bring me down. I would do as I wished and no one would stop me.

He's coming back, I thought, panicking. The killer hadn't left me here to die, yet. I glanced over my shoulder at Tiffany's broken body, and prayed that wasn't his intention. Deciding it would be better to know what he had planned, I closed my eyes and took a deep breath, steeling myself against the fear that roiled in my stomach.

I shouldn't come back here so soon. He may find me out, but I can't help it. I need to smell her fear and hear her beg for her life. I heard her scream a minute ago, so I know she's awake. Did the other girls frighten her? Or is she just hurt? I can't help it, I must know. I have time. He won't find me here now. He knows the others are searching. He'll stay away for awhile.

The double sensation of panic and relief surged through me. The killer had heard me, but maybe someone else had, too. If I could only keep him talking to me, maybe someone would find me. I concentrated on taking deep breaths; I would need my wits about me. I couldn't let myself get out of sorts.

I heard him above me and the rock above moved as if it were light as a feather. I was bathed in blinding light. I blinked up at the man who squatted near the edge of the hole. As my eyes adjusted, I looked up in shock at the familiar face with a silver streak of hair. Emotions mixed and twisted inside my head. Shock and fury ran through me as I looked up at Reuben.

"I see you are awake," Reuben stated, as if he had just met me in the store and asked how I was doing.

Disbelief won over every other emotion as I stood there and gaped at him, not sure what to say. What do you say to a sadistic murderer? Hi, nice day, isn't it? Why ruin a perfect day with murder? I hear it's going to rain tomorrow and my schedule is free...

"I suppose you've met my other girls?" he added conversationally, a slight smile curving his lips.

All the little bumps of things in the water with you are people. Dead, murdered hikers. Well, not all hikers. I turned and looked again at Tiffany's torn body, biting my lower lip to try to hold the hysterical scream back that threatened to tear from my throat.

"Why are you doing this?" My voice shook, and I hated myself for sounding so weak. I had to keep him talking so someone could find me. I squared my shoulders and lifted my chin stubbornly and glared up at him.

"Well, my dear. You wouldn't stay out of the way, so I had to take care of you. I could not have you mess up my plans. You threaten too much that I hold dear. With you out of the way, no one would ever have to know what I am—who I am." His smile was getting more eerie by the second.

"The Trail Killer," I shivered.

He laughed. It was a short, loud burst that didn't at all sound amused. "Yes, that's what they call me. But I'm so much more. They don't have any idea of everything I am or the power I hold."

Okay, so he was a lunatic *and* a sadistic murderer, I decided. I tried to keep my voice level and strong, in spite of my body that was still quivering. "My sister. What have you done with Emily?"

"Oh, your little brat is fine. I didn't have to touch her" he scoffed, waving his hand down as my little sister were nothing but a trivial matter. "She was only bait to get you to leave the game. Being a Keeper for as long as I have, you learn that sometimes you can make your Seer see things that aren't precisely true, especially if you concentrate hard enough. I've done it with Jenna White Hawk for years. All I had to do was concentrate and think about abducting your little brat and that's all you saw. The hardest part was getting that teddy bear so you would get close enough to the trees. I didn't think she would ever leave it where I could snatch it. I finally did, though, and then everything was so simple. You believe everything you see so easily."

Relief flooded through me that Emily was safe, and all the tension left. I was the only one in danger, so I could deal with this. I would find a way to get out of this deep, dark hole. Adam would find me, and then this man in front of me would have hell to pay.

Keep him talking. You need to find out more, I reminded myself.

"Where am I and what is this place?"

"Well, my dear, you are in a hole, in case you haven't noticed. And it isn't all that far away from your house. I happened upon it years ago when I was leaning against the rock and it gave a little. I pushed it, and discovered the nicest little hiding place. I knew no one would ever find anything here, being as it's close to the edge of a Deadland," he said, seeming rather satisfied. "I haven't had to worry much, since your grandmother was so old. When she died, I made sure I was given the house at the rental agency to watch over. There hadn't been any trouble until you showed up. Now, all of a sudden, the leader of the pack decides to travel this way on a daily basis. At least this stone blocks their scent." He peered down triumphantly at me.

"Why Tiffany? Why is she here? She wasn't one of the hikers. What had she done to you?" Sure, she had made everyone in school mad at her from one time to another, but I couldn't make a connection from the hikers to her to *him*.

Sudden rage flared up in his dark eyes. "She was after the boy, but it was only because of you. She would never have bothered with him if you hadn't ..." he broke off and his head snapped up, as if he had heard something.

Now was my chance, someone was coming. "Help! Help me, please!" The sounds of my screams were cut off as he jumped to his feet and had the massive stone slid back in place in a mere second. My last word bounced and echoed against the walls, as if it were as trapped as I was.

Once again, I was left alone in my dark, watery prison. Now that I was aware that there were many more bodies down here than just Tiffany's, my skin became super-sensitive as it felt the brush of things that bumped against my legs. I propelled myself backwards, trying to get to more shallow water. I took small, shallow breaths through my mouth in an attempt to ignore the overwhelming smell of rot and decay.

The opposite wall was closer than I judged and once again I whacked against the solid rock, whooshing out what air I had, and bumping the back of my head. If I hadn't already had a goose egg where he hit me earlier, it probably wouldn't have hurt as much. But being as it had already been hit once, the slight tap sent bright white spots whirling in front of me. My eyes watered and I slid down the wall to crouch, waiting for the pretty white spots to leave me and the darkness to surround me again.

Adam, where are you? I need you so much. Why can't you find me? I gave in and cried. I brushed the tears away after a few moments, irritated that I felt so helpless. For some reason the Keepers couldn't find me, so I would have to help them somehow. Maybe brain waves didn't carry through solid rock. I was going to have to try to get out again, and then maybe they would find me.

I waited another minute for my head to quit throbbing, before I attempted to stand. My mind raced as it replayed the conversation with Reuben. Who was *the boy*? Whoever he was, Reuben seemed very protective of him. If I couldn't get out before he came back, maybe I could use that angle to gain some sympathy. I doubted it would work, but I was ready to try anything. Only his mention of *the boy*, had given him any emotion that seemed human. And human was the only part that I would be able to bargain with. Leaving my mental walls completely down in case he came back, I decided my best bet was to try to climb up the mud again and get as close to the opening as I could manage.

This time seemed easier than the first, and the closer I got to the opening, the clearer the voices and thoughts bounced into my head.

Did he hear her? If he did, there's only one thing I can do.

Where is he? I could have sworn I thought I heard someone scream.

The first voice I knew, without a doubt, as my abductor. The other had me more perplexed. It wasn't one of the Keepers. I knew their thoughts and voices. Each of them had a different feel that made them individual and pointed out who they were. I crawled closer to the crack and strained to hear more.

Worry took over all at once, flooding every cell in my body as my heart raced, threatening to beat out of my chest. My breath started coming in short gasps as if I had been running as fast as I could go, pushing myself harder than I had ever gone before.

Where is she? I can't find her, Adam's voice fuzzed brokenly through my mind, like a radio station with bad reception filtering out the voices I heard seconds earlier. Then, a bright flash blinded me.

I was racing ahead of the pack. I had to find her. I had always known where she was until now. I felt her at the football game, then I felt her fear, and then there was nothing. How could there be nothing? I never should have left her and went searching so far away.

The other four wolves raced behind me. Feeding off my fear, they bounded through the trees faster than they ever had before. We had to get back. Something was so very wrong.

Small clips of thought from the other four worked into my head. All worried and wondering where I was and if I was still alive. And one passing thought, that if I wasn't, they would have to lay Adam to rest beside me, because it would kill him, too.

"Oh, no," I said as I dug my heels further into the mud and shoved my face next to the crack. "That isn't going to happen. I'm getting out of here."

My nose pressed against the crack, I screamed for all I was worth, taking every bit of worry and energy that I had left in my body to be as loud as I could manage. Most of the sound reverberated back from the rock and blasted into my own ears. But surely, someone had to have heard me.

Something shuffled above me. I jerked. The movement caused me to slide back in the mud a couple feet. I scrambled to dig in and keep from falling. I still was concentrating on keeping my place, hands dug down deep into the muck like suction cups, when the rock moved again.

"Click, click, snort. Humph," a familiar voice grumbled down.

The moon cast an eerie light on the biggest, hairiest, most beautiful, massive beast I had ever laid eyes on.

"Chewy, I'm so glad to see you!"

"Humph," the Sasquatch snorted as he peered down at me. He made a high keening sound as he spotted Tiffany behind me.

"Yeah, I know. He's a monster, but he won't get away with it. Adam is on his way," I said gleefully as I dug in made my scramble toward freedom.

I made it to the top and grasped the edge of the hole. My hands grasped bunches of full, dark grass. I pulled myself up. I sat on solid ground, physically and mentally pulling myself together. I took a deep breath and looked up at my hairy hero, who had backed up a few feet and was keeping a wary eye on me.

"Thank you." I smiled at him. He grumbled, a low and vibrating sound. Then he looked over the top of my head and started to fidget as if he sensed someone coming toward us. He took one more look at me, as if to make sure I was out of the hole and able to escape, then turned and disappeared into the trees.

She's too loud. I know I heard her scream that time. I have to go back and finish her off. I hope he didn't hear her and that I can do this in time. How dare she mess everything up? Anger seethed out of his mind and into mine, and I knew I had to get up and run, because this was it. There wasn't going to be any talking him out of anything, he was coming in to kill, not to talk.

My body was aching and stiff as I struggled to my feet. Then, he appeared. I froze, somehow rooted to the spot and unable to move, even though everything in me told me I should be running. A silver mist was shrouding his body, causing it to sparkle and shine. If I hadn't known he was deadly, he would have looked beautiful. He stalked closer, his dark eyes changing and slanting. His hands flexed into fists at his sides and a low, menacing growl came from his snarled mouth.

Well, this is it. I'm gonna die now, my mind told me, resigned to the fact that there wasn't any need to run now. I had waited too long. I wondered if he would throw me back in the hole after he killed me. Of course he would. I shivered. Adam had to know, he would avenge me.

Adam, its Reuben. I wish you could hear me. Please, please, hear me. It's been Reuben all along.

So caught up in my little broadcast of information, I never saw the huge black and white wolf jump in front of me until it landed, snarling and growling, and looking totally ticked off as it slammed one huge front paw heavy into the earth, then did the same to the other for good measure as if daring anything more to happen. I had half a second where I was frozen until I looked up and realized that Reuben had stopped where he stood and looked nearly as stupefied as I was. Obviously this wolf was not him, and it did not like what Reuben's intentions were toward me.

It snarled again, baring its sharp fangs as if daring him to come closer to me. Reuben stared at it, indecision flickering across his face as if he were facing a major dilemma and couldn't figure out what to do. The enormous wolf turned and nuzzled my hand, whining.

Are you okay? a worried voice asked.

"Yes," I said. The wolf looked at me thru sapphire blue eyes that held worry and guilt. He looked more like a Siberian Husky than a wolf, I decided. The black intermingled with the white in his thick fur and his eyes sparkled in contrast.

"Who are you?" I asked, as if he could open his long muzzle full of razor-sharp teeth and answer as any person could.

He winced and put his enormous head against my stomach and gave a gentle, but rather solid push, as if to tell me to go. Then he turned and squared his shoulders to meet the enemy, and a deep, challenging growl seemed to vibrate the very earth I stood on.

"You know you don't have to do this," Reuben said. His face had partially changed while we hadn't watched, and now he was speaking through a pile of sharp teeth. "You don't need her. We can get rid of her, and no one would know. You've needed someone to show you what it is that you are. We always hunt better in packs. You won't be alone, son."

Son? I gaped at the wolf. Was it Darren? The boy who everyone assumed would be the sixth Keeper? I looked at the wolf again, and then looked over at Reuben. Somehow I didn't think the little scrawny kid I had seen at the Res was this massive, beautiful—and deadly—wolf in front of me.

I saw Reuben look up at me and snarl, and then a flash blinded me as he projected his memories into my mind.

She was so beautiful, laughing and talking with her friends by the bleachers. She swung her long, chocolate-brown hair back over her shoulders. I wanted to go talk to her, but I was so nervous and afraid. What if she laughed at me? After all, I was one of the guys from the Res. We didn't exactly fit in. I shifted nervously from foot to foot, wanting to follow her and keep her in my sight. But I didn't want to confront her. Not yet.

It was getting to where all I thought of was her, and the weird part was that I always knew where she was. I could find her anywhere. I wasn't sure what to do, especially when I found myself at her bedroom window, hoping to catch a glimpse of her. I only wanted to be near her.

Her friends left her. She waved to them, and then started to walk around the bleachers, on her way home. The wind blew softly, carrying her scent to me on a light breeze. It was intoxicating. I breathed it in deep and watched as the wind blew her skirt tight against her thighs, showing every curve, every detail of her tanned, slender legs. My breath caught, and I knew now was the time for me to gather my courage before she left.

My wolf had stirred at her scent, and I drew upon it for its courage and bravery, since my own had abandoned me. I gave myself over to the animal and let it have its way in return for the strength it gave me to follow her.

She rounded the bleachers and I moved silently behind her, reaching my hand out. It brushed through her warm, silky hair and she turned around, startled. The animal was in complete control now, and there was only thing it wanted to do.

I watched as her beautiful eyes widened, as she realized what was to come, and what I was.

"Brian," I whispered, knowing now who the wolf was in front of me with the sapphire blue eyes. It was his father who was trying to kill me.

Brian hesitated in mid-growl when he had heard me say his name, and I watched as his tail dropped between his legs in shame. Reuben picked that instant to try to leap over his son to me. As soon as his feet left the ground, he changed into a huge silver wolf. His teeth bared, he was coming for my throat. Brian launched himself off the ground and slung his full weight into the oncoming silver wolf. Teeth snapped mere inches from my skin, and then Brian managed to roll both of them away from me.

The ground shook, as the huge ball of black, white, and silver fur rolled. I backed up. I didn't know whether to run or to stay. The part of my brain that was in charge of self-preservation was telling me that I was definitely the weakest one here and that I should be running for cover.

But I couldn't do it.

My feet were frozen to the ground as I watched the two wolves face off and circle before they attacked again. Brian seemed to be stronger and bigger than Reuben, but what he lacked in muscle, Reuben made up for in experience. Brian charged, snapping towards the other wolf's neck in an obvious attempt to end it once and for all. Reuben leapt to one side and sunk his teeth into Brian's back hip.

Brian yelped, but turned to snap again, this time to be rewarded with a mouth full of silver fur from Reuben's side.

You won't hurt her, I won't let you. Do what you can to me, it doesn't matter, but this will end here, Brian's voice was calm in my mind, which seemed at odds with the snarling, black and white wolf with bloodstained fangs.

Blood oozed in the coats of each wolf, matting their silky fur. Each seemed oblivious to the pain as they attacked, then squared off and circled again and again. Brian's goal, it seemed, was to kill Reuben. He snapped each time in a spot that would injure the smaller wolf the most.

Reuben was clever with his attempts. Each movement seemed to have purpose, which was to disable, not kill, his son.

Yips filled the air as fangs sank into flesh, and growls echoed. It seemed I had stood in the same spot for years watching them fight. One was desperate to kill me, while the other wanted to save me.

Nikki, I'm coming. I know where you are. Hold on, Adam's relieved voice soared into my brain loud and clear.

I nearly went limp with relief. If Brian could fight just a little longer, help would be here and it would all be over.

Brian seemed to be holding his own, and it almost looked like he was wearing the older wolf down. As if knowing that the others were on the way, Reuben lunged towards Brian's neck. A split second before it would have been too late, Brian turned and his father ripped out his shoulder. Bone crunched and blood sprayed.

My hero went down.

Reuben backed up, and sat, satisfied, and watched as his son tried again and again to stand. Each time he fell back down, unable to stand and face his attacker. Nothing human remained in the silver wolf's eyes, as he sat panting and watching. Blood dripped from his fangs. The silver wolf that would have been beautiful, now looked only like a thing made of nightmares.

He got up and padded slowly over to the injured wolf, and circled him slowly, as if taunting him. Only an animal remained, and the prey was lying in front of him helpless.

You are nothing like me. I tried to teach you the way, but you wouldn't listen. You aren't worthy of the skin you wear, and so now you must die, and the girl will be next. His voice snarled in my head.

As if he knew the end was near, Brian turned his head and looked at me with sad blue eyes. He whined softly.

I'm so sorry, Nikki. I failed you. I couldn't stop him.

"No," I whispered. I wanted to stop this, but I didn't know what to do.

Reuben stood over Brian's head, baring his teeth in a bloody, triumphant smile. He looked as if he were ready to strike. The, he stopped, the wolf leaving him in a quick mist as he straightened and stood human once more.

"No more," a clear, firm voice said beside me.

The animal was gone from his eyes, as Reuben looked longingly at the woman who stood beside me. The black pistol in her hands was raised and pointed straight at him.

"Anita," his voice was a hoarse whisper as he took a step closer, and in that instant I felt such a sense of sadness, that it blocked out every other emotion that was inside me.

In the flip of a coin, he had lost his life. At least it felt that way. A bet against fate, if such a thing could be done. Well, he had done it, and rather unknowingly. The only problem was that he didn't recall wanting to gamble the life that he had. He hadn't known the price he would pay, that eventually he would lose the very essence that made him who he was. Every time he drew on the animal for its strength and courage, he let every bit of himself go. Each time less and less of himself came back. Finally, there was so little of what made him human that it rarely ever surfaced in his mind. It was just a tiny shred of humanity that hardly ever showed, buried so far inside that sooner or later, it would die just like everything else.

Until now.

Now, all the longing and sorrow was etched in his face as he looked at the woman who was once meant to be his. He took another step toward her, his arm outstretched.

"Stop," Anita whispered, and a fine tremble ran down the length of her arms, causing the end of the gun to waver the slightest bit.

So transfixed in looking at her, Reuben didn't seem to realize the moon, full and round, had come from behind the clouds, and the magic that had been his own, was slowly leaving him. The silver mist would have flowed across his body to transform him into his wolf was now seeping out of every pore of his skin and moving up to float above his head like a shining silver cloud.

The cloud hovered above him, shimmering slightly as each drop of silver joined it. As the last of the mist left his outstretched arm, all of the magic that had made him one of the Six left, too. His body looked older, his posture slightly drooped. His eyes, however, still shone bright with unshed tears.

The silver cloud moved over Brian's head. In his next breath, it went through his mouth and nose. It moved so fast that it looked like a shimmering blur that had pierced him. His eyes flashed a brilliant blue and his back arched as he threw his head back in a soundless howl.

Unaware of what had happened behind him, Reuben shifted, as if to take another step toward Anita.

"Anita, I…" A black and white blur slammed into him and razor-sharp fangs ripped out his throat.

The bundle of fur and man landed a few yards away from us. Then, the wolf jumped up on top of the man's chest and hurled out a ground-vibrating growl as if daring any more threats to come from him. As he saw the blood bubbling out of his neck, he yelped and skittered backward a few feet and sat down rather abruptly.

Wary, Anita kept her gun pointed at Reuben as she walked slowly over to where he lay. Blood pooled under his head, and wet, sloppy air sounds escaped from his neck as he tried to breathe.

The threat gone, Anita holstered her gun and squatted down next to Reuben's head. His eyes never left her face as his lips tried to form the words he had tried to say. As his body slowly died, he took a final ragged breath, and forced them out in a ragged whisper, "I'm sorry."

Anita made her way to where Brian sat, blood soaking his muzzle. His eyes still locked on the dead man.

"Brian," she said quietly, "it's alright now."

Realizing his mother stood near him, Brian changed back from his wolf and looked down, as if ashamed. She brushed back the hair from his forehead, and put her tiny hands on either side of his face and forced him to look up at her.

"Whatever else you may be, you are always my son and nothing will ever change that," she told him firmly.

He wrapped his arms around her and she crouched, rocking him back and forth as if he were just a small child, murmuring small soothing noises in his ear.

"Nikki!" The shout had me jumping nearly out of my skin as Adam bounded to me and grabbed me up close to him. He squeezed me, and then he sat me down and took me by the shoulders. His amber eyes looked frenzied and worried, "Nikki, how? I couldn't…" He gave up, shook his head, and scooped me back up into him so tight that it was hard to breathe. He never set me back down as he took in Reuben's still form, and the woman and boy sitting in the grass a few yards away.

I wrapped my arms around his neck. "I'm okay, Brian saved me. He's your sixth Keeper," I said into the warm, dark silk of his hair.

He tightened his grip around me yet a little more. "I swear, I'm never leaving you again. Ever. I'll never let you out of my sight."

He gave a small, involuntary start, and somehow the next instant I found myself planted firmly behind him, with the other guys flanking him on either side of me.

Now what? I couldn't stand much more excitement. My body started to shake uncontrollably.

It's okay. We won't let anything happen to you. I can hear your heartbeat speeding up and feel you shaking. I'll keep you safe I promise. Stay close to me, Adam's voice soothed through my mind as he reached behind him to take my hand.

I took his hand, "What's wrong? Is he still alive?" I edged around a little and took another look at Reuben, who hadn't moved a muscle and seemed to be as dead as he was moments before.

"No," Adam said, "look over there." I peered in the direction he faced.

Three sleek cats seemed to materialize as from thin air. They sat calmly at the edge of the clearing, a couple of them stretching lazily as if they were quite bored. Only their long tails belied the fact that they were ready for any excitement, as they twitched to and fro. One sat before the others, watching us with calm interest.

The wolves stayed silent, waiting for Adam's lead. I waited to feel him tense beside me, for him to change as the wolf took over to protect us.

But he didn't.

The cats slinked toward us, low to the ground, as if on a hunt. Within a few yards from us, the air seemed to change direction and blew toward them, stirring up sand that seemed as magical as the cats themselves. Before it covered them completely, the lead cat bared long, white fangs at us in a snarl. Then the glittering sand blocked them from sight. The Keepers moved restlessly, and someone let out a barely audible, still human, yip.

The wind died as quickly as it had started, leaving the clearing completely silent.

"You're early," Adam said casually to the boy standing in front of us who would have been the lead cat. All three of the boys standing in front of us looked ferocious, their heads shaved but for a single strip of hair down the middle that was spiked straight up in a Mohawk. They stared at Adam with hard expressions. They seemed bigger than the Six, more heavily muscled. I chewed my lip nervously and watched as they seemed to multiply before my eyes. The world seemed to sway just the slightest bit, then tilt back to normal.

No one moved for what seemed an eternity.

The lead boy looked over at Brian and Anita, then back over and locked eyes with me. His deep green eyes seemed to pierce straight into me, and the world quit tilting and swaying. Just as suddenly, he blinked, and the spell broke when he took in the mud, blood and vomit splattered and caked all over me. His nostrils flared, and he snorted out once.

"I don't smell that great. Sorry," I mumbled, not sure if I was supposed to apologize before I was eaten.

He grinned and shook his head, sending a row of golden earrings tinkling and swaying in one ear, as he looked over at Adam, "You know we love a party. It kinda looks like we're late, not early."

Adam returned the grin, and clapped the boy on the shoulder, "It's good to see you, Rune. I'm glad you're here."

Whoops of excitement broke out from both sides as the tension left and everyone started talking.

Then everything went black.

SEVENTEEN

I AWOKE, BLEARY-EYED, to a clear plastic bag that hung over my head on a pole. A dripping liquid ran down a clear tube that attached to my arm.

Flailing, I tried to sit straight up and was rewarded with a resounding thump, as if my heart had decided to change location and took up residence in the back of my skull. I thought my head was going to explode.

"Easy, Nikki," Brian sprung up from his spot beside my bed, "It's okay, just lay back there."

There seemed to be a hospital bed, and since it seemed to be a relatively safe place at the moment, I did as I was told and eased back against the pillow.

Everything's okay, just take it easy, I'm just outside in the hallway, Adam's voice whispered through my aching head, *I'm right here if you need me, but I let Brian come in first. He needed to see you were safe.*

I nodded slightly as if he could see me through the wall, and turned my head to look at Brian.

"I require drugs," I told him solemnly, as I looked at him through one eye, since both of them didn't want to focus at the same time together.

He laughed. It had been the first time I had seen him smile in what seemed forever. He almost looked normal again, like my old Brian. My best friend. I tried to smile, but it made my head hurt worse. Frowning didn't help, either.

"I'm quite serious, you know. I really could use a Tylenol," I hinted, hoping either he or Adam would go and find a nurse.

"I'd say you need more than that," he smiled, reaching over my bedrail, and pushed the nurse's button for me.

I caught his hand and gave it a squeeze. "So how bad is it? Am I dying?"

His blue eyes were locked on our clasped hands as I heard his voice whisper in my mind, *No, but I would tell you anything if you'd never let go.*

"You've got a heck of a concussion, as you can probably tell from the big lump on the back of your head, and you've got scrapes and bruises literally from head to toe..."

"And you're about to start feeling a lot better," a smiling nurse interrupted him as she came through the door, wielding a large syringe full of painkillers.

"Please tell me there's an easier way," I fidgeted on the bed, looking at her through my one open eye.

"Of course," she laughed, stabbing my IV line, thankfully, instead of me, "You let me know if you need anything else, but I doubt you'll be awake much longer."

I nodded and she left. Relief washed through me, numbing me from head to toe as the medicine began its work. I let out the breath I hadn't realized I had been holding and started to relax. Cautiously, I slit one eye open, and then the next, and was rewarded with only one Brian.

"Better?" he asked, with a small smile that didn't reach his sapphire eyes.

"Oh yeah," I sighed, squeezing his hand again. "How about you? Are you ok?"

*Other than the fact that I've learned my father, who also raped my mother, was also a killer of so many girls they haven't even figured out how many yet? Oh yeah, and let's not forget he also turned into a monster...the worse kind of monster...*his voice whispered brokenly in my mind.

"Yeah, sure. I'm fine," he mumbled, dropping his head so that his dark hair fell forward hiding his eyes.

I killed him. I'm not sorry I did it. I'd do it again, for he deserved to die. So, now, I'm the killer. I'm the monster. I don't want to be like him. Please, don't let me be like him.

Silent tears ran down his cheeks as he pulled his hand away from mine and I felt his heart break.

"You're not like him at all. You saved me, Brian. If you hadn't been there, I'd be dead now." I sat up and reached out to him. "You're strong and you're good. You have such a good heart, just like your mom. And you only did what you had to do. Look at me. Please?"

Slowly he lifted his head. His blue eyes were shining with tears.

"Thank you for saving my life." I smiled. "I wouldn't be here without you."

He nodded, and then brushed his hair back from his eyes. "I don't know, you're pretty tough, you'd have figured out something. You found a way out of that hole. From the looks of things, I don't think anyone else did. You're a survivor."

"Nah, that wasn't me that was Chewy." I dismissed it with a slight wave of my hand.

"What's a Chewy?" he asked, frowning slightly.

"He's a Bigfoot. He moved the rock for me so I could crawl out. I think he was returning the favor since we helped save his baby." I yawned, starting to feel the drugs take effect.

"There's no such thing as Bigfoot," I heard him say before I closed my eyes and began drifting off.

Well, why not. I turn into a huge, black and white wolf. Bigfoot could be real. Why did she name him Chewy? His voice sounded amused.

"'Cause it fits him," I whispered, smiling at the sound of his soft laughter, then I gave in to sleep.

I woke later with a huge pair of beautiful golden eyes staring back into mine. Adam smiled, then leaned over the inch that had separated us and kissed me as long as he dared. I felt warm and fuzzy, way better than the shot of whatever it was had made me feel. It was as if I could just melt into a happy puddle of contentment. The air swirled and snapped warmly around us.

"I'm so glad to see you," I smiled.

"Not nearly as glad as I am to see you." He grinned, causing his eyes to sparkle, the little onyx specks glinting and swirling in them.

"Where's Brian?" I asked, looking over at the chair where he had sat.

"He's gone home to check on his mom. He's pretty shaken up. I hope you didn't mind I let him come in first, but he looked like he needed to see you, and he looked a lot better when he came out of here." Adam leaned forward to rest his forehead next to mine. "How's the head?"

"Feels like a wrecking ball hit the back of it. Other than that, though," I shrugged a little. "I'll be fine."

"Your mom and Emily just left a few minutes ago to find something to eat. She warned me if anything happened to you while she was gone it would be my fault." He dropped his eyes from mine and picked aimlessly at a loose strand of thread hanging on my blanket. "I think she was joking. But if she wasn't, I can't say that I blame her. I'm the reason you're in here."

"None of this is your fault, Adam. I'm fine, really. I'll be as good as new in a couple days." I reached over and brushed a long strand of hair from his face.

"I never should have left you." It was a statement that didn't invite any opposition. He wasn't going to ever let himself let it go. I saw it in the little wrinkle between his brows and the firm set of his mouth. I knew it wasn't his fault, but I didn't think I would be able to convince him any differently. I had to try.

"It's done now and I'm okay. Reuben's dead, the mystery of the trail killer is solved, and now you won't have to go searching anymore Deadlands. You can stay right here all the time." I grinned as far as my face would stretch.

A small smile tugged at one side of his mouth as he looked back up at me. "You'd better count on it."

As it happened, they kept me in the hospital for the rest of the week and he rarely left my side. My mom was the only one who seemed to hold the power to ward him off. She made him go home in the evenings. But the next morning, he would be there the moment the nurses let him in. I wondered how much trouble he was getting in since I knew he was skipping school.

Every day, another member of the pack would drop in to see me. It was during these visits, I learned from Ed, Erik, Tommy and Michael everything that Adam hadn't told me. They hadn't actually told me, I just more or less picked it up since they had all been projecting their thoughts so clearly.

From Ed, I had learned the most. He had sat beside me, still flexing his hand that had gotten the briar in it when we searched the Deadland.

"Is it okay?" I asked, pointing to it.

"Oh yeah, it's fine." He quit flexing and folded his hands in his lap, and smiled, but it didn't quite reach his dark eyes.

Still feels weird, but it's not like anyone's going to understand. It feels like dark magic running inside me, but it could just be all the weird stuff that's been going on, his brain contemplated to himself, and conveniently, to me, as he thought of everything that had happened.

I sat back, closed my eyes, and went for the ride his memory took me on, starting with finding me by the huge hole, wet and covered in vomit and blood. I frowned and tried not to pay attention to the details there that he seemed to remember so vividly. I tuned out and barely watched his memory until I saw Wynter's image pop into my mind.

She had shown up at the underground pit after I had been taken to the hospital. She had basically ignored Erik, who had taken command of the pack since Adam went with me, and showed even less interest in the three giant cats that stood by.

After walking around the rock that had covered the opening, she circled it a few times, and then over to where Reuben's body lay. She abruptly left, having never uttered a single word.

When the police arrived, the scene they had found had been very different from the one I had left. The bodies of the missing women were found only to have broken necks, from their supposed fall into the cavern. All were ruled as accidents, even Reuben, whose missing throat somehow had become whole again. They were saying he had a heart attack after finding the bodies and rescuing me from what surely would have been certain death.

The bad guy was the hero.

Well, that sucked, I thought, jerking myself out of Ed's head and leaning back to pretend sleep so he'd go home.

I didn't tell Adam that I knew what had happened. I was ready to try to forget about all of it, even if my subconscious wouldn't let me. Night after night I woke in a cold sweat, feeling as if the walls were closing in on me. I couldn't even sleep with covers on. It felt as if they were choking and trying to drown me.

The nightmares eased up a little after I got to go home and life started going back to normal. Adam reluctantly started setting up for the Powwow with Rune and the others after school. But on evenings he didn't come to see me, I began visiting Penny as she worked the gift shop. She always kept me up to date on each day's happenings and filled me in on what was happening with the Powwow. On one visit, I found her working on a dress.

"I will be one of the dancers at the Powwow," she told me, as she threaded beads on the leather strips.

I knew I wouldn't be a dancer, but it was then that I got the weird idea to search the upstairs attic for a dress to wear to the Powwow.

After all, my grandmother was Cherokee. I might find something pretty cool up there.

Or I could just borrow one from Penny, I thought, as part of me tried to persuade myself that I didn't want to go poking around in a dusty, old attic that no one had been in since before my great-grandma had died.

But the thought of an unexplored section of house had me reaching for the little loop of string that would pull down the small, rickety wooden steps and lead me up into the unknown. I wasn't sure why I thought there should be something in the attic, it just felt like there was something up there for me to see. That feeling had me tugging on that string harder than I needed to.

The old steps groaned as they stretched down to me and made rather scary cracking noises under my weight as I climbed up and stuck my head directly into a huge cobweb.

"Ew," I squealed as I batted at the sticky mess that covered my head like a shroud.

Still whacking at my hair, I took a step back and slipped backwards, landing flat on my back looking up at the ceiling. With a disgusted snort, I sat up and decided to look around while still sitting before I got up and accidentally killed myself by some other unknown peril.

The small windows at either end of the attic let in surprising amounts of sunlight. Dust motes swirled and sparkled around in the air giving the area a feeling of enchantment. Huge pieces of sheet-covered furniture loomed above me. With the sun shining behind them, it gave the appearance of giant white ghosts, with subtle hints of skeletal wooden bones beneath their thin coverings.

Getting slightly unnerved by my own imagination, I stood up and started jerking the sheets off, uncovering a large desk, and a big oval mirror. In an attempt not to die of dust inhalation, I quickly jerked the collar of my sweatshirt over my nose, as clouds of dust rose around me in puffs for what seemed like forever. Figuring I was going to die if I didn't get oxygen soon, I hurried over to the far side of the attic and took a deep breath, let go of my shirt and yanked the window open.

Clean, crisp air flooded in, and in seconds the dust settled, and I took a better look around. It wasn't all that crowded for an attic. I had expected piles of boxes, crates and mountains of ancient garbage to surround me, but there really just wasn't much there. A rickety old rocking chair sat nearest me, not far from the window. The opposite wall was clear all the way to the mirror, where a couple of large trunks sat in front of it.

I walked slowly over to them, even though the dust seemed to have completely dissipated. Sitting in front of the first one, I flipped the latch, and the lid swung up all on its own, as if it had waited for me to free it. Frowning, I looked behind it, searching for springs that must have popped it open. The only thing I saw were tarnished brass hinges.

"Weird," I muttered to myself, eyeballing the trunk carefully before getting the courage to peek inside.

It was a treasure trove. An old family album sat on the very top. Forgetting my earlier caution, I dove in, got the old book out and started flipping through. The first page was a picture of my great-grandparents. They stood in front of the steps of the house. Neither smiled as they stood stiffly side by side, staring at the photographer. My grandpa was tall, yet trim. His white hair had been brushed straight back from his forehead, leaving his face open. I stared at him closely, wondering what he had been like. I had never met him and the picture didn't give away any details as to his personality. He seemed to stare straight back at me from the album. I turned my attention to the slight woman, whose head only came to her husband's shoulder. My grandmother's salt and pepper hair was pulled back into a loose knot at the back of her head. She, like her husband, stared solemnly at the camera.

"Geez," I said to myself as much as to the picture, "I'm glad we don't do pictures like that anymore."

A tiny sound that sounded like soft laughter, barely registered in my brain, as a soft breeze blew through the open window. Jumping nearly out of my skin, I snapped the album shut and looked around, but didn't see anything out of the ordinary.

"You're nuts. There isn't anyone up here but you," I warned myself, setting the old book down beside me, as I reached back into the trunk. I pulled out a few old books and stacked them on the album, and sorted through a few odd trinkets, before my fingers felt the crinkled paper-covered bundle.

I took it out and unwrapped layer after layer of the yellowed, old paper until I felt something soft. A beautiful white buckskin dress lay folded in my hands. I got up and let it unfold in front of me. Small blue and black beads decorated the long strands of leather around the neck and the hem of the dress. Nearly giddy with excitement, I peeled off my sweatshirt, and kicked my jeans off, then pulled the soft buckskin over my head.

I smiled at my reflection in the mirror. It fit perfectly. The wind blew thru the window, causing the old rocking chair to creak as it rocked.

Across from the chair, something at the corner of the wall glowed. I spun around, half-expecting everything to change, but the chair still rocked, more rhythmically, creaking and groaning, and the small patch of wall still glowed. Cautiously, I walked over to inspect it closer, and saw that it was a small part of the paper that covered the wall that had come unglued, and whatever lay beneath the ancient, crinkled paper was what was glowing in a faintly-tinged blue light.

I don't know why I did it, when my subconscious was screaming to run back downstairs to safety, but I reached down and pulled the corner of the paper. It turned like a giant page of a book and I stood looking at a wall that looked like glassy, blue water. I reached out and touched it, expecting my finger to come away wet from the liquid wall. Small ripples spread where I had touched, then they flashed, and I watched as the kitchen downstairs was replicated on the wall in front of me.

My great-grandmother stood at the sink, sleeves pushed up to her elbows, washing dishes. She was older than in the picture, her body was more stooped and her movements were slow and rigid. She hummed softly to herself as she worked. She stopped suddenly, and turned slowly to face something that I couldn't see.

"For being as old as you are, you still haven't learned manners. I don't recall hearing you knock." Her sharp, keen eyes seemed to stare directly at me.

My mouth dropped open and no sound would come out, which ended up being a good thing as the scene continued to unfold before me without any help on my part.

"When one's door is opened, one should have no need to announce her presence, especially amongst friends." The musical voice like raindrops echoed in the attic as I watched Wynter come into view.

"Hmph. Friends, is it?" My grandmother's dark eyes hardened and narrowed to slits. "What is it you want?"

"Your grandson and his family. They have a hand in destiny. You must call them here soon." Wynter looked at the old woman sadly. "Their presence is required."

"I'll not be calling them here for the likes of you. I don't owe you anything, and I won't have you interfering..."she broke off in a cough that doubled her over, her hand on her chest.

"Your time is nearly come. I could ease the pain, should you only ask." The offer came with a slight shrug.

"I don't need you or your magic. Whatever it is you're wanting, you won't be getting it from me or my family. We owe you nothing and we never will." Fury etched in the deep lines of my grandmother's wrinkled face. "Get on out of here!"

Wynter sighed, then turned her giant blue eyes to stare out of the wall directly at me. "She has come before, she will come again. I cannot stop her. There is only one who can. I hope she makes haste."

Thousands of tiny electric currents seemed to run over the surface of my skin, and something furred seemed to slide along my bones as something awakened from deep inside me. My body shook harder, and I caught my reflection in the mirror as a sparkling, iridescent white mist hovered around my body. I fought as I felt my bones shift, as muscles tried to realign, pain seared through every nerve ending.

I fought the urge to scream as panic rioted through my body, as something so not *me* tried to take over. A low growl tore from my lips, and I watched as the mist covered me, and a single thought from the animal inside me whispered in my mind,

I am White Wolf.

Other Titles

By KR Thompson

The Keeper Saga:

Once Upon a Haunted Moon (Book 2)

Wynter's War (Book 3)

The Wolf (Prequel)

The Untold Stories of Neverland:

Hook

Nerida

K.R. Thompson was raised in the Appalachian Mountains. She resides in southwestern Virginia with her husband, son, three cats, and an undeterminable amount of chickens.

An avid reader and firm believer in the magic of books, she spends her nights either reading an adventure or writing one.

She still watches for evidence of Bigfoot in the mud of Wolf Creek.

Stay up to date on all of her newest releases on her website:
http://authorkrthompson.wix.com/thekeepersaga
And on Facebook:
http://www.facebook.com/thekeepersaga